after
midnight

after midnight

A YOUNGBLOODS NOVEL

LYNN VIEHL

Woodbury, Minnesota

First Edition
First Printing, 2011

Cover design by Kevin R. Brown
Cover illustration by Juliana Kolesova
Cover images: horse © iStockphoto.com/Cliff Parnell;
    woman © iStockphoto.com/Quavondo;
    man © iStockphoto.com/Factoria Singular;
    moon © iStockphoto.com/Ufuk Zivana;
    clouds © iStockphoto.com/Niilo Tippler;
    decorative accents © iStockphoto.com/appleuzr and Fred_DL

Flux, an imprint of Llewellyn Worldwide Ltd.

Library of Congress Cataloging-in-Publication Data
Viehl, Lynn.
  After midnight / Lynn Viehl—1st ed.
    p. cm.
  Summary: Fifteen-year-old Catlyn Youngblood finally learns her family's secret, that they are descended from legendary vampire hunter Van Helsing, when, after she and her brothers settle into tiny Lost Lake, Florida, she feels an overpowering attraction to Jesse Raven, a vampire.
  ISBN 978-0-7387-2632-8
  [1. Brothers and sisters—Fiction. 2. Vampires—Fiction. 3. High schools—Fiction. 4. Schools—Fiction. 5. Moving, Household—Fiction. 6. Orphans—Fiction. 7. Florida—Fiction.] I. Title.
  PZ7.V6668Aft 2011
  [Fic]—dc22

                                    2010050130

                                       Flux
                           Llewellyn Worldwide Ltd.
                             2143 Wooddale Drive
                           Woodbury, MN 55125-2989
                               www.fluxnow.com

                    Printed in the United States of America

For my daughter, Katherine Rose,
with all my love—as promised.

One

Family secrets are like terrible birthday gifts. They're always stuff you never wanted but have to keep anyway because someone you love gave them to you. Like a black velvet painting of Justin Timberlake or a jean jacket with a sequined unicorn on the back. You can stick them under your bed and pretend they're not there, but someday you know someone nosy will find them, and laugh at you, and tell everyone.

Then there are the secrets that are so terrible that your family hides them from you. Funny thing is, no matter how well they keep those secrets, you still know they're there. You can hear them in the conversations that stop as soon as you walk into the room. You can see them when they won't look you in the eye. You can feel them, like monsters hiding under your bed, waiting for you to find them.

No matter what kind of family secrets you have, the one thing they never do? Is go away.

My alarm went off at six a.m. on my first day at Tanglewood High School. School didn't start until seven-thirty, but I wanted an extra hour to work on Trick. I'd rehearsed everything I planned to say the night before in the shower; like how tired I was of going to a new school every year, all the problems we could avoid if he home-schooled me, and how much I could help out with the horses and around the house if he didn't make me go.

If that didn't work, I had a Plan B. I was almost sixteen, practically an adult, and old enough to drop out of school if I wanted. Trick couldn't stop me.

It wasn't because I hated school. I just didn't see the point in going to another one that I'd have to leave in six months or a year when we packed up and moved again. I'd already gone to fourteen different schools since first grade, and I was sick of forever being the new kid.

It was time for me to take charge of my life.

I went downstairs and found Trick in the kitchen, fishing black-edged waffles out of the toaster. He was five-ten, like me, but twice as wide and fifteen years older, so people always thought he was my uncle or something. Working outdoors with the horses tanned his skin pretty dark, and kept the muscles in his arms and legs huge. He shaved his head and wore a plain gold ring in his left ear, and no matter how hot it was, he always dressed in a black T-shirt and black jeans, like a priest on steroids. Trick said it was because black hid stains, but all his clothes were black, and he wasn't that messy.

We never talked about it, but I think before Mom and Dad died my brother had been a biker.

Trick didn't turn around or look at me, but when I opened my mouth he said, "Put the orange juice on the table, Cat, and go wake up your brother."

He sounded like he was talking through a mouthful of gravel, and only one thing did that. He'd been up all night again working out in the barn while he worried about stuff. Trick hadn't done that once since we'd moved here.

I decided I could argue about going to school tomorrow. "What's wrong?"

"Nothing."

"Come on." It must be pretty bad, I thought. "No way you're getting a cold." Trick never got sick. Ever.

He turned away so I couldn't see his face. "I'll tell you when Gray's up."

My brother Grayson lived in what had been used as the garage by the previous owners. Trick had converted it to a bedroom because the farmhouse only had two bedrooms and he said we all needed our privacy. That was fine with me. Of course Gray's room was five times bigger than mine, plus he had a private entrance. He also didn't have to climb the stairs a hundred times a day to get to his room like I did; he only had to walk through the laundry room. But he had no closet, and had to sleep with the water heater, the well pump and the noisy window shaker Trick had put in that mostly blew around the hot air.

Gray didn't care. If Trick would have let him, he'd have slept out in the woods or in the barn with the horses.

I knocked on my brother's door three times before I tried to open it and found it locked. I couldn't yell—one of Trick's house rules was no yelling at all no matter what—but as long as I used my fist I could hammer as much as I wanted.

So I did. "Grim." He hated that more than Grouch, Gross, Gripe and all the other nicknames I'd given him, but I pounded the door three more times just to be sure. "Get up."

I heard a low groan, mattress springs springing, and a jingle of keys, and stepped back.

The door opened a crack, and a single blue eye buried in a lot of messy blond hair glared down at me. "What?"

"School. Trick says we're going." I folded my arms. "He's in the kitchen burning breakfast right now." I looked over my shoulder before I lowered my voice and added, "He was up all night again."

The eye closed. "Great." The door thudded shut in my face.

I wasn't offended. My brother Grayson made brick walls look friendly and talkative.

I took my favorite pair of jeans out of the dryer before I went back to the kitchen. Trick had piled two plates with his singed waffles and some sliced peaches. At his place were a cup of black coffee and the weekly issue of *Lost Lake Community News*, a free local newspaper he picked up whenever he went into town for supplies.

"How come Grim and I have to eat breakfast and you don't?" I asked as I sat down and began trimming off the burned parts of my waffles.

"I had breakfast earlier." Trick came over with a bottle of syrup for the waffles. He looked at the jeans I'd draped over the back of my chair. "You're not wearing those old things to school."

"I can't go in my underwear." I sipped some juice. "Think of all the detentions I'll get."

Trick sat down and opened the paper. "I just bought you five new pairs of jeans."

That he had, along with five new T-shirts and five new flannel shirts. Unless Trick let me wash them a couple hundred times, I wasn't planning to wear them anytime soon.

"They still have the tags on," I mentioned. "If you let me stay home this year, you could return them and get your money back."

Two brown eyes looked over the top of the paper. "You're going to school, Catlyn."

I really hated my name—everyone thought you were supposed to pronounce it like Caitlin or Kaitlin, and forget about spelling it right—but the only time Trick used it was when he wanted me to know that what he said, he meant. It was better than him yelling or swearing at me, which he never did.

Sometimes I wished he would—yell, of course, not swear. Trick never lost his temper, or made a mistake, or did anything wrong. No way was I ever going to be half as perfect as he was.

A shadow fell over the table as Gray came in, sat down and began to eat. He ate like he did everything, fast and in total silence.

When he wasn't sleeping Gray spent every minute he could outside, so his tan matched Trick's, and the sun had streaked his blond hair and turned his eyebrows and eyelashes white. He hated getting his hair cut—among the ten thousand things he didn't like, strangers touching him ranked pretty high on the list—so he wore it in a ponytail or shoved it through the back of one of his baseball caps. Gray had been taller than me since the fifth grade, and bigger than Trick since two Christmases ago. I had a fuzzy memory of him being skinny like me when we were little, but that hadn't lasted.

Since we'd become teens the kids at school had started teasing my brother and calling him things like The Hulk and Terminator, but he didn't care. The only things that mattered to Gray were food, sleep and being left alone.

I felt a little better when Grayson was around. He might have been a big, moody grouch, but he never made me feel like I wasn't good enough.

When Trick got up to refill his coffee, I slid my plate over to my brother, who forked the scorched waffles I hadn't eaten onto the pool of syrup left on his plate.

I waited for the big announcement, but Trick just stood gazing out the window at the south pasture. I knew he really liked this place; he'd been in a decent mood all summer.

Finally I couldn't wait another second. "So do we need to start packing?"

"No."

If we weren't moving, then it had to be about money. "Are we broke or something?"

"I've been saving up for a couple years. We're okay." He drank some of his coffee. "It's time we put down some roots." He glanced over his shoulder. "We're staying here, Cat."

Because of Trick's work, we'd never stayed anywhere. For a minute I didn't know what to say. "Why here?"

"I think it's a good place for us."

We'd lived in other good places, like California and Wyoming. Very good places, in fact. So why would he think living in a backwoods country town in the middle of Nowhere, Florida was better?

"What about your job?" I asked. Trick had worked for a big computer company that had sent us all over the country. They never needed him to stay at a branch office longer than six months.

"I resigned a couple of weeks ago." He turned around to face us. "Working the farm and breeding horses is going to be my job from now on. The barn's almost ready, so I'll be buying more stock."

I bit the inside of my lip. Wherever we'd lived, we

always rented a little house in the country, with a barn and stalls and pasture for our horses, but I'd thought that was only because Trick hated the city and didn't want to sell the horses. He'd never once mentioned breeding them for a living.

"You check it out?" Gray asked.

Trick nodded. "Nothing but corn fields and cattle ranches."

They were talking around me again, the way they did whenever they meant something I didn't know about or understand. Sometimes I had the feeling that Grim and Trick kept a lot of stuff from me; probably because I was a girl or the youngest. It wasn't fair because Gray was only a year older than me, plus I hated being treated like the baby of the family.

"What did he have to check out?" I asked Gray. When he didn't answer, I turned on Trick. "Well?"

"Just the neighborhood, Cat," my brother said mildly.

I shoved my chair back from the table, but before I could stomp out of the kitchen I heard a faint mew from outside. I went to the window and saw a little shadow hiding behind the gardenia bushes we'd planted around the porch.

"If you keep feeding him," Trick said, "he'll never go away."

"Hear that, Grim?" I smirked at my brother. "You're going to live with us forever."

I grabbed a paper plate and the bag of cat food I kept stashed in the pantry and went outside onto the back porch. As soon as I closed the door the little stray crept out of the bush and jumped up beside me. He purred as he rubbed against my legs and tried to get his head under my hand. That made me spill some of the cat food, and I bent down to scoop it back onto the paper plate.

"Look what you made me do," I scolded, and then laughed as he jumped onto my lap and butted me in the chest. "Okay, okay. I'm glad to see you, too."

He was dirty, smelly and thin, and his ears had bald spots from rubbing against the wrong things, but he had the sweetest gold-green eyes. A tiny fleck of white fur on his chin always made me think of a soul patch. He wouldn't touch the food until I went inside, so I took a minute to give him a gentle scratching around the ears and under his neck.

"Now eat your breakfast," I told him after I put him down and stood. He always tried to follow me inside so I had to slip into the house quickly. Even when I closed the door he sat outside on the doormat as if waiting for me.

"Don't leave that cat food sitting out there like you did yesterday," Trick told me. "I saw raccoon tracks in the yard. Once they smell it they'll start coming here every night to scrounge."

"Sorry." I saw Gray had already gone back to his room. "Are you taking me to school?" Sometimes Trick's motorcycle, an ancient Harley that was forever breaking down, wouldn't start. With a little luck I might get to stay home anyway, and then I could find out why after all these years of bouncing from town to town he'd decided we needed to settle in Lost Lake.

Trick ruined that idea, too. "I have to go look at a couple of brood mares today. Gray will take you."

That was another thing that seemed so unfair. Grim already had a license and had been driving for almost a year. Trick wouldn't even let me take the test to get my learner's permit.

"When am *I* going to be allowed to drive?" I asked for the hundredth time. "When I'm thirty?"

For once Trick didn't say yes. "Bring home straight A's this semester, and we'll talk about it."

"Seriously?" I couldn't believe it. He knew I always got straight A's. "Will I have my own car? Do I get to pick it out?"

"We'll see what we can afford." Trick glanced at the clock. "Go and get dressed now. You don't want to be late."

Not anymore, I didn't. I grabbed my jeans and ran upstairs.

———

I didn't have much in the way of nice clothes. We weren't poor, exactly. Trick worked hard and always made sure we had what we needed. It had more to do with me being the youngest and the only girl in the family.

Up until last year Trick had bought all my clothes, which had been tragic because he really had no idea what girls were supposed to wear. When I was little I didn't mind the jeans and the T-shirts he bought, but by fourth grade I started noticing that the other girls at my school didn't dress like me. I wasn't crazy about skirts, dresses and the frilly lacy stuff some of them wore, but I didn't like looking different, either.

Things changed when my sixth grade gym teacher sent home a note asking Trick to buy me some bras because I was "blooming" and starting to show through my T-shirts. I had to explain the blooming part, which really embarrassed me and him both. That night he took me to Wal-Mart, handed me a bunch of money and left me in the lingerie section. Luckily there was an older lady clerk working there, and when I asked her about the sizes she measured me and helped me pick out what I needed.

"Your mother should have come with you," the clerk said as she took me back to the dressing room.

"I don't have a mom," I told her. "I mean, she's dead. So's my dad."

Her stern face softened. "Oh, you poor thing. Who's taking care of you?"

"My oldest brother, Patrick." I didn't like to talk about our parents because all people really wanted to know was how they died. I didn't remember the car accident and my brothers never talked about it, so I didn't really know much. Plus strangers never seemed to have a problem with asking a kid for all the gruesome details. I held up one of the stretchy sports bras she'd given me to try on. "Does this come in beige?"

Since then Trick let me buy my own clothes, and I had a couple of dresses and skirts, but I was too self-conscious to wear them often. I definitely didn't want to show off how skinny my legs were on the first day of school, so I put on what Trick called my uniform: faded jeans, a white T-shirt and a blue plaid flannel shirt. I didn't have pierced ears, and the only jewelry I owned was an old silver St. Christopher's medal that I wore on a chain tucked under my shirt, so after I put my sneakers on I just had to do something with my hair.

Unlike Grim I didn't inherit my mother's fine, fabulous blond mane; my dad had stuck me with his thick, stick-straight dark brown hair. I wore it parted on the side so it fell over my left eyebrow, which I thought looked better than parting it in the middle, but that was about all I could do with it. It wouldn't hold a curl or a wave unless I slept in wet braids, and even then the crimps would fall out as soon as I showered.

I didn't mind my hair so much, even if it was ordinary and boring. Back when my chest started "blossoming" I would pull my hair over my shoulders to hide the embarrassing little bumps. The one time Trick did cut my hair short in elementary school people thought I was a boy. It took three whole years to grow it back out, and now it hung down to my waist. I wanted to grow it so long I could sit on it. Trick didn't care what I did as long as I kept it clean and neat.

I went into the bathroom to finish getting ready. I wasn't allowed to wear makeup yet, so I couldn't do anything about my face. The pimples I'd gotten in seventh grade had finally cleared up, so my skin looked okay. I didn't like my straight dark eyebrows, my long nose or my pointed chin, but my ears weren't too big and my mouth was kind of pretty. I thought my eyes, which were big and almond-shaped, could have been my best feature if they'd been sky blue like Grim's. Instead mine were hazel, a dark olive green with tiny light brown streaks and spots in them.

I used some SPF 50 lotion on my face—my skin always burned really easy—and then put on some cherry-flavored lip balm to give my mouth a little more color. There was nothing else I could do but brush out my hair and decide between loose, braid or ponytail.

If I wore it loose I'd have to take a brush with me, and I usually braided my hair only when I went riding. A braid would make me feel like I was nine years old again; Trick had always kept my hair braided when I was little so he didn't have to brush out knots, which we both hated.

Gray's face appeared in the mirror above mine. "Are you ready yet?"

"Give me a minute." I held the elastic band between my teeth as I gathered up my hair, and glanced around for my backpack, which I'd left by the door. I could be really spacey; I constantly misplaced things, and sometimes I completely forgot about them. "You really want to stay here?"

"I guess." Gray picked up a white elastic from the

counter and used it to pull back his golden locks into an untidy tail. "Don't you?"

"I don't know." I looped the band around my hair twice and ran my brush through the trailing ends. Before he'd turned into the Incredible Brooding Hulk, Gray and I used to tell each other everything. I missed that more than I wanted to admit. "It seems kind of sudden. We don't know anybody here."

"Trick says it's okay." That was good enough for my brother. "Come on, let's go."

Two

When Trick first told us back in May that we would be moving from Chicago to Lost Lake, I went to the library to find out more about the place. The town didn't appear on any maps of Florida, not even the one in the huge U.S. atlas they kept on a pedestal in the reference section. It also wasn't listed on Yahoo, Google, or any of the search sites I checked on the library computer. Then I tried to find it in books written about Florida, but the only time it was mentioned was in a book about historic buildings, and only then in a footnote about Freemasons. Tampa was supposed to have the oldest Masonic temple in the state, but the footnote said one might have been built in Lost Lake twenty years before it.

Might have been? I thought. *Couldn't they call and check?*

I asked the reference librarian if she knew why Lost Lake wasn't listed anywhere.

"It's probably a small town," she said as she pulled up something on her computer terminal. "Or perhaps they've been annexed by a larger community." She studied her screen. "According to the state's list of cities and town, Lost Lake, Florida has a current population of seven hundred thirty-one. That's a *very* small town." She smiled up at me. "Are you and your family planning to visit there?"

"No, ma'am." Rather than explain I was actually moving to this dinky place, I added, "Would there be any magazine or newspaper articles written about it?"

"The population report is the only thing showing on my system." She tapped her lips with one finger as she thought for a moment. "You could write to the state visitor's bureau and request some information from them. They usually provide free booklets with points of interest and that sort of thing."

She printed out an address for me and I wrote to it, but all that came in the mail was a big splashy tourist's guide to all the big theme parks and attractions in Orlando. It also mentioned some of the cities in the area, like Silver Springs and Ocala, but nothing about my new town.

Wherever Lost Lake was, it just wasn't that interesting.

We packed up and drove to Florida as soon as Gray and I got out of school for summer break. It took a week and a half to make the trip because we brought our stock horses, Sali, Jupiter and Flash, along with us in a rental trailer. Sali, a big Tennessee Walker Trick had bought for me when I turned eleven, was used to traveling and didn't mind the long hours in the trailer as long as we made regular stops to water, feed and exercise her. Jupiter, Trick's white stallion, was also pretty good about moving, although he always got cranky about being put back into the trailer after a rest stop.

Gray's gelding Flash, a golden palomino who was as quick as his name, was what Trick called our "problem child."

Flash hated traveling. On moving day Gray had to put his blinders on before he led him out of the barn, because as soon as Flash saw the trailer he'd rear and run off. It took both my brothers to coax him up the ramp and get him loaded, and then once he was inside he'd really start kicking up a fuss.

We made the inside of the trailer as comfortable as we could for the horses, and even put some feed in their buckets to keep them occupied when we started out, but Flash didn't care. He would kick at the sides of the trailer, butt his head against the windows and ceiling, and neigh and tromp around so much you'd have thought he'd gotten a snootful of red ants. Trick put up a steel grate partition between Flash and the other horses to keep him from injuring Sali and Jupe, but Gray usually had to ride in the trailer for the first couple of hours we were on the road to keep Flash from tearing it apart.

We'd never been to Florida, so I did look through the pictures in the guide the state bureau sent. In between the advertisements for the theme parks there were some nice panorama shots of white-sand beaches, groves of trees studded with huge oranges, tall, exotic palm trees, and flocks of pink flamingoes. All the families in the pictures were in bathing suits or tank tops, shorts and flip-flops, and looked like they were having a blast, too.

Too bad we didn't move to *that* part of Florida.

I started watching the scenery as soon as we crossed the over the Georgia-Florida state line, but trees or cement walls were all I saw on either side of the interstate. When Trick got off the highway and started driving west, the cement walls disappeared but the trees became clusters of ficus, scrub pine and acres of bushy brush.

For the next thirty miles all I saw were a couple of dirt roads, miles of wire and post fencing, and thick blankets of kudzu draped over everything. Where the trees ended, huge tracts of cleared land stretched out as far as the horizon. I noticed some cows and goats grazing in a few places, but most of the land sat empty, growing nothing but weeds.

"This can't be Florida," I told my brother. "There aren't any oranges or palm trees. Are you sure we're not in Alabama?"

"Positive." Trick pointed at my window. "That's an orange grove right over there."

I looked at the thin-branched, scraggly trees, which did not resemble the photo in the guidebook. Weeds had grown up so high around the trunks that you could hardly tell that they had been planted in rows. Some of the trees looked dead. "They don't have any oranges on them."

"You can't see them yet," he told me. "This time of year, they're little and green."

"Oh." We passed another scattering of black cattle. "Why are there cows? This isn't Texas. There were supposed to be flamingoes."

"You can't milk a flamingo," Gray said from the back seat. "Or grind it into bird burgers."

"Thank you for that visual, Grayson." Trick glanced at me. "Don't worry, Cat. It'll be better in the lake country."

Trick was wrong; it didn't get better from there. It just got darker and wetter. The empty weed fields vanished under miles of thick brush surrounding chains of creeks, marshes and ponds. Forests of huge black-trunked oaks with long twisted limbs and impossibly tall, spindly-looking pines started crowding toward the road, until they marched along both sides of it. From practically every branch hung long, pale gray bunches of Spanish moss, like dirty cobwebs or stretched-out dust bunnies.

Suddenly I knew why they called it "lake country." No one would come here if they called it "swamp land."

When we finally left the road and drove through some hills and rediscovered civilization, I thought Trick had taken a wrong turn. Barely two miles wide, the town we drove through was made up almost entirely of two story wood-frame row houses jammed together and painted pastel candy colors. It looked like the kind of place fussy old ladies would love, with all the fancy white gingerbread stuff hanging from the roofs, tiny balconies surrounded by dainty scrolled wrought iron railings, and hand-painted wooden window boxes filled with bright red geraniums and purple tulips. I didn't spot a single fast-food place, clothes boutique, or discount shoe store, though.

I'd never been much of a mall rat, but even I could see this town was in a permanent shopping coma.

The houses that had been converted into little businesses each had a two-sided sign hanging from an angled bracket beside the entrance. Someone had hand-painted them with cutesy names like *Maude's Porcelain Emporium*, *Something Old Something New*, and *Johnson Junktiques*. Old stuff crowded the shop windows and sat out beside open doorways: rickety-looking spinning wheels, faded patchwork quilts, rusty dented tins and crackled china vases.

If it looked like it should have been donated to a thrift store ages ago, some place was selling it.

Most of the people walking around downtown had silver or white hair and wrinkly faces. A couple were so old they used canes and walkers as they shuffled along, their shoulders stooped and their eyes squinting against the glare of the sun. All of them had on the usual grammywear: loud Hawaiian shirts or pastel polos (the grampas) and tees with dogs, flowers or hearts made of sequins or rhinestones (the grammas). From the waist down everyone looked the same; knee-length baggy shorts, white half-calf socks and clunky sandals. Some of the ladies had on bright purple T-shirts and wore big red hats with lots of frou-frou stuff around the brim, and went from shop to shop in small groups, like girlfriends on a mission.

Why old people dressed like that, I didn't know. Maybe after a certain age they got cataracts. Or mirror phobia.

I didn't panic until Trick parked the truck on the street in front of a bright yellow and pink realtor's office. "Why are we stopping here?"

"This is it." He gestured toward the center of town, a fountain surrounded by purple azaleas and two red hat ladies with cameras. "Lost Lake."

"We can't live here." Not in the Village That Fun Forgot. "We're like *fifty* years younger than everyone else."

"This is the business district, and those people are the tourists." He nodded toward the north. "Our place is in the farming community outside town, where most of the locals live."

"Oh, yeah?" I wasn't convinced. "Just how *old* are these locals?"

Trick smiled. "You'll meet plenty of kids your age in no time."

Since then we'd been pretty busy unpacking, setting up the house and taking care of the horses. Our nearest neighbor was seven miles down the road, so I hadn't had a chance over the summer to meet any of the local kids.

To be honest, I hadn't really tried.

I wanted to make friends, but I didn't have the personality—okay, the nerve—to walk up to someone I didn't know and start talking to them. My brain had its own special on-off switch. When I was alone it stayed on, and I could think of a million clever things to say to a complete stranger. As soon as I met one? The switch flipped off, and I ended up standing there saying *Uh-huh* and *Okay* and looking as dumb as I sounded.

It was just easier to hang out with my brothers, who didn't care what I said.

Not like anyone in Lost Lake was in a hurry to be my new best friend, either. We saw people when Trick took us with him when he went into town for groceries and things, but hardly anyone spoke to us. There was only one grocery store, so there were always people shopping there, but while they stared at us, no one said hello or waved or anything. On those trips I saw four or five other farms near our place, and they had cars and trucks parked by the houses and plenty of stock in the pastures, but not one of those neighbors stopped by our place that whole summer.

Trick said the people in town were just shy, and the farmers were probably too busy with their animals or the summer planting to come visiting. I believed him, mostly. We'd lived in other towns where we'd been treated like outsiders or the locals had kept to themselves. It just seemed a little odd that no one came near our place.

Now driving through downtown with Gray on the way to our first day at school, I saw a couple of kids walking toward Tanglewood High. Their backpacks were new, but their jeans looked as old and faded as mine. The boys had uniformly short, neat haircuts, which made me glance at my brother's gilded mane before I checked out the girls. Long loose curls, poufy crowns and uneven, slanted bangs seemed to be in fashion; so did tiny barrettes, polka-dot head bands and what looked like black velvet bows.

Not one girl wore a ponytail, though. All my doubts came rushing back to me and sat like a boulder on my chest. "What if we don't like it here?"

Gray didn't say anything, but then, he hated everything.

Since we were playing Silent Jeopardy, I rephrased the question into an answer. "Okay, we've already lived here two months and we haven't met anyone else. Now what if we don't fit in at school and everyone avoids us like they have all summer and we end up…" I didn't know what to call what we'd been at every other school we'd gone to.

"Lepers?"

"No." Surely it hadn't been that bad. "I don't know. Outsiders. Loners. Friendless."

He made a turn into a parking lot filled with small pickups, compact cars and a couple of old, primer-patched heaps, and passed a group of kids hanging out behind a mud-encrusted Jeep and a gleaming metallic gold Impala. Of course they all turned to watch us park.

I hunched down a little and inspected at the dashboard. I hated the first time kids noticed us; they always stared.

Gray put the truck in park, shut off the engine, and sat there as if he didn't want to get out, either. Then he said, "Trick's tired of moving around, and I think breeding horses has always been his dream. He wants this to work."

I glanced to one side and saw the kids had walked from the parking lot across the street and into the school's main building. Sometimes, like now, I felt bad that our older brother had been stuck with raising us. He should have been off living his own life instead of playing Dad to two teenagers.

Grayson never said much, but when he did make it usually made more sense than I could with an hour of arguing.

"All right." After all Trick had done for us, I could deal with this. How bad could it be? "At least this will be the last time that we're the new kids."

My brother handed me my backpack. "Until college."

"Shut up." I slung one strap over my shoulder and climbed out.

———

The first bell rang as Gray and I walked across the street to the big double doors leading into the main building. Tanglewood looked like every other school we'd been to: green lawn strips bordering cement walkways, closed white blinds lining all of the tall, narrow stacked windows, fake rose brick mortared over gray stucco, steel doors painted a boring brown. As I reached out for the handle, both doors flung open and I had to jump back to keep from getting smacked in the face.

A short, red-faced boy ran between me and Gray, and when I turned my head I saw the backside of his jeans were dark and dripping, as if he'd peed in his pants. He darted around the corner of the building so fast he was gone before I could blink.

"Maybe they haven't opened the restrooms yet," I said to Gray.

He stared after the boy. "Maybe they have."

Inside we walked into the expected first-day chaos: kids going in a dozen different directions and teachers zigzagging around trying (and failing) to herd them along. The air smelled of old floor wax, pencil lead, disinfectant and new sneakers. No locker doors banged— they wouldn't be assigned until next week—but plenty of doors, desktops, and books did. And all around us, swamping us, was the noise. Voices pressed in on my ears in a wall-to-wall jabber of talking, laughter, yells, whispers and echoes.

Gray bumped my shoulder to get my attention. "Office is down there." He nodded toward the end of the front hall.

My brother walked in front of me, not to be obnoxious but to clear a path. The usual thing happened; everyone took one look and got out of his way. I noticed a couple of girls turning around and stopping to stare after Gray, which was not the usual thing.

It had to be the long hair. The boys I saw in the halls had the same clean-cut style I'd noticed on the kids walking to school.

A shriek and the sound of flushing water made me stop at the corner of another hall. I couldn't see much over the crowd of kids blocking it off, but I heard guys laughing and some wet, slapping sounds before the crowd parted and a boy came running at me. I stepped back against the wall and as he passed me I saw the seat of his pants were soaking wet, just like the other kid who had run out of the school.

"Where's the next noob?" a mellow, laughing voice called from inside a restroom, and I saw a couple of older boys dressed in brown and white sport jerseys file out. The kids backed away a little as the jocks went around and checked through the crowd for someone.

I didn't know what a *noob* was, but it was clear no one wanted to be one.

"Come on," the same voice said, and a boy the size of a grown man came out. His brown and white varsity jacket had the number eight and the name BOONE spelled out in block letters across the shoulders. "Bell's about to ring."

Not quite as tall as my brother, Boone had almost the same build as Gray, except he was a little leaner in the chest and arms. Everything about him said rich kid, from the gilded brown hair that fell in precise razor-cut layers over his ears down to the brand-new designer sneakers he'd already scuffed. Even the dark sunglasses he wore looked like they cost a small fortune.

He wasn't especially good-looking, but that didn't seem to matter to all the girls around him. They stared at him like he was some rock star.

"Got one here," one of the jocks yelled. He dragged by the collar a small, white-faced boy out of the shuffling crowd. "Know whatcha use a urinal for? No? Time to learn." He shoved him toward Boone.

"You're a real runt." Boone circled the younger boy like a shark. "You fall in, we might never see you again."

Some of the kids chuckled, and suddenly I could guess why the other boys' pants had been soaked. Boone and his friends were making the freshmen sit in the urinals while they flushed them.

"Aaron Boone."

A couple of kids turned away and hurried off as a frowning older woman in a bright pink suit pushed her way through to the center of the crowd.

"Aaron Boone," the teacher repeated, "what do you think you're doing here?"

"Morning, Mrs. Hopkins." Boone slung his arm around the younger boy's shoulders. "Me and some of the guys are just showing the freshmen a few things. You know, like how to use the boy's room." He looked down. "Right, kid?"

The pale boy made a strangled sound.

"Indeed." Mrs. Hopkins folded her arms. "Four students

with soaking-wet pants have come into the office in the last half-hour, asking for permission to go home and change."

"That's too bad." Boone bared his teeth. "I guess we missed them."

As the kids around the teacher choked back their laughter, Mrs. Hopkins's face turned almost as pink as her suit. "Bullying younger children is cruel and unnecessary behavior, Aaron. You and your friends could be suspended for this."

Boone took a step toward the teacher. "Has someone accused us of bullying them, ma'am?" he asked in a soft voice.

I expected Mrs. Hopkins to take the boy by the arm and march him down to the principal's office. Instead she seemed to shrivel a little, hunching her shoulders and raising one hand as if to hold him off.

She was a teacher. Why was she scared of him?

"No." The bell rang, and she cleared her throat before she spoke to the kids watching them. "Go and report to your homerooms now."

Someone behind me snickered, and Boone turned his head. I didn't realize he was staring at me until he reached up and took off his shades. His eyes weren't blue or brown but a light, cold green, like sea ice. Gazing into them gave me goose bumps, especially when he started walking toward me.

"Cat." Gray appeared next to me. "What are you ... " He stopped as he saw Boone coming at us. He stepped in front of me, and over his shoulder I saw Boone stop in his tracks. Gray stood there until the other boy retreated. "Come on." He gave me a nudge. "We're going to be late."

Three

"Everything appears to be in order," Miss Renda said as she looked through the paperwork Trick had filled out when he'd registered us at the school over the summer. She handed me then Gray a couple of papers. "These are your class schedules and a map of the campus. Freshmen have first lunch period, and sophomores have second and third."

My schedule listed all the classes I wanted—English Comp, Biology, Political Science, and Calculus—along with Ceramics and PhysEd as electives, and second period lunch. I handed it over to Gray, who was trying to read it from the side. I wondered which year Boone was in; he had looked old enough to be a senior.

"When do the juniors and seniors have lunch?" I asked.

"Most of them leave campus for lunch," she said, "or take a dinner period."

"I'm a junior," Gray pointed out, "and I'm scheduled for third lunch."

The guidance counselor frowned. "I forgot, this is your first year at Tanglewood. Half of our juniors and all of our seniors attend an evening session, the first classes of which begin after your sixth period. A few of our special-needs upperclassmen matriculate by taking classes on their home computers."

The school hadn't looked that overcrowded to me. "Why would you need to have two sessions instead of one?"

"At the moment we're experiencing a teacher shortage." Miss Renda stacked some papers before smiling at us. "Do either of you have any other questions?"

"Yeah. Can these schedules be changed?" Gray asked. "My sister and I don't have any classes in the same building, or the same lunch period."

She shook her head. "We keep siblings separated. In general it creates fewer problems."

My brother didn't like that, but the news made me pretty happy. Gray was a year ahead of me, but from middle school on we'd always had some class or lunch period together. I think he planned it that way; ever since we'd become teenagers he'd been acting as over-protective as Trick. It was nice to know that for one year I wouldn't have to worry about him hovering around.

Outside the office Gray checked his school map.

"We're not even on the same side of campus all day." He scowled at me. "You're glad."

"No way," I assured him. "I'm depressed. Seriously." I pressed the back of my hand against my forehead. "How will I ever make it through the lunch line without you?"

"Brat." He trudged off.

The map Miss Renda had given me of the five buildings on campus also showed the room numbers in each, which made it simple to find my first class, English Comp. As I joined the queue filing into the class, a girl barely five feet tall and dressed in brightly-colored, mismatched clothes tugged me out of line.

"Hi," she said, peering up at me. "Your name's Catherine, right?"

"Uh, no." I tried not to stare at the wide streaks of blazing fuchsia she'd dyed in her dark brown hair. "It's Catlyn."

"Ooo, I like that better." The girl grinned, displaying a heavy-duty set of metal braces. "I'm Barbara Riley. Everybody calls me Barb."

As if to confirm this, a couple of girls said "Hey, Barb" as they passed us, and she smiled and fluttered her fingers at them.

"I'm Cat." When I saw the amount of eyeliner she had on—a good half-inch plastered around both eyes—and the bright, mismatched patterns of her layered top and Capri pants, I realized she was a "scene" girl, one of the kids who liked to dress like a colorblind Goth. "Nice to meet you." I turned to go inside, but she caught my arm again.

"Didn't Miss Renda tell you? I'm going to be your student mentor for the first week. I get to show you around, keep you out of trouble, and introduce you to everyone."

"Better clear your schedule, new girl," a skinny boy said as he edged around us. "Barb knows everyone. When they need the names and numbers to print a new telephone book, they just call her."

Barb elbowed him smartly before she beamed at me. "You'll have to tell me your life story, of course."

"Of course." I followed Barb inside, where she led me to a seat beside her in the middle rows and asked to look at my schedule.

"We've got four classes together, that's good," she said as she handed it back to me. "I don't take Ceramics or PhysEd, but I have second lunch, too, so we can sit together. So where are you from?"

"We moved here from Chicago." I went to hang my backpack over my chair and saw Boone sitting at the desk two rows behind mine. "Does this teacher assign seats in alphabetical order?" I asked Barb.

She shook her head. "We can sit wherever we want. Ms. Newsom is on major anti-depressants so she doesn't care. It's because Mr. Newsom..." She mimed someone drinking out of a bottle.

"How do you know all that?"

"I have eyes everywhere." Her braces glittered. "Like

when I saw you earlier with that really big blond guy. Is he your boyfriend?"

That startled a laugh out of me. "No, that's my brother, Grayson. He's a junior."

"Really? You two don't look anything alike." She darted a look over her shoulder before she whispered, "Oh, my, God. Do you know that Aaron Boone is watching you?"

The hair on the back of my neck knew. "Who?"

"Aaron Boone," she repeated, leaning closer to whisper more. "Okay, he's the quarterback of our football team, and the cutest guy in school, and he hangs out with all the jocks. Every girl in Tanglewood has a dire crush on him, but he's totally unavailable." She giggled. "Did I mention he's the cutest guy in school?"

Mrs. Newsom called for everyone to settle down, which ended the conversation, but for the rest of the period I felt uneasy and had a hard time focusing on the teacher. When the bell rang, I sat and waited for Boone to leave before I got up from my seat and followed Barb out.

In between classes my new friend introduced me to practically every other kid we passed in the hall while at the same time filling me in on Boone and his friends. They were sophomores like us, but they were all football players who came from wealthy families. According to Barb, Boone's parents owned ten of the largest cattle ranches in the state, and lived in an enormous mansion in one of the exclusive gated communities outside town.

Boone's parents were famous for spoiling their son by doing outrageous things like giving him a brand-new sports car for his sixteenth birthday.

"He got held back one grade in middle school because of mono," Barb explained later as we walked into the cafeteria. "That's why he's already sixteen and can drive. He should really be a junior."

"Why do Boone and his friends pick on freshman?" I asked her later as we walked to the cafeteria.

"Everybody bullies the noobs a little," Barb said. "I guess Boone and the other jocks are pretty awful, but it's the way they are. Did you bring your lunch?" When I shook my head she steered me around the tables to the line of kids waiting for trays. "Don't ever get the meatloaf, the chili, or the casserole surprise. Mr. Jennings made us use lunchroom food last year to grow mold cultures. Those three turned green and hairy in like only one day."

"I'll start packing my lunch tomorrow," I told her as I picked out a large green salad, a bowl of fresh fruit and a bottle of cranberry-grape juice.

"I wish I could eat healthy." She sighed and looked down at her tray, which she had loaded up with pizza, nachos, and sugar cookies. "Maybe when they invent diet pepperoni."

We sat down at one of the empty tables, which was round shaped and had built-in seats attached. While we ate, some of Barb's other friends stopped by to say hi to her, but none of them sat with us. Barb didn't seem to mind being marooned with me, and while we ate she pointed out several kids from our classes while she told me who was dating who, who had broken up with who, and who was on the rebound. I paid attention to the names but not the gossip; it was basically the same thing at every school.

"Anyone sitting here?" A thin, dark-skinned boy in an oversize green T-shirt advertising a lawn service and worn black work trousers dropped his tray next to mine. He had a PB&J sandwich and a small carton of milk. "Besides me?"

Barb sighed. "Ego."

"No one else is going to sit with her." The boy tore open his milk carton and chugged it.

"Cat, this extremely rude person was my friend, Diego Valasca. Ego, for obvious reasons." Barb threw the rolled-up paper from her straw at him. "It's Cat's first day here. Be nice."

"I am being nice," Ego told her. He peeled a slice of cheese off the outside of his sandwich. "Why do they stick processed cheese on PB&J? It's not nutritional, it's disgusting." To me, he said, "So what's Cat short for?"

Now I sighed. "Catlyn."

"Where do you live?" When I told him, he began to fire questions at me. "That's a big farm. You don't look like a farmer's daughter. Are your parents farmers? Do they make you work the fields? What crops are they planting?"

I held back a laugh. "You ask a lot of questions."

"Oh, he's just getting started." Barb rested her forehead against her hand. "Why couldn't we be scheduled for third lunch?"

"Because her brother has it," Ego told her before he grinned at me. "He's in my Trig class. Big blond guy. Doesn't look like you, Cat. Weird name, Grayson." He checked the big chunky watch on his thin wrist. "Gotta go." He stuffed half the sandwich in his mouth, put the other half in his shirt pocket and picked up his empty tray. Through the PB&J he said a muffled, "See you around" and took off.

"Ego's harmless," Barb assured me. "He's really nice, and super smart, too, but he has issues."

I knew the lunch he had was the one they gave to kids who were on the free lunch program. "Why is he dressed like that?"

"He's on a work program, you know, you go to a real job half the day and they give you vo-tech credit for it." She brushed some crumbs from the front of her blouse. "His parents were pickers who came here to work in the groves when he was little. When they moved on to the next job, they left him behind." She scrunched up her face. "Never came back for him."

"Wow."

"Yeah." Barb sighed. "He has nice foster parents, but being dumped by his real folks, well, it's a lot to deal with. I told him he should talk to this therapist I see sometimes, but he got very huffy about it. Oh, and I'll warn you now: Ego likes to play practical jokes. He hasn't gotten caught yet, but one of these days . . ." she trailed off as a group of girls in brown and white cheerleader uniforms surrounded us. One of them, a petite redhead with big blue eyes and a sulky expression, glared down at Barb.

"This is *our* table," the cheerleader told her. "Move it somewhere else."

Barb instantly got to her feet and grabbed her tray. I was tempted to stay where I was—there were plenty of other open tables around us—but I decided it wasn't worth the trouble. The cheerleaders wouldn't step out of the way, so I had to elbow my way through them. Then something caught my right ankle and made me stumble. I managed to hang onto my tray, but the half-finished bottle of juice on it tipped over and splashed all over the redheaded girl's immaculate white uniform top.

Time seemed to stop for a second as we all froze in place. Then the cheerleader shrieked, and every kid in the cafeteria stopped talking and turned around to look at us.

"Oh, no." I grabbed the bottle, but most of it was already spreading into a huge purple stain down the front of her uniform. "It's all over you. Here." I tried to hand her some of the paper napkins I hadn't used, but she shoved my hand away. "I'm so sorry—"

"You've ruined it, you idiot." She pushed me back. "Get away from me."

I retreated, blindly following Barb to the tray drop-off. Everyone stared at me. When I looked back at the cheerleaders they stood huddled around the girl I'd doused.

"I tripped," I told Barb as she hurried me out of the cafeteria. "It was an accident."

"I know it was." She gave me a sympathetic look. "It'll be okay. She'll probably forget about it after she calms down. In a few months. Or years."

I understood why everyone had stared at us, but the silence didn't make sense. When something like that happened, kids usually laughed. "Who is she?"

"Tiffany Beck. Head of the cheerleading squad, and the most popular girl in school." Barb tried to smile. "She's the reason Aaron Boone is totally unavailable. They've been going steady since fifth grade."

———

After that I didn't think my first day at Tanglewood could get any worse. I'd attracted the attention of a bully and dumped juice all over his girlfriend. For the rest of the day every kid I passed gawked at me, and everyone in my classes whispered around me. At least Barb kept talking to me, but she stopped calling people over to meet me in the halls. I'd obviously made a major mistake.

I couldn't wait to get out of school, which was why after my last class I practically ran to meet Gray at his truck. But when I turned around the corner of the hall, I almost walked into Aaron Boone.

I looked up from the brown and white jacket to his

face and tried to go around him, but he stepped in front of me. "Excuse me."

He didn't move. "What's your name?"

Tiffany must have told him what had happened in the cafeteria. I went the other way, but he blocked me again. "I really need to go."

His upper lip curled. "Want me to show you where the girl's room is?"

I thought of what he and his friends had done to the freshman and shuddered. "No, thanks." I wrapped my arms around my books a little tighter and tried to think of what to say. "My brother's waiting for me." I hoped.

"Let him wait." He moved closer, and his sneer softened into a smile. "Relax. I only want to talk to you."

"Catlyn." Gray appeared out of nowhere and stepped up to Boone. His eyes never left Boone's as he said to me, "Go and get in the truck."

Boone's expression turned sulky. "I'm just having a little private conversation with your sister."

"No." My brother's hands tightened into fists. "You're not. Cat."

"I'm going." I hurried off toward the parking lot, looking back every couple of steps. My brother and Boone just stood there, staring at each other like a couple of cavemen.

I waited by the truck for five minutes before Gray came out of the school. He didn't say anything when he walked over and unlocked my door for me. "What happened?"

"Nothing. He won't bother you anymore." He went around and got in behind the wheel.

"What did you do?" I knew from past experience just how over-protective my brother could be. "Did you threaten him? Did you get into a fight with him?"

"Forget about it."

I checked his knuckles and his face, but I didn't see any bruises or cuts. Whenever Gray had defended me at school in the past I never saw what he did, and afterward he refused to talk about it. Whatever happened, whoever had been picking on me never tried it again.

Even if Gray's intimidation tactics worked this time with Boone, there was still Tiffany Beck, and Barb's prediction: *She'll probably forget about it after she calms down. In a few months. Or years.*

It wouldn't have been so bad if we'd be moving away by Christmas or next summer. But thanks to Trick, we were staying put and settling down in Lost Lake. I'd be going to Tanglewood until I graduated. And I'd just embarrassed the most popular girl in school in front of her friends and half the students in our grade.

Yep. I was doomed.

———

Trick was sleeping when we got home from school. After Gray dropped his stuff in the house he said he was going for a ride and went out to the barn to saddle Flash. That left me alone to do my homework and start getting stuff ready for dinner, which was fine by me. When Trick got up he was going to ask me about school, and I needed time to think up some convincing lies.

It hadn't been that bad, I thought as I filled out the endless stack of forms Trick would have to sign later. All my teachers had seemed okay. Barb had been nice to me, and in his own way so had Ego. Cheerleaders had to have more than one uniform, and it wasn't like I was going to hang out with Tiffany Beck or her posse. Hopefully Gray had scared off Boone for good.

I hadn't gotten one of my bad headaches, the kind that made me so dizzy and tired that I had to go to bed. And I knew the knot in my stomach would go away. By Christmas.

I decided to make Italian for dinner, and was searching through the freezer for some ground beef when Trick got up. He still looked tired but his voice sounded better, and he didn't grill me too much about school. Still, he knew something was wrong. Trick always did.

"You want to tell me about it?" he asked as he watched me chop onions for the sauce.

"I just did." I dumped the onions in with the ground beef. "It's a good school. I like my teachers. My student mentor is great." I glanced at him. "All right. The truth is I skipped school, shoplifted cigarettes, met a cute married man and now I think I'm pregnant. Happy?"

"If he's getting a divorce. Smoking's bad for the baby." He got up, came over and kissed the top of my head. "If you ever do need to talk about anything, I'm here."

"I know." That was something he didn't have to say, but the reminder was nice.

He finally went out to the barn to shovel out the stalls and fill the feed buckets, which gave me time to finish making the sauce and put it on to simmer. I took an early shower, folded the laundry and had the table set by the time my brothers came back to the house.

I had learned to cook by getting some easy cookbooks from the library, and watching some shows on television, but my cooking was only average. Lucky for me Trick and Gray weren't picky, and they always cleared the table and did the dishes for me. I tried to read for a while that evening, but I kept seeing my juice splashing all over Tiffany's uniform, and the shock and hatred on her face as she shouted at me. Whatever happened because of this, I wasn't drinking anything at lunch but water for the rest of the school year.

Because we had to get up at dawn to take care of the horses, we all went to bed pretty early. I said good-night to Trick and Gray at ten, and spent the next hour staring at the ceiling before I gave up on sleep. I changed out of my nightshirt and shorts into my riding clothes, tiptoed down the stairs, and stuck my head out into the hallway. Trick's bedroom door was shut, so he'd gone back to bed. Nothing short of a train wreck outside his door would wake up Grayson.

I slipped out of the house through the back porch door and walked to the barn. I wasn't supposed to go riding at night. I could repeat word-for-word the lectures Trick gave me about it, too: *It's too dark out here in the country. You can't see where you're going. If the wildlife don't come after you, Sali could step in a hole you don't see, throw you and then you'd be in a bad way. We wouldn't know you were missing until morning.*

I never argued, but I didn't agree with him. Technically I had never promised him that I *wouldn't* go out at night on Sali. Besides, when I couldn't sleep, riding was the only thing that tired me out. Trick didn't know it, but I had great night vision and could see everything ahead of me, even on new moon nights. Sali was steady as a rock; nothing spooked her, even the things that should have like snakes or sudden sharp noises. As for the wildlife, I'd never run into anything bigger than a stray cat or a possum.

The only time I ever felt right with the world was at night, riding my horse under the stars.

As soon as I went into the barn Sali put her head over her stall door and whickered to me. The color of bittersweet chocolate with a big white blaze on her nose, she was darkly gorgeous, and she knew it. She also knew I only came out this late when I wanted to sneak out with her, and I think she liked it as much as I did. Jupiter came to his door, too, but when the big white stallion saw it was me he snorted and stomped a little. Some people thought horses were too dim-witted to understand human beings, but not me. I suspected Jupe always knew exactly what I was up to and, like Trick, he didn't approve.

Flash ignored all of us to sulk in the corner of his stall. He was so much like Gray sometimes it was spooky.

I strapped my bareback riding pad on Sali before I bridled her and led her out of her stall. I didn't use a saddle or stirrups when I rode at night, mainly because riding bareback added to the sense of complete freedom—but also because in the morning Trick might notice that the underside of my saddle was damp (the pad I could hide). I looped the reins over her head, stepped onto the mounting crate and boosted myself onto her back.

At eighteen hands high Sali was a big mare, but I was no shrimp, so we fit each other. I kept her to a slow walk as we rode out of the barn and out into the back pasture before I eased up on the reins and let her quicken to a lope. Trick had bought Sali for me because she had a smooth, gliding gait, and her breed was famous for being gentle and comfortable to ride (all desirable traits for the eleven-year-old I was when I got her). I loved to ride Sali because her running walk was faster than most horses' canter, and she had incredible stamina; she never seemed to get tired.

The nights had grown a little cooler since July, and layers of thin mist hovered over the open pastureland and swirled around the nubby dark trunks of the bordering trees. Some of the black oaks on our land were over a hundred years old, Trick had told me, and had survived tornadoes, hurricanes and countless wildfires. He thought they were beautiful, but I liked the maples and the ficus trees better. They didn't remind me of nightmares I could barely remember, or bad Halloween movies I couldn't forget.

Along with the house our farm included a hundred and forty acres. About half of it had been cleared sometime in the past for use as pasture and planting, and the rest were woods and groves that formed a natural boundary area between our land and the closest neighboring parcel. The other property, about three times the size of ours, was mostly woods and wetlands (another polite name for swamp). The realtor in town had told Trick that no one had lived on it for years, which made me wonder why someone had posted so many *No Trespassing* signs along the outer tree line.

Once we were far enough away from the house, I leaned forward, urged Sali into a full gallop, and let her race into the back forty. Her hooves ate up the ground and flung clods of dirt and grass into the air behind us. The coarse black hair of her long mane whipped against my cheeks, but I didn't care. With the mist parting around us and the stars glittering just above the black billowy shapes of the oak canopy, I felt like we were flying instead of riding.

I felt the other rider before I saw or heard him, to the left of me, coming up as fast as Sali and I were galloping. I spotted a gap in the trees a hundred yards ahead, where

Trick had installed the new barbed wire and post fencing he'd been working on all summer.

The other rider was heading straight for it.

I reined in Sali, but she didn't have brakes like a car and we broke into the clearing just as I saw a big black blur burst out of the pines. The stallion must have seen the fence at the last moment, but he wasn't a jumper, because he swerved away instead of trying to clear it. As I caught my breath the huge black reared and bucked off his rider, who landed on the fence and collapsed it.

"Hold on," I called, and urged Sali over to the fence. I swung over and jumped down, looping her reins over the post before I ran over to the fallen rider, who was struggling inside a tangle of wire and splintered wood. "Are you okay?"

He lifted his head, and his long black hair fell away from a pale, angry face. "I will be fine." He grabbed at the wire wrapped across his chest, and then hissed and pulled his hand back. "Go back where you came from, girl."

"I live here," I told him, and crouched down to start untangling him. "Hold still or you'll just make it worse. Did you hit your head on anything? Does anything hurt when you move?"

"Stop." He took in a sharp breath. "I can do this myself. You may go."

I may go? Was he kidding?

He looked to be about my age, maybe a little older,

but it was obvious he wasn't getting out of this without help. So I ignored him as I tugged and pulled and worked each length of wire free. Trick had special-ordered the fencing, which was studded every couple of inches with clusters of long, sharp iron spikes. I tried to be careful, but by the time I freed the last length from the boy's legs both of my hands and forearms were cut and bleeding in several places.

Other than rips and tears in his clothes, and some thin slashes in his skin from the barbs, I didn't see anything wrong with his arms and legs. That didn't mean anything.

"Does your head hurt? What about your back?" He started to get up and without thinking I put an arm around him. "Take it slow. You might have broken something."

When he got to his feet he was a head taller than me, and had a long, lean form with broad shoulders and streamlined muscles that made me think of Olympic swimmers and speed skaters. Dark stains mottled the long sleeves of his white shirt, and he was covered in grass and dirt, but he didn't stagger or fall again. In fact, he stood so still all I saw move were his eyes as he looked around.

"The last time I rode here there was no fence." He regarded me. "Is this your doing?"

The way he was talking made me blink. I'd only heard people speak like that in movies. But maybe he was from another country, or English wasn't his first language. "My brother put it up this summer. You *are* on private property, you know."

"Am I." He didn't seem worried about it as he inhaled slowly. "You've been injured."

"It's only a couple of cuts from the wire." I looked up and saw his face clearly for the first time. His skin looked like moonlight, he was so pale, and his eyes were the color of marcasite, the darkest shade of silver. He had long, dead-straight black hair that gleamed with tiny blue and purple lights, and spilled over his shoulders as if it were liquid. Add to that the fact that he had the most beautiful face I'd ever seen on a boy.

The anger faded from his expression. "Are you in pain?"

"I'll be okay." No, I wouldn't. Not in this lifetime.

He took my arm from around him and held my wrist up so he could look at my hand. "You're bleeding." He took a cloth handkerchief from his pocket, folded it and pressed it against my cuts. He wasn't looking at my hands or my face now, but stared over my head. "Thank you for your help."

Maybe the sight of blood made him feel sick.

"You're welcome." I heard a buzz in my ears and felt dizzy, and had to brace myself with my other hand against his chest. I hadn't realized my heart was pounding so fast, and then I felt his heartbeat under my palm, thumping as fast and as hard as mine. I moved my fingers until I touched his skin through a tear in his shirt, where I felt something cool and wet mingle with the blood from my cut hand.

That was when I realized how good he smelled. Like spices and herbs simmering in honey.

My skin felt tight and hot, as if it were shrinking, and my face practically blazed. I was behaving like an idiot, and probably bleeding all over his shirt, but I didn't care. I focused on the feel of his heart, and listened to my own.

The beats slowed, grew heavier, and then melded together, until there was no difference in the rhythm. His heart was beating with mine, exactly in sync.

"We can ride back to my house." The way my head was whirling made it hard to speak. "My brother can call for some help. I think I'm going to faint."

"I have you." He put his arm around me. "Tell me your name."

"Catlyn."

He repeated it but he made it sound wonderful, like it was something besides my name, and then covered my hand with his. His fingers felt deliciously cool against my fiery skin. "You are so warm. Do you feel that, Catlyn?"

All I could manage was a nod before the night started crowding in on me. Then I was falling, and he moved, so fast, lifting me off my feet and up into his arms.

I wanted to tell him I'd be okay, that I just needed a minute to rest and get my head straight, but the world dwindled away and stars filled my eyes. I should have been frightened, and on some level why I wasn't confused me. All I knew was a sense of feeling safe and protected, the way I did when I curled up under a warm, soft quilt on a bleak, stormy night.

The last thing I remembered was the rider carrying me. Not to Sali, and not toward home, but into the shadows.

Four

A crick in my neck and the sound of biting and chewing woke me from a dead-to-the-world sleep, but when I opened my eyes I discovered that I wasn't in my pajamas, my bed or my house. I'd been sleeping sitting up, propped against the trunk of a big black oak. I hadn't gone back to the barn, hadn't hidden my bareback pad, hadn't rewarded Sali with an apple cookie.

I was still outside.

I lifted my head from where it had been drooping to one side (which explained the neck crick) and saw Sali tethered to a low-hanging branch a few yards away. "Sal? What am I doing here?"

She lifted her head, snorted, and went back to cropping grass.

A couple of stars still twinkled in the dark sky over

my head, but a widening ribbon of purple rising over the tops of the trees promised the sun was on its way. It was almost dawn. I'd spent the whole night out here.

I'd never been thrown from a horse, ever. Still, my first thought was that Trick's warnings about night riding had finally come true, and Sali had gotten spooked and dumped me. Once I'd carefully moved my arms, legs and neck to make sure none of them were broken, I looked out at the fence where the dark boy had fallen.

Dark boy. It sounded silly, but I didn't know what else to call him. He hadn't told me his name.

The fence was not smashed to pieces, but completely intact, as if last night had never happened. When I checked my hand the cuts I'd gotten from untangling the dark boy from the barbwire, they had likewise disappeared. I didn't even have a bump on my head.

But if the whole thing had been a nightmare or a concussion, who had tethered Sali to the oak tree?

I stood for a minute to see if I was going to pass out. I felt a little light-headed, and dew had left my clothes uncomfortably damp, but nothing else seemed wrong. As I walked to Sali she lifted her head again and watched me, her big dark eyes as calm as ever. I ran my hands over her to check for any injuries or signs that she'd taken a spill, but she didn't have a scratch on her. She nuzzled my palm and bumped my chin with her nose when she didn't find a cookie. For Sali, it was way past cookie time.

"Who tied you up, girl? Was it him?" What was his name? Not knowing it made me feel a little nervous. He could be anyone, live anywhere, and I wouldn't know until I saw him. He could even be our next-door neighbor. And why did thinking about him make me feel so jumpy?

Once I felt sure Sali was all right, I left her and walked over to the section of fence where the dark boy had been bucked off his mount. At first glance it seemed fine, but on closer inspection I saw three of the cross ties had been replaced with less weathered boards, and the wire had been tacked into place with carpenter's nails instead of the heavy-duty staples my brother used. Someone had gone to a great deal of trouble to repair the fence but make it look as if nothing had happened.

Again, why?

I glanced down to see if I could find any broken bits of wood, blood, or anything more to confirm what I remembered, and saw a cool sparkle in the grass by my left foot. When I bent down to pick it up, it turned out to be an old silver man's ring with a broad band and a scroll-edged oval filled set tiny, flat red and black stones. The darker stones had been set in the silver to form the shape of a flying black bird. It felt heavier than my dad's broad gold wedding ring that Trick sometimes wore. That was the only jewelry my oldest brother owned besides one small gold earring; Gray didn't like wearing anything, not even a watch.

I closed my fingers over the ring, squeezing it in my palm as a peculiar, hot sensation unfolded in my chest and crawled up my neck to boil over onto my face. I'd put my hand against the dark boy's chest, and our hearts had beat in time. He'd caught me when I'd fainted and swept me up in his arms, and then... I didn't remember anything else.

It *had* to be his ring. More importantly, it proved that I hadn't dreamt a thing.

A shaft of sunlight streamed through the trees, making the black stones glitter. My anxious flush cooled and my head finally cleared. It was near dawn. The sun would be up in a few minutes.

So would my brother Trick.

Sali didn't want to stop munching on the pasture grass, but once I untied her and mounted I promised her two cookies, which persuaded her to get moving. As we rode back to the barn I thought of every explanation I could give Trick as to why I was up so early. Inventing a story was not an option; my brother could always tell when I was lying. Explaining how I'd helped the dark boy also meant admitting to sneaking out of the house and riding alone in the dark; two things that would get me grounded until Christmas, maybe Easter. No, I'd have to be very careful about what I said, and pretend the silver ring sitting in the bottom of my hip pocket wasn't there.

I took care of Sali, rubbing her down and watering her before I tried to sneak back into the house. I thought I had made it when I slipped into the empty kitchen and started toward the stairs, only to be stopped in my tracks by Trick's voice.

"What are you doing up this early?"

Although the hall was dark, I put on my grumpy morning face before I turned around. "I took Sali for a ride." I had to change the subject before he asked me when. "What's for breakfast?"

"Oatmeal." Trick looked a little guilty. "I know, you hate it, but we're out of everything else. After looking at those mares yesterday I was too tired to run into town. I'll get some more groceries this afternoon after I pick up my order from the feed store."

Normally I'd make a fuss about the oatmeal, but my heart just wasn't in it this time. "It's okay." Then, just so he wouldn't become suspicious, I added, "If I choke to death on it, say nice things about me at the funeral."

I went upstairs to my bedroom, and to keep up appearances I let the door slam just a little. Then I waited and listened, but all Trick did was go down the hall to knock on Grayson's door and tell him to get up.

I washed up and changed as fast as I could before I went to join my brothers for breakfast. Gray ate his oatmeal without complaint, but I made a few faces as I picked out all the disgusting raisins. I hated oatmeal, but I'd happily eat ten pounds of it ice-cold than swallow a single wrinkled grape. The only thing worse than raisins were prunes.

Trick drank his coffee and read the paper. *Everything was going to be fine*, I thought, and then Gray's voice made me jump when he said, "I want to try out for the football team."

Gray had been born without a sense of humor, so

I knew he wasn't joking. "Seriously?" Because we had moved around so much, neither of us had ever joined clubs or tried out for anything. "You? Football?"

Trick looked over the top of his paper and asked my third question for me. "Why?"

"I want to," Gray told his empty bowl. "You said we were staying here."

Our older brother put down his paper. "What brought this on?"

In typical Gray fashion, he only shrugged.

Although Trick and I occasionally watched NFL games on TV, and we always had a little Superbowl party every year, we weren't really football fans. I couldn't imagine my brother in a uniform running around a football field. He'd hated group activities ever since he'd started getting really big, back at the beginning of middle school. He wouldn't even pose for class pictures.

"Don't they have a size limit or something?" I asked, and got a blue-eyed glare in return. "Come on, Grim, be realistic. The first time you make a tackle, you'll probably turn the guy into a crunchy pancake."

"Catlyn." Trick gave me the *shut up* look. To Gray, he said, "You've never shown any interest in football."

"I've watched some games." He took his bowl over to the sink and came back to stand by the table. "I know how to play it."

I remembered some football players in a class at my last school grumbling about having to spend most of July going to practice. "Didn't they already hold tryouts over the summer?"

Gray shook his head. "The county cut back their funding. All the smaller schools around here are starting later and playing shorter schedules." He glanced at Trick. "It's just tryouts. I might not even make the team."

I almost swallowed a raisin. "Right." When he wanted to, Gray could run down a horse, lift a hundred-pound sack of feed with one arm, and beat both me and Trick at darts, horseshoes and hoops. I noticed how my brothers were looking at each other, as if I weren't even at the table. "If you do make it, I'm not going out for cheer-leaders. They already"—I couldn't say *hate me*—"have enough of them."

"You have no experience playing team sports, and I need you to help me with the new horses when I buy them," Trick said finally. "I'm sorry, Grayson. Maybe you can try out for a college team."

"Yeah." My brother's chair screeched across the lino-leum as he shoved it back and got up to stomp out of the kitchen.

I didn't understand why Gray wanted to play foot-ball, but I felt sorry for him. "Trick, couldn't you just let him try out, this once?"

"I could," he said. "I think it would just be a replay of what happened to him in fourth grade."

Gray doesn't play well with others, his teacher had once written in the margin of his report card next to the "U" for his unsatisfactory behavior. He'd earned it because of what he'd done to three older boys who had jumped him during recess. According to every other kid in Gray's class, he hadn't hit anyone, but had flicked them off like gnats. One boy had fallen on his arm and sprained his wrist; another had broken his nose when he hit a chain link fence face first. I still remembered how angry Trick had been when he'd come to school to have a conference with that teacher.

"Gray's older now," I reminded him. "I know he'd be more careful." I heard the sound of a car pulling up the drive out front and frowned. "Are you expecting someone?"

"No." Trick got up and went to the front room.

I followed him, and through the front windows saw a black-and-white patrol car marked with a stylized logo that read *Lake County Sheriff*. The big, dark-haired man who climbed out of the car was wearing a khaki uniform with a shiny gold badge on the breast pocket.

Oh, no. I knew he was here for me. The boy I'd met last night must have told his parents about getting bucked off into our fence, and they'd called the police, and now I was going to be arrested because I'd ... helped him? Passed out? Spent half the night under a tree?

The bulge in my pocket suddenly felt as big and heavy as a brick. *Stolen his ring?*

"Morning," our visitor said as he came around the car and stood between it and the front porch. "I'm Jim Yamah, the local sheriff." The mirrored sunglasses he wore gave him a menacing look, aided and abetted by his thick mustache and broad, heavy build. He didn't smile or offer Trick his hand but inspected us in a distinctly unfriendly fashion, as if he'd found us at the scene of a crime we'd just committed. "You'd be the man of the house?"

Trick didn't step off the porch. "Patrick Youngblood." He rested a hand on my shoulder. "This is my sister, Catlyn." As Gray came out of the house, he added, "My brother, Grayson."

"Just the three of you, then?" Yamah asked.

"Yes." I felt Trick's fingers flex against my shoulder before he took away his hand. "Is there a problem, Sheriff?"

"I received a report of an incident out here last night." The mirrored sunglasses turned to Gray. "You boys get into a tussle with anyone? Maybe someone you caught trespassing?"

As my brother told him no, I bit the inside of my cheek. No one had seen me out riding except the dark boy, I was sure of it. But if his parents had caught him sneaking back into his house, and saw his torn and bloodied clothes, they'd have wanted some answers.

Had he told them about me?

"How about your horses?" The sheriff turned and nodded toward the barn. "Any of them wander off last night?"

He didn't know what had really happened, I realized. He was fishing for details, and glaring at my brothers as if he suspected they'd caught the dark boy on our property, and had worked him over or something.

"We had a quiet, uneventful night, and none of our horses have gone missing," Trick said calmly. "You want to tell me what this is about, Sheriff?"

Instead of answering his question, Yamah changed the subject. "I expect you don't know about the curfew." He hooked his thumb in his belt. "Minors are required to stay at home indoors from eleven p.m. to five a.m. No exceptions."

"Our realtor mentioned it," Trick said. "But my brother and sister were here all night, and we didn't have any visitors at all."

"Just so you know," Yamah said, looking at me for the first time, "any minor caught out after curfew is given a week of community service under my direct supervision. There's always plenty of trash on the roadways and around the lake that needs cleaning up."

The prospect of spending seven days being watched by Sheriff Yamah's spooky sunglasses while picking up garbage around town erased any lingering guilt I felt. No way was I saying a word in front of him about my curfew-violating midnight ride, or the boy.

"You don't have to concern yourself with my brother or sister," Trick told the sheriff. "They're good kids."

As much as I resented being called a kid, and as little as I deserved the praise at the moment, I put on my angelic face. It usually worked on everyone, but it didn't seem to impress Jim Yamah.

"Whatever you say, Youngblood." He smiled at me, his teeth very white against his tanned skin, and I thought of a shark getting ready to bite something dangling in unsafe waters. "You youngsters had better get going now, or you'll be late for school." With that he got back into his car, and after giving us all one last, long stare, drove off.

"Were you out last night wandering the woods again?" Trick asked Gray.

"No. I was asleep." My brother went back inside, and this time he slammed the door.

I heard Trick mutter some words I wasn't allowed to use under his breath, and knew this was the moment I should confess. In fact, I should have told Trick the truth when I'd come in this morning. This whole thing was my fault.

As I thought of how to tell him, I stuck my hand in my pocket, and felt the ring, cool and smooth against my fingertips.

Do you feel that, Catlyn?

I couldn't tell him, not now. I'd never kept secrets from my brothers, but I still didn't know exactly what had happened to me last night. Until I found the dark boy and talked to him about it, not knowing all the details might get me into more trouble than keeping quiet. I knew it was wrong, but I'd think up a suitable punishment for myself, like doing all the dishes or eating oatmeal for the rest of the week.

Trick put his arm around my shoulders. "Don't worry about it, Cat. You know in small towns like this they always go after outsiders first."

"Yeah, I guess." He thought I was scared because I *hadn't* done anything wrong.

I'd have to eat a lot more oatmeal before I felt better about myself. Maybe even with raisins.

———

The next week at school was better than my first day, thanks to Barb, who stuck by me every day and treated me as if I were her new best friend. When we went to lunch, she picked a table as far away from the cheerleaders as we could sit and still be inside the cafeteria, which also helped. Her friends all still kept their distance, but by the middle of the week she had coaxed some other kids, mostly freshman, to sit with us.

I should have tried to be friendlier, but I had a lot on my mind. At home Trick and Gray were barely speaking to each other, thanks to my own silence. Then there was the dark boy, who I just couldn't find.

I spent every moment I could hunting around the school for him, first in all of my classes, and then checking out the faces of the kids who passed me in the halls. I never spotted him once, and by Friday I was beginning to wonder if he was somehow avoiding me.

"Who are you looking for?" Barb asked as she caught me inspecting the kids sitting at the tables near ours in the cafeteria. "Aaron Boone? He goes off campus with the other jocks for lunch, you know."

"No." Hearing that name killed my appetite, and I

looked over at Ego, who had already wolfed down his lunch. "You want my apple?"

He grinned, flashing his chipped tooth. "Only if you don't want to see me fish it out of the trash can after you throw it away."

I handed it over while Barb complained about how unfair it was that underclassman weren't allowed to leave campus during lunch period. I wouldn't tell Barb, but I was glad the jocks shunned the cafeteria. Every other time I saw Boone I caught him watching me. I also noticed him following me and Barb a few times in between classes. When Barb saw him and said "Hi, Aaron" he just smiled at us, and once when she got the giggles he rolled his eyes at me. My mentor made it clear that she thought he was the cutest boy in school, but I didn't like or trust him.

Then there was Tiffany Beck, my other stalker.

Boone's girlfriend and I only had one class together, in which the teacher made us sit in alphabetical order, so she was in the second row while I sat in the very back. The first time I walked by her seat in class, she tried to trip me (which was also the last time I walked by her seat). If the teacher called on me and I answered, she'd whisper something rude and all the girls around her would crack up. When we passed each other in the halls, she'd do something with her face: glare, scowl, or smirk. If I didn't get out of her way, she made a point to swerve into me to step on my foot or bang her shoulder into mine.

Tiffany seemed to be a pro at how to harass someone without getting caught, and I knew better than to
react to it. Complaining about her bullying would only
make things worse, too, so I put up with it in silence.
All I could hope was that eventually she'd get bored and
move on to torment someone else.

"Cat?" Barb's hand waved in front of my eyes. "Are
you awake? I said, who are you looking for?"

"Uh, just a guy." I hadn't told her anything yet about
the dark boy; Barb was a nice girl but a dedicated gossip,
and I didn't want her spreading any rumors about him
and me that Gray might overhear. At the same time she
did seem to know everyone at the school, judging by how
many kids she talked to on a daily basis, and I wasn't getting anywhere finding him on my own. "I saw him out
riding the other day."

"Someone from school?"

"I think so," I said, trying to sound casual. "I don't
know his name, but he's about our age, with dark hair
and eyes."

"It was probably me," Ego said. "Don't look so surprised. I go riding all the time."

"Yeah, on your bike." To me she said, "You mean
someone riding a horse, right?" When I nodded, Barb
grinned. "I know everyone who goes here. Describe him
to me."

"Well, he's tall and slim, kind of pale, and his hair is
um, straight and dark. About down to here." I touched the

appropriate spot on my arm. "He was riding a big black stallion."

"Not counting your brother, most of the boys around here don't wear their hair long." She glanced around. "Not too many of them ride, either."

"Are you sure it was a boy and not a girl?" Ego asked. "Darla Hamilton has long brown hair, and she's been in riding competitions since sixth grade."

Barb wrinkled her nose. "That girl always smells like the inside of a barn."

I resisted the sudden urge to sniff myself. "No, I'm pretty sure it was a boy. His hair is probably black, not brown."

Barb asked me a few more questions, but I had to keep my answers vague so she wouldn't become suspicious.

"It might have been one of the pickers' kids," she said. "They don't go to regular school so they can work with their folks full-time in the groves. Some of them have long hair, too, don't they, Ego?"

He nodded. "Haircuts in town are too expensive for them."

I remembered the boy's strange accent. "Do they have access to horses?"

"Only if they steal them." Ego dropped the core of my apple into his lunch bag and crumpled it up. "Maybe that's who your mystery guy is, Cat. A horse thief."

Had he stolen the horse? Was that the real reason the sheriff had come out to the farm? Why did that possibility make me feel as if someone were hammering a three-inch nail into the side of my head?

Barb leaned close. "Are you okay?"

I needed to find him, and talk to him, so much that I was starting to make myself sick over it. Without thinking I took the ring I'd been carrying around in my pocket out and held it out to her. "He dropped this while he was riding across our property. Does it look familiar?"

"Wow." She took the ring and studied it. "No, I've never seen it before." She peered at the stones and then sat back. "You know, with this bird design, it might belong to one of the Ravens."

Was he part of a gang? "What are the Ravens?"

"Not what, silly, *who*. They're the oldest family in town." Barb tried on the ring and admired it for a moment before slipping it off. "They're descended from some circus people who came here from Europe about a hundred years ago and bought up most of the land. The circus people built the town and started a bunch of cattle ranches and horse farms. When my mom was in high school the Ravens had this huge mansion built on the island. That's where the family lives now."

I wanted to snatch the ring back from her, and I didn't know why. "What island?"

"The one that's right in the middle of Lost Lake," she said, running her fingertip over the ring's gleaming stones. "The Ravens have serious money, you know. The family still owns just about every shop in town, plus most of the ranches and farms around here. The land next to your farm belongs to them, too. I'm pretty sure they have a son, but I've never met him."

"His name is Jesse," Ego put in. "But it's not him."

Jesse Raven. Just thinking of the name made me feel better. "Why not?"

"Because the Ravens are snobs who think they're too good for this town," Ego informed me. "They wouldn't lower themselves to mix with the riffraff. You know if they want something, they make my foster dad buy it and bring it out to them when he goes to work."

"That's right, your foster parents work for them," Barb said. "I forgot."

"Yeah." Ego scowled. "They wanted me to work on the island, too, mowing the lawns and doing the landscaping, but I said no way. That place gives me the creeps." He glanced at me. "Seriously, Cat, it couldn't have been Jesse Raven. He doesn't even go to school. Marcia—my foster mom—said he takes all his classes by computer. Pretty sweet deal, if you ask me."

I tried to hide my disappointment. "Okay, so he doesn't go to Tanglewood, and he lives on an island. It still could have been him out riding."

"You don't get it, Cat," Ego said. "Jesse Raven doesn't just skip coming to school. He never leaves the island. Neither do his parents."

Five

Thinking about Jesse Raven, his rich family and how they'd marooned him on their private island preoccupied me for the rest of the day. So did wondering if he was or wasn't the dark boy, which didn't help the headache I'd gotten during lunch. By the time I met Grayson after the last bell I needed an aspirin, so as soon as I got in the truck I raided the first aid kit Trick kept in the glove box.

Gray watched me rummaging through the band-aids. "What's wrong?"

"Raisins. Quantum physics. Mint green polyester stretch pants." I found a little packet marked *pain reliever*, but all it offered were two chewable orange-flavored pills. My big bottle of extra-strength aspirin, the only medicine Trick let me take whenever I needed it, was at home in the bathroom cabinet. "Don't you have anything stronger than this baby stuff?"

"Not in the truck," my brother said, "and I meant, what's wrong with *you*?"

"That's a much longer list. If I tell you we'll be sitting here all weekend." I tore open the packet and popped the pills in my mouth. "Don't worry, it's just a teenager tension headache."

He just sat there watching the other kids walking out to their cars. "What made you tense?"

"High school, Dr. Grouch. It's the gift that keeps on giving." The orange flavoring didn't do much to cover the bitterness of the pills, and I made a face. "Would you drive by the lake on the way home? I want to see something."

Tanglewood High had been built on the outer east side of town, and I'd thought the lake was on the far west side. After Gray drove down two blocks of candy-colored shops that constituted downtown, I saw I was wrong. The business section of Lost Lake had been built on a rise which blocked the lake from view. Once my brother made a turn onto an unmarked, curving street lined with bigger, older houses I finally saw the glitter of water.

The lake was so close I could have walked from the school to the edge of the water in three minutes.

I spotted a sign that read *Public Docks* and pointed to it. "Can you park over there for minute? I want to take a closer look."

Gray eyed me. "You don't like boats, water, or fish."

"I'm not planning to sail, swim, or catch anything."
I sighed. "Someone at school told me there's an island in
the middle of the lake. Come on, I just want to see it."

My brother pulled the truck into the small empty lot
by three rickety-looking piers. "Make it fast. I've got stuff
to do."

"Be right back." I climbed out and walked around
the truck toward the first pier.

Lost Lake wasn't just big. It was huge.

At least five times as large as the town, the lake
stretched out like a scallop-edged looking glass, the far
side disappearing beyond the horizon. Although clouds
filled the sky overhead, here and there the sun shone
through and made the murky lake water look like dia-
mond-studded quicksilver.

I shaded my eyes with a hand as I looked out toward
the center of the water, where a gray and dark green
smudge lay surrounded by some kind of low-lying mist.
If that was the island, it had to be at least a mile from
shore. I saw no sign of the fabled Raven mansion, but
the mist around the island was so thick that only the very
tops of tall, leafy trees were visible. They appeared so
close together they seemed to be growing into each other.

Was he out there? Was my dark boy Jesse Raven?

"Help you, miss?"

I jumped around and saw a balding, tanned old man
in a brown uniform embroidered with *Lost Lake* above
the right pocket and the name *Ray* above the left. "No,
sir. I just came down to look at the water."

"If you want your folks to take you out on the lake, they can charter a pontoon over at Gladys's boat yard," he said, giving me a patient smile. "The old girl charges about twenty dollars an hour."

"I'm not a tourist; we moved here over the summer." I pointed toward the center of the lake. "Do you know the name of that island out there?"

"Raven Island." All the friendliness left his expression. "That's private property, miss." Without another word he walked away and disappeared behind a boat shed.

I heard Gray tap his horn twice, and glanced one more time at the island before I walked back to the truck.

As soon as I got in Gray reversed out of the lot and drove to the main road leading out of town.

"You're speeding," I pointed out. When he didn't slow down I glanced sideways and saw that he had both hands on the wheel and his jaw set. "Sure, ignore me now. When you have to explain to Trick why you need ninety bucks to pay for a speeding ticket, you'll wish you'd listened to me."

That worked.

I lifted a hand to rub my temple, only to realize my headache had vanished. "Other than most of the civilized world, something bothering you?"

His hair shook a little. That was Grayson-speak for "I can't talk about it."

My brother didn't confide in me very often, so I wasn't surprised. Normally I would try to annoy him by guessing out loud whatever was on his mind, but after meeting the dark boy I understood why Gray might want to keep some things to himself. "If you change your mind, I won't say anything to Big Brother." I drew a cross over my heart.

"Has Trick been talking to you about me?" He didn't sound especially interested.

I pretended to think. "He mentioned selling you and Flash the next time there's a stock auction." I grinned. "I told him no one can handle Flash's temper or your food bills."

All my brother did was grunt, but his grip on the steering wheel relaxed and he didn't try again to break the land speed record for pickup trucks. When we got home I found a note from Trick saying that he was going to look at a stallion for sale and wouldn't be home for dinner.

No point cooking a big meal for just the two of us, I thought as I folded over the note. I still didn't have much appetite, either.

"You want soup and sandwiches?" I asked Gray, who shrugged before he dropped his backpack and headed out to the barn. A few minutes later I glanced through the kitchen window and saw him riding Flash out toward the woods.

Gray liked to ride as much as me, but usually he did his homework before he jumped in the saddle. Something must have been seriously bothering him to put off Trig and World History. Maybe he was still sulking over the vetoed football tryouts.

I got a soda from the fridge and sat down to sort out my own schoolwork. After my first week at Tanglewood I was having no problem keeping up with my classes, although I suspected that Calculus and English Comp were both going to be a yearlong bore. One problem with switching states and schools so much was that I often repeated the same lessons over and over. According to the syllabus my English teacher had handed out, my class was going to be reading and analyzing Harper Lee's *To Kill a Mockingbird*. Which I'd already done at my last two schools. Still, I hadn't forgotten Trick's promise to let me test for my driver's license if I brought home straight A's, so it was good to know I'd ace at least one test.

I started reading over the notes I'd taken in Calculus, but the formulas and derivatives began fading away as I thought about the dark boy.

If he was this Jesse Raven, how had he gotten off that island? Where did he keep his horse? Why did he ride on our neighbor's property? Why did he ride at night?

Everything Barb and Ego had told me about the Ravens echoed in my head, answering my questions. *You know if they want something, they make my foster dad buy it and bring it out to them ... The family still owns just about every shop in town, plus most of the ranches and farms around here. The land next to your farm belongs to them, too.*

As for riding at night, I could imagine why. Maybe the only time Jesse Raven could get away from his parents was while they were sleeping. He'd run less risk of being seen by anyone, too.

I felt the bulge of the ring in my pocket and took it out to look at it again. Boys at school usually wore only their class rings. Something this old and expensive had to belong to his dad or his grandfather. If it was a family heirloom, he'd definitely want it back. So why hadn't he come to look for it? Didn't he realize he'd lost it?

I sat studying the pattern of the red and black stones for a while. I couldn't keep it, but I didn't know how to get it back to him. I couldn't exactly drop by a private island on the way home from school. If I tried to call his house his parents would likely answer the phone, and then I'd have to explain who I was, what I had, and how I'd gotten it. They'd probably ground Jesse for life. I didn't even know how to mail it to him; what could be his address? Jesse Raven, huge mansion, Raven Island?

Finally I put the ring down on top of my notebook and unfastened the chain of the St. Christopher's medal I wore around my neck. I felt embarrassed as I slid the ring onto the chain; I shouldn't be wearing it as if we were going steady or something. But as soon as I fastened the chain and slipped it under my T-shirt I felt calmer, as if the weight of it against my heart lifted some of the worry off my shoulders.

"What are you doing?"

I jumped and turned around to see Gray standing in the doorway. "Homework, obviously. Cough or something next time, will you? You almost gave me a heart attack."

He made a point of glaring at the wall clock. "It takes you forever to do homework now?"

I didn't believe him until I saw the time: six-thirty. Outside the kitchen window the sun was starting to sink behind the tops of the trees, and my back and leg muscles suddenly felt stiff, as if I hadn't moved for hours.

That was just it: I hadn't. Nor had I started my homework, made dinner, fed the horses or done any of my chores. All this time I'd just been sitting and thinking about Jesse Raven and his ring.

For three straight hours.

"I guess I got sidetracked," I said as I got up and winced. "Can you take care of the horses for me?"

"Already did." He went to the fridge and took out some cold cuts and cheese. "I'll make the sandwiches. You do the soup."

I retrieved a couple cans of soup and emptied them into a pot. My brother was being awfully forgiving. "Aren't you going to complain about how starved you are, or rag me about wasting time daydreaming?"

"I'll wait until Trick gets home." He dodged my elbow. "Or maybe someone will do my laundry tonight and I'll forget about it."

"Fine." I loved my brother, not that I'd ever admit that to his face. "Blackmailer."

He grinned. "Slacker."

———

Trick got home a few hours later, and came upstairs to say good night. "Anything happen while I was out?"

"Just the usual." Not counting the three hours I'd zoned out thinking about Jesse Raven, which I was in no hurry to discuss. "We had soup and sandwiches for dinner. I think there's some ham left if you're hungry."

"Thanks, but I grabbed a burger on the way back." He eyed the book I was reading. "*To Kill a Mockingbird*, huh? You must have that memorized by now."

"Almost," I said. "But it could be worse. It could be *Moby Dick* again. After reading that book seven times, I'm starting to cheer on the whale."

"I think I would, too." He chuckled. "'Night, Cat."

"'Night."

Skimming through three more chapters of the book didn't bore me enough to make me sleepy. Neither did burrowing under the covers and keeping my eyes shut. All I could think of was Jesse Raven and the dark boy. Maybe they were the same person, maybe they weren't. The two names began spinning in my imagination, blurring into each other: Jesse Raven, dark boy, dark boy, Jesse Raven, Jesse Raven, dark boy, dark Jesse, Raven boy—

Stop.

I tried to distract myself by listening to the familiar sounds of Trick fixing the coffeemaker, checking the locks, and shutting off the lights before he went to bed. I counted all the little creaks the old house made and the ticking of my alarm clock like sheep. Every time I moved, the rustle of the sheets seemed overloud. Then the night got so quiet that I heard the sound of my heartbeat, faint but steady, pulsing in my ears.

The dark boy's heart hadn't been faint; it had beat under my hand like a drum, or no, more like a jackhammer. Such an ordinary thing, a heartbeat, but the skin on my palm tingled as I remembered how amazing it felt.

Okay, how amazing *he* felt.

Being alone in my room made it okay to think about him; there was no one around to see me turn red. Touching him had felt like scary and thrilling and magical, like nothing I'd ever done. Not that I had a huge amount of experience with putting my hand on a boy's chest. I didn't exactly go around touching strangers. And then, when I'd toppled over and he caught me in his arms…

Like that will ever happen again. I turned onto my side and tried to find a cool spot on my pillow. *Jesse Raven lives on an island. He's seriously rich. His parents don't even let him go to school. If he is the dark boy, you'll never see him again.*

I'd *never* see him again.

I sat straight up, pushing the covers off me as I climbed out of bed. I didn't know why I had to see him again, but I didn't really care. Not knowing who or where he was felt worse than any trouble I might get into trying to find him. I had to go back to where we'd met.

There had to be something else there to help me find him.

I pulled on a pair of jeans and a T-shirt, but I felt too hot to put on a jacket. I wanted to run to the stables, but

I forced myself to slow down and make no sound as I crept downstairs. The last thing I needed was for Trick to catch me sneaking out of the house.

At the barn Sali stood quietly as I got her ready.

"I wish you had wings," I told her as I led her out of her stall. "Then you could fly me out to that island." I ran my hand down her long neck, letting her warmth and strength soothe me. "Let's go back out there. Maybe he dropped something else."

I walked Sali from the barn out to the back of it, where I jumped up on her. I'd never mounted her without using a step-up, so finding myself straddling her made me go still and look down at the ground. I didn't know how I'd done it. It was as if my legs had grown invisible springs, and I'd simply bounced up onto her.

The night air felt good against my hot face, and cooled some of the sweat on my scalp. Sali shuffled under me, and I saw that I had the reins in a white-knuckled grip.

"Sorry, girl." I eased off and patted her side. "It's not you."

I rode her along the same path I'd followed that first night, and the closer I came to the spot where I'd seen the dark boy fall, the calmer I became. I slowed Sali to a walk so I could check the ground, but I didn't see anything else he might have dropped. By the time we reached the back fence I was beginning to feel a little foolish.

"No wallet, no ID, no helpful note inscribed with his phone number." I guided her over to the fence where I dismounted and tethered her to one of the boards before I moved to the spot where I'd found the ring in the grass. Nothing else was there. "Looks like we're out of luck, girl."

Two little shadows padded over to me, flanking me as the moon reflected in their slanted eyes. One was the kitten with the soul patch; the other an older, tough-looking tabby that I'd also fed a few times who I'd nicknamed Terrible. They reached me and meowed as they tried to get their heads under my hands.

"What are you guys doing out here so late? Hunting for something interesting?" I ran my hands over their arching backs before I stood and looked around. The cats both sat down on their haunches and gazed up at me. "I think all the mice were smarter than us and went to bed."

Terrible turned his head, hissed at something and then scampered off. Soul Patch stood his ground for a minute before uttering a short yowl and following his friend.

"Go ahead, abandon me." I watched them disappear into the trees before I felt something, and turned to see a much larger shadow vault over the fence.

It was him.

My heart skipped a beat as I watched him land. He'd jumped a five-foot fence like it was a parking curb. He walked toward me, and I almost reached out to him before I caught myself. Behind him, I saw the big black he'd been riding the other night stood tethered on the opposite side of the fence.

He'd come back here, like me. It didn't seem real. I wondered if I'd just gotten an enormous compliment. Or I needed my head examined.

The moon appeared to get brighter, and painted him with its silvery-white light. I'd been so sure he wouldn't be as stunning as I remembered; no teenager I knew had flawless skin and hair like polished black silk and gleaming gemstone eyes.

But this close, I could see that he looked exactly as I remembered, just as tall and pale and perfect as before. The only difference this time was that his long black hair had been pulled away from his face. Seeing those dark marcasite eyes and the sheer beauty of his features made my throat tight. He must have been riding the stallion, and yet he didn't have a single strand of hair out of place.

Compared to him I was a hot, sweaty, rumpled mess.

"Catlyn."

"Hi." Hearing his voice made me smile. Which was silly, but it was better than giggling. "I didn't expect to see you out here again."

"I hadn't planned to return." He took a step closer. "You are well?"

"I'm okay." From what I could see, he didn't have any visible bumps or bruises on him, especially on his forearms, which I recalled the wire had been slashed in several places. "How about you? That fall you took was pretty bad."

He smiled a little. "I'm not hurt."

"Good. I was worried. I mean, I thought maybe your

folks caught you coming back, and saw how your clothes were torn up, and they'd grounded you for life or something." I waited for him to confirm or deny that, but he only watched my face. "So, is your name Jesse? I mean, are you Jesse Raven?"

"I am." He inclined his head. "How did you learn my name?"

"I didn't tell anyone about what happened," I said quickly. "I just described you to some friends at school."

"Why did you come back here, Catlyn?"

"I felt like taking a ride." He wasn't smiling anymore, and I felt anxious and annoyed at the same time. I had wanted to see him and talk to him so badly; didn't he feel the same? "This *is* our property, you know. I *am* allowed to ride on it."

"You are?" He looked skeptical. "By yourself, in the middle of the night?"

"No," I had to admit, "but I couldn't sleep, and, well, it doesn't matter. Why did you come back?"

"I lost something. You shouldn't come here again." He turned his back on me. "It's dangerous to ride in the dark."

For me, he meant, not him. "You're the one who got bucked off into a fence."

He didn't look at me. "I should go." But he didn't move, either.

"Maybe you should. There's just one thing I want to know." I walked around him to face him. "What happened after I passed out that night, Jesse?"

Six

Nothing." Jesse studied my face. "You think that I did something to you? To hurt you? I would never."

"In case you forgot"—I pointed across the pasture—"you left me over there. Unconscious. Alone. Under a tree."

"I left you only to go and retrieve what was needed to repair the damage I caused." He gestured at the fence. "When it was finished, I stayed with you for as long as I could. I could not wake you." He hesitated, and then added, "I would have taken you home, Catlyn, but I didn't think it would be wise."

"Good call." Even if he could have held me while riding—no way was he strong enough to carry me on foot all the way back to the house—he would have had to leave Sali behind. I didn't even want to think about how Trick would have reacted to finding a strange boy carrying my limp body up to the front door. "You could have tried harder to wake me up, though. What if a bear had come along and decided I'd make a great late-night snack?"

"There are no bears out here," he assured me. "Even if there were, they would not try to cross the barbed wire."

"That's another thing." I showed him my palms. "You remember how I cut my hands, getting you untangled? When I woke up that morning, the scratches were gone. And you, you were all torn up, worse than me, and now you look like it never happened. I know I didn't dream any of it because you just said you repaired the fence. So how did you fix the two of us?"

"I did nothing." He gave me a suspicious look. "I thought it was something you did."

"I saw you get thrown from your horse, I helped you out of the wire, I passed out, and I woke up under the tree. That was it. So." I spread out my hands. "Wasn't me."

"I've told you everything that I did," he assured me. "I feel as frustrated as you. I can't stop thinking about that night. That's why I rode out here tonight. I thought if I did, I'd find something that would make sense of it."

"I've been driving myself crazy, too." Now I felt guilty for snapping at him. "Did your parents catch you coming in late? Were they angry?"

"I didn't disturb them." He shrugged. "If they knew, they wouldn't be angry."

"You can't be sure. Maybe your mom found the blood on your clothes and thought you got into a fight." As he gave me a sharp look, I added, "The sheriff showed up the next morning to talk to us. He acted like he knew something about your accident, and even implied one of my brothers might have been responsible. I thought maybe your parents had sent him over."

"James Yamah came to your house." He said it oddly, as if he didn't believe me.

"I didn't say a word," I assured him. "I haven't even told my brothers. Which, by the way, makes me feel like a real jerk. I think the sheriff believes one of my brothers had found you trespassing and beat you up."

"If he thought that were true, he wouldn't have come to talk to your brothers," he told me. "He would have arrested them."

I rubbed the back of my neck. "That makes me feel so much better."

The black stallion squealed, and Jesse and I walked over to where he was tethered on the other side of the fence. Jesse calmed him by stroking his nose and murmuring to him in a strange language.

I could have stood there and listened to him play horse whisperer for the rest of the night, but there were a few more things I needed to know. "Why do you think the sheriff came out here? Did you tell anyone about that night?"

"No, but Yamah knows that I sometimes come to the mainland to ride." Jesse adjusted the black's bridle. "He doesn't trust outsiders, and he's very protective of my family and our privacy. He believes that our wealth attracts the wrong sort of attention."

Now I felt very glad I hadn't admitted anything to the sheriff. "Is that why your parents don't let you go to school? Because you're so rich?"

"I cannot attend school because of my condition." He touched his fingers to his jaw. "If I go outside during the day, my skin burns."

"So does mine," I told him. "Haven't you ever heard of sunscreen?"

"It would not help," he said. "For me, the sun is like fire. Any direct exposure to its rays would kill me in a few minutes."

"Are you serious?" I'd never heard of such a thing. "That's horrible. Isn't there some kind of medication or treatment the doctors can give you?"

"There's no cure." He looked up at the stars and then at me. "You ride by moonlight, and live in the sun. When do you sleep, Catlyn?"

He often talked the way the old poetry sounded when someone read it out loud, but I was starting to get used to it. "I don't do this all the time. Only when I feel restless."

"Are you tired now?" When I shook my head, he held out his hand. "Will you walk with me? I want to show you something."

I had my hand in his before I thought about it, and

shivered a little as I felt his cool fingers curl around mine. "I can't leave Sali alone too long. She doesn't like it."

"Neither does Prince." As Jesse said his name, the black snorted. "But we won't go far."

As we walked away from the horses, part of me stood off to one side and shrieked silently in my head: *You're alone with a boy. You're holding his hand. This doesn't happen to you. Boys don't notice you. Boys don't like you.*

That last part wasn't true, or at least, I was almost sure it wasn't. Having a boyfriend was impossible when you moved across the country every six months. Besides, Jesse wasn't my boyfriend. He was a boy I'd met twice. A boy I'd helped. Who was holding my hand, which I knew would start sweating all over his any second now.

Why couldn't I have been born beautiful and brave and boy-familiar? Or turned into a supermodel just for, say, the next fifteen minutes?

He led me along the fence line, ducking his head now and then before he stopped near some vines hanging down from a tree branch. The vines had formed a web between the oak and the fence, latching onto the ties and wire with tendrils that had curled clockwise in tight coils. It was probably a weed, I thought, until I saw the big splashes of white against the broad, heart-shaped leaves and smelled a soft, delicious perfume.

"What are these?" I touched the petals of one of the snow-white flowers with my fingertip, tracing the five-pointed star the inner folds formed.

"*Ipomoea alba,*" Jesse said.

The Latin made me chuckle. "Do you know that in English?"

"Moonflowers."

"Really. Star flower would have been a better name." I bent over to breathe in the bloom's fragrance, which smelled better than any perfume I'd ever tried. "I've never noticed these before now."

"You wouldn't. This variety only blooms after midnight." He plucked one flower from the vine and held it up beside my cheek. "I thought so."

"You thought what?"

"Your skin." He tucked the bloom in my hair. "It's almost the same color as the petals."

If anyone else had said or done such a thing I would have been stuttering with embarrassment, but Jesse made it feel natural. As if I went around every day having boys put flowers in my hair and pay me outrageous compliments. "Hmmmm. I think that makes me Snow White."

"Only if you have a wicked stepmother, small friends, and a taste for bad apples," he joked.

I was not going to babble or giggle, no matter how badly I wanted to. "So how do you know all this stuff about moonflowers?"

"My mother grows them on the island," he said. "She's a devoted gardener." His eyes shifted. "What is that?"

I followed his gaze to a bunch of dry-looking white bulbs hanging in a bunch around the top of one fence post. "Garlic. My brother believes in using organic pest control."

"Pest control?"

I nodded. "Trick always hangs bunches of them on the fences wherever we live. The horses don't like the smell, so they stay clear of the wire, and it keeps termites from infesting the wood. He hangs it all over the place."

"The wire he used for the fence is made of iron," he told me. "Why did he choose that?"

"I don't know. Maybe it was cheaper." I tried to remember what Trick had said about the fencing, but it wasn't something we'd really discussed. "I think he special-ordered it before we moved here."

"Did he." Jesse moved away from the moonflowers, from me. "You should go home now, Catlyn."

He didn't like that Trick had fenced in our property; maybe he wanted it to stay open so he could ride wherever he wanted whenever he wanted. But we had the right to protect our land and horses, and Jesse had plenty of property to use on the other side of the fence.

As I turned away to start walking back to Sali, I felt the lump of the ring under my T-shirt, and reached up to tug the chain out.

"I have something I think belongs to you." I fumbled a bit with the clasp before I released it. Once I slid the ring free, I held it out to him.

He stared at it. "You found my ring."

"You must have dropped it in the grass when you fell. I showed it to my friends at school," I added. "That's how I found out your name. They said it might belong to your family."

"You carry the protection of St. Christopher." He held up my medal, turning it over before he glanced down at me. "Are you a believer?"

"You mean, do I go to church and pray and all that?" I shook my head. "Do you?"

He didn't answer, but reached for the ring. I turned my hand over, and then somehow our fingers meshed and we were both holding it. After a few seconds I tried to let go, but I couldn't. It was as if my hand and the ring belonged to him now.

The ring grew warm between our palms as we looked at each other, and the perfume of the moonflowers grew thick as more of the flowers unfurled and opened.

His fingers tightened. "Catlyn."

"I know." I felt it, too, just as I had the first time we met. Everything about this had been accidental, unplanned, and yet I had the strangest feeling of finally arriving at something important. As if everything in my life had happened simply to bring me here so that we could meet and be together. Meeting him had turned my world upside down ... and made it right. "What is this, Jesse?"

"If I knew, I'd tell you." He sounded as confused and unsettled as I felt, and abruptly took his hand away. "It would be better if you forget about me, Catlyn. I can't come here again."

Now I felt angry. "Why not?" I knew he'd felt the same connection I did. Why wouldn't he admit it?

He didn't answer me, but walked away and vaulted over the fence. He mounted his horse with one easy, fluid movement, glanced back at me, and then rode off.

My blood pounded in my ears as I hurried over to Sali, untying the reins and swinging up onto her back. I'd never tried to jump a fence with her but I was pretty sure she could clear it. Or I could ride around to the front gate and go out that way. It would be safer for both of us. I'd have to ride fast to catch up with him, but then—

What am I doing?

I lowered the reins and closed my eyes for a moment. I felt so furious that I was shaking. I had every intention of going after him, of chasing after a boy I didn't know, a boy who didn't want to know me.

I was behaving like a lovesick idiot.

I turned Sali and rode her at a slow walk back to the barn. I'd let myself get some kind of silly secret crush on Jesse Raven; that's why I was acting so crazy. I'd always pitied girls who mooned over boys who hardly knew they were alive, and now I'd turned into one.

Well, at least he'd said that he wouldn't be back, so I'd never have to see him again. Or listen to his poetry voice, or look into his shadow eyes. Everything in my life could go back to normal. I'd forget about Jesse Raven, settle down and focus on what was really important: the farm, school, friends, having fun...

By the time we reached the barn I felt so tired I

could have fallen off Sali and slept wherever I landed. It made me awkward as I dismounted, and I pulled the pad askew, but Sali just swung her head around and gave me a mildly reproving stare.

"Sorry, girl." I got my feet under me and leaned against her for a moment. "It's okay. We'll be okay."

"Not if Trick hears about this."

I looked over Sali's back and saw Gray standing just inside the barn doors. The sight of him shocked me so much I could hardly speak. "What are you doing out here?"

"Waiting for you." He came and took the reins from me. "Come on. We have to talk."

"Talk about what?" I followed him as he led Sali back to her stall. "I'm going to bed."

He looped Sali's bridle to a stall rail and unbuckled my bareback pad. "Trick told you, no riding at night."

I grabbed the pad away from him. "No, he said it's dangerous. I agreed."

"Same thing." My brother tossed a towel at me. "Dry her back; she's sweaty."

I could bicker with him, or I could make peace. "It was just this once, okay?"

"No, it wasn't."

"How would you know?" I rubbed the towel over Sali's back. "You never get up at night."

Gray didn't say anything else until we finished with Sali and put her in her stall. Then he caught my arm before I could walk out.

"Listen," he said. "I won't tell big brother, as long as you do something for me."

"Let me guess: your laundry, forever?" I imagined myself folding his T-shirts, jeans and boxers for the rest of eternity. "I'd rather be grounded, thanks."

"I need a copy of my last physical," he said, astounding me again. "The one I took right before we moved."

"That's probably in with our school transcripts," I told him. "Get it yourself."

Gray shook his head. "He keeps our medical stuff locked in his desk."

Suddenly I understood. He didn't just want me to get his physical, he wanted me to break into our brother's desk and steal it. "You've got to be kidding."

"I need it, Cat."

"For what?" I demanded. "You've had all your shots. You're not sick. All it probably says is *surly, oversize grump in need of a haircut.*"

"I have to turn it in with some forms." His expression grew stubborn. "I'm going to try out for football."

My jaw dropped. "Trick already said you couldn't." And Gray never defied our brother. Not once in my memory.

"Yeah. The same way he said no riding after dark." For someone who was behaving like he'd been possessed by mind-controlling aliens, he seemed remarkably calm. "You should understand why."

"What?" I stared at him. "Who *are* you, and what have you done with my brother Grayson?"

93

He made an impatient sound. "We always do whatever Trick says. He wants to move, we move. He wants us to live in the country, we live there. He makes all the decisions and we just go along with it."

"That's because he's our guardian, stupid," I said. "We have to do what he says."

"I'll be seventeen in a couple of months," Gray said.

He had a point there. "Then wait another year, until you turn eighteen," I told him, "when he can't stop you and you don't have to lie to him and make me steal stuff."

"No."

I couldn't believe he was being this stubborn about, of all things, *football*. "If you do this, he's going to find out, Gray."

"I don't care."

He didn't; I could see that. I also suspected that if I didn't help him he'd make a mess of it. "All right. I'll do it. When Trick finds out he's going to ground you until you graduate, but that'll be your problem, not mine." As he grinned I held out my hand. "By the way, this makes us even. Forever. Promise."

He shook hands. "I promise."

Seven

After being rejected by Jesse Raven and caught by Gray, I expected to toss and turn until dawn. Instead I fell asleep as soon as my head touched my pillow. I also dreamed, of riding through the night down an endless stretch of dark land between armies of gigantic black oaks. This time I was chasing a shadow instead of a boy. The shadow had no shape, so I couldn't tell what it was, but it moved like nothing I'd ever seen.

When Sali and I finally caught up to it, I saw that it was flying, not running, and its wings were coal black and edged with tiny silver stars. I reached out and caught some of its feathers, only to see them dissolve into dark gray smoke that puffed out through my fingers as the shadow flew on ahead of us.

I knew I could catch it; I just had to ride faster.

Toward the end of the dream, I pulled my feet out of the stirrups and crouched, my boots somehow balanced on two flaps that had grown out of my saddle, ready to spring as soon as Sali closed the gap. She held steady, her hooves pounding in a staccato four-count beat, her sides bellowing in and out beneath me. I heard another rapid thumping sound in my ears and thought it might be my heart, rocketing out of control. Just before Sali's nose touched the edge of the shadow I jumped—

—and landed on my bedroom floor, yelping as my hands and knees smacked into the wooden panels. The wild tangle of my hair blinded me for a minute until I freed myself from the twisted mess of my sheets. As I sat up, I squinted at the window, saw the sun hovering over the treetops and groaned.

"Cat?"

I glanced over my shoulder to see Trick standing in the doorway. "Morning."

"I didn't mean to startle you," he said. "But it's after eleven."

"No problem." The thumping sound I'd heard in my dream must have been him knocking on the door. I got up, wincing as my knees let me know how sore they were. "I guess I forgot to set my alarm last night. Can you write me a note for school?"

"You don't need one. It's Saturday." He came around the bed and helped me up. "You sure you're feeling okay?"

"Uh-huh."

"Why do you smell like Sali?"

I was glad my hair was hanging in my face. "I also forgot to take a shower last night."

He nodded. "Put that at the top of your to-do list."

"Sure." All I wanted to do was fall back in bed and sleep, but Trick would want to know why I was so tired. "Sorry I overslept."

"You deserve a late morning every now and then." He put me in my robe and tied the belt as if I were still six years old and all thumbs. "Just don't make a habit of it, or I'll think you're trying to avoid my cooking."

I managed a weak smile. "I'd never do that."

Trick had saved me some slightly mushy, underdone pancakes, which I finished cooking in a skillet during a pretense of warming them up. Once I finished my belated, repaired breakfast, I washed all the dishes and fed the cats waiting on the back porch. Soul Patch and Terrible had a brought another friend with them this time, a small, delicate-looking orange-and-white marmalade kitty with one green eye and one blue.

"You're telling the other cats about the free food here, aren't you?" I asked Soul Patch, who tried to make himself into a furry ankle bracelet.

I sat down on the edge of the porch to watch the cats eat. At once all three abandoned the food I'd brought out and tried to climb into my lap.

"Do I look like a couch?" I protested. The little marmalade marched over the much larger, meaner tabby and promptly sat on his head as she nudged my chin. "Okay, Princess." I lifted her up on my shoulder to make room for the other two, and sighed as she licked my cheek with her sandpapery tongue. "You're welcome."

Princess tugged something out of my hair, and the mangled remains of a moonflower fell on to the ground.

Your skin . . . it's almost the same color as the petals.

Gently I removed the cats, stood up and went back inside. I was not going to spend my weekend moping about Jesse, the wonderful things he'd said, or the awful way he'd shut me down. I'd solved the mystery of who he was, I'd returned his ring, and now I had to pay for the privilege. After I stole what Gray wanted from my brother's desk, I'd never have to think about Jesse Raven again.

If I kept telling myself that, I might even stop reliving every second I'd spent with him last night.

I took a shower, got dressed and threw myself into my chores. It was my weekend to vacuum and dust, but that hardly took an hour. To keep busy I went ahead and did my brother's chores, too, and by the time I cleaned the kitchen, the bathroom and mopped the floors I felt a little less Jesse-obsessed.

I saw that I'd worked through lunch, and went into the kitchen to see what I could put together for dinner. By the time my brothers came in I was putting the finishing touches on a big salad and toasted roast beef and cheddar sandwiches.

"That smells great," Trick told me as he washed up at the sink. He glanced down at the spotless counters and floor. "Kitchen looks nice, too, but I thought it was my turn to clean it."

"I was bored." I didn't look at Gray, who was setting the table. "The bathrooms are also done."

"You've been busy." Trick tugged at the end of my ponytail. "Keep this up and I'll let you sleep in every weekend."

I made a scoffing sound. "That'll be the day."

My brothers plowed through dinner with their usual enthusiasm while I picked at my salad and listened to Trick talk about repairs to the barn stalls that had to be made before he bought our new breeding stock.

"I spotted some dead patches of what looked like Johnson grass while I was riding today out by the west pastures," Gray said when he'd finished eating. "You should take a look at it tonight."

Eating Johnson grass—a toxic weed that grew on cultivated land—gave horses serious bladder infections and weakened their hind legs, making them stagger as if they were drunk. When the weed died it became even more poisonous, and had been known to kill cattle, horses, and other grazing livestock.

Trick frowned at the window. "We don't have much daylight left."

I was about to agree when I caught Gray looking at me. He was giving me the *time to steal for me* glare.

"You should go take a look," I said to Trick while I kicked my idiot brother's shin under the table. "I'll clear and do the dishes."

Now Trick eyed me. "What's gotten into you? You hate house work."

"Temporary insanity," I assured him. "Enjoy the madness while it lasts." That sounded awfully harsh, even to my ears, so I softened it with a sigh. "I'm just feeling restless."

That seemed to reassure him, and he patted my cheek. "Don't repaint the house while we're gone."

I carried my dishes over to the sink, and Gray met me there with his plate. As he handed it to me, he slipped a key into my hand. Trick kept his key ring on a rack in the kitchen; Gray must have slipped it off while our brother was out working in the barn. "We'll take care of the horses when we get back, Cat," he said, loud enough for Trick to hear.

That meant they'd be out of the house for at least an hour; long enough for me to do the dirty work. "Take your time."

———

Once my brothers left the house I shoved the key in my pocket and finished tidying up while I watched through the window. I didn't relax until I saw Trick and Gray ride away on Jupiter and Flash.

"I can't believe I'm doing this." I waited another minute just to be sure they weren't coming back for some reason, and then left the kitchen and walked down to hall.

Trick's bedroom was easily twice the size of mine, but since he also used it as his home office it was much more cramped for space. In addition to his king-size bed, night stands and bureau, he had his computer station, printer stand and four bookcases packed with manuals and boxes of printouts. I knew he worked with codes to design programs, but nearly everything he did was so beyond me that his papers might as well have been written in Sanskrit.

Beneath the only window was his desk, where he had a phone, a big calendar blotter, a can filled with pens and pencils and an accordion file where he put bills and things. The desk had five drawers; two stacked together on either side and one long, narrow one in the center. All of them had individual locks, and for the first time I wondered why. My brother didn't keep a lot of money in the house, and other than the horses, Trick's motorcycle and Gray's truck we didn't own anything that was particularly valuable.

I pulled out the key and unlocked the center drawer first. Inside were some boxes of pens, extra keys to the truck and the bike, a bunch of rubber bands and a couple of books of stamps. Feeling foolish for holding my breath, I closed and locked it before I sat down in the swivel chair and turned to the right stack of drawers.

"Please," I told the desk. "Make this easy on me."

The top was half-filled with envelopes stuffed with credit card receipts, utility bills that had been paid and copies of old tax forms dated by year. There were also some newspaper articles Trick had cut out, folded and bundled together with a rubber band. The one on the outside showed a grainy photo of a bunch of cop cars parked along a wooded area and had a headline that read, "Hikers Attacked on Trail."

I took off the rubber band and sorted through the articles, all of which were about other wild-animal attacks. Forest rangers, campers, farmers, joggers and even some homeless people had been found injured or killed during the night in remote, wooded areas. The articles mentioned the authorities blaming bears, cougars, boars and even wild dogs for the attacks, which seemed logical given the circumstances, but I couldn't understand why Trick was saving the grisly reports. Then I started looking at the locations, and realized that the attacks had happened in or around the country towns where we had lived.

Had he been worried about something like this happening to me or Gray? Was this the real reason he'd been so adamant about me not riding at night?

I put aside the articles to finish looking through the drawer. I found an envelope all the way at the back marked "Deed" in Trick's scrawled writing, and I peeked inside. The address on the deed was for the farm here in Lost Lake, but it was old and yellowed, and dated 1949. Then I saw the name on it: not Trick's name, Patrick Robert Youngblood, but *Thomas Patrick Youngblood.*

Our father's name was Thomas Patrick. *Dad* had owned this farm?

In the envelope with the deed was a letter dated less than a year ago from a law firm in Orlando. I didn't understand all the legal jargon, but it mentioned a title search and transfer of ownership from our father to my brother.

Things that hadn't made sense before now began clicking in my head. Trick had gone to see a lawyer in Chicago right before we'd moved to Lost Lake, and he'd had to get a bunch of documents notarized. I remembered because I'd gone to the bank with him that day, and he'd made me sit in the lobby and wait while he got them signed. Now I knew why.

So we hadn't bought the farm; my brother had inherited it. But why hadn't he told us this place had belonged to our father? What reason would he have to keep something like that a secret?

I loved knowing that our dad had once owned this land. It instantly made the farm feel more like my home instead of just another place in a strange town surrounded by people who didn't know us and didn't care about us. Lost Lake must have meant something to our father or he wouldn't have lived here.

Had he lived here?

Slowly I put the documents back in the envelope and replaced it in the back of the drawer. Trick might be an ex-biker computer geek with the heart of a cowboy, but he wasn't a compulsive liar. If he'd kept this from me and Gray, he had to have an excellent reason. At least now I understood why he kept his desk locked up all the time.

I opened the lower drawer to find it packed with file folders, and began thumbing through them. Each label had an alpha-numeric code and contained contracts, schematics and other computer program specs that must have been from his job. Toward the back I found three files with our names on them, and copies of our birth certificates, shot records and other medical reports. I found Gray's most recent physical and took it out, placing it on the desk before I closed the drawer and locked it.

I did what I promised, I thought, looking at the last two drawers I hadn't opened. *The sensible thing to do would be to just walk out of here now and forget about this.*

When had I become so sensible anyway?

The left-hand-side top drawer held a jumble of tabs and labels along with some plastic boxes filled with tacks, paperclips, ink cartridges, and mechanical pencil leads. Nothing scary about them.

In the drawer beneath it were reams of blank paper, a couple of notebooks and a battered metal box. I looked at the box for a long time before I took it out and lifted the lid, making the rusty hinges creak. Inside the box were a pile of school photos of me and Gray, and some older black-and-white pictures of my mother and father. Beneath those I found an old-fashioned iron key and a large bundle of envelopes tied together with a faded purple ribbon.

The shamrock-shaped end of the key had been stamped with the letters *AVH* and stirred a vague memory of an old black trunk that had been lost during our many moves. The topmost envelope in the bundle of letters had the name *Thomas* written on it in beautiful hand-written script. I slid it out from under the ribbon and lifted the open flap, which was embossed with a scrolled letter *F*. As soon as I took out the delicate pages I smelled roses.

My mother's name had been Rose, and she had always worn rose-scented perfume. Cliché, maybe, but kind of sweet. The embossed *F* on the flap must have stood for her maiden name, Fanelsen. She'd written these letters.

A gossamer sorrow wrapped around me. I always felt a little fragile and sad whenever I thought of Mom.

As the youngest I had the fewest memories of her, but when I thought hard I could recall a blurry image of her face. She'd had a gentler version of Trick's dark eyes, and wore the golden hair she'd passed along to Gray in curls she'd piled on top of her head. I was pretty sure I had her mouth, which I mostly remembered being pink and smiling. My mother had always been so happy, right up until the day she and my father had died.

To have something that belonged to her in my own hands made my heart ache.

The first letter was dated thirty-one years ago, I saw as I began to read the first page.

Dear Thomas,

I dreamed of you last night, and it felt so real that when I woke up I expected to see you there, sitting beside me and telling me another story about Rio or Paris or London. You've traveled to so many wonderful places, and hearing you describe what you've seen there makes me feel as if I've visited them, too.

Despite the formal language my mother sounded so young and sweet, like a girl from a Victorian novel. She'd used a fountain pen, judging by the appearance of the ink, and her fine handwriting reminded me of the calligraphy on fancy invitations.

As wonderful as it was to meet you, I'm frustrated because there is still so much that I don't know about you. You never said why you came to Virginia or how long you plan to stay. Do you have family here? If my parents know them, then I think we can arrange to be properly introduced.

"*Proper* introductions required," I murmured. "You really were old-fashioned, Mom."

I know, that sounds horribly quaint, but my parents are from Holland, and I guess over there they were very strict about that kind of thing. I keep telling my mother that because I was born here so I should go to school and be like other American kids, but she says the old ways are best for us.

My grandparents had been Dutch? Trick had never told me that. Once, when I'd asked about them for a school project, he'd told me that our grandparents on both sides of the family had passed away before Gray and

I were born. Our parents had been their only children, so we had no other living relatives. The next day he'd called the school and my teacher had given me a substitute project that didn't involve family.

It seemed odd that the sum total of what I knew about the Youngbloods and the Fanelsens would have barely filled half a sticky note.

I wanted to read the rest of what Mom had written, but a glance at the desk clock told me that my brothers would be returning from their ride soon. I put the old trunk key back in the box, and almost added the letters, but I hesitated. Trick had no reason to check the box; because he kept it locked up he probably never looked in it anymore. Besides that, my mother's letters belonged to all of us, not just to him. It wasn't fair that he'd hidden them for so long.

I left Trick's room and went to mine, where I put Gray's report in a school folder and tucked the bundle of letters under my mattress. Just in time, too; I heard the kitchen door as it opened and my brother's voices drifted down the hall.

I sat on my bed and pretended to read while I waited for Gray, who knocked and came in a few minutes later. As soon as he closed the door behind him, I handed him the folder and the key to the desk.

"Thanks." He frowned. "What's wrong?"

"Nothing." Everything. "How much did Trick pay for the farm?"

"He never said." His shoulders hunched. "Not a lot, I guess. Why?"

Gray could do a lot of things, but lying well was not one of them. His reaction told me that he probably knew the farm had belonged to our father.

Which meant *both* of my brothers had kept it from me.

"I just wondered if he has enough money left to buy me a decent car." Now I didn't feel so bad about taking Mom's letters. "Maybe when he grounds you for life I'll ask him if I can have your truck."

He scowled. "You'd better not tell him."

"In case you forgot, I'm your accomplice, blockhead," I reminded him. "Telling on you means I also have to confess to my part. I still can't believe you made me do this for something as stupid as football."

"It's not stupid," Gray said flatly. "It's important to me."

"Whatever you say." I shrugged. "I hope it's worth spending a year or two in your room."

"Someday you'll understand." Without explaining that, he left.

Eight

Once I heard my brothers go into their rooms I tiptoed over to the door, listened, and gingerly turned the button lock. Then I took out the bundle of my mother's letters and began reading them.

There were twenty-eight of them, and I actually meant to stop reading after two or three to make them last, but the things she wrote fascinated and puzzled me. When I finished one, I found myself automatically reaching for another.

Her first letters were short, merely one or two page notes signed only with the letter *R*, as if she were afraid someone might find them. Because none of the envelopes were addressed or stamped I knew she hadn't mailed them; maybe she had passed them to someone to give to my father. Then, in the fifth letter, I discovered how my parents had been communicating.

> *Every morning I ride out to the old mill hoping that I'll see you, but you're never there. You must leave for work very early. I've been tempted to come back in the afternoon, but I'm afraid one of the farm hands working in Rucker's orchards might see me there (Mr. Rucker is nice but his wife is a busybody, and I know she'd mention it to my mother). That's why I go as soon as I've left my letter for you in your saddlebag. The only safe time for us to see each other is after dark.*

"So *that's* why I like to sneak out at night," I muttered as I turned the page. "It's in the chromosomes."

My mother didn't say much about her life at home, but some of the things she mentioned here and there made me think that she was unhappy. She didn't like being homeschooled, and often disappointed her parents with her lack of interest in her studies. She loved to read, but hated the books that her tutor assigned, all of which sounded pretty dull to me, too.

> *My tutor wants me to finished four chapters of my political history book tonight. Four chapters on medieval European law, Thomas! I can barely keep awake long enough to read one. Yes, you are to blame for some of that, but I don't mind. I'd rather*

*yawn my way through my lessons than give up the
few happy hours we spend together.*

I didn't understand everything Rose wrote, and some
of the references she made completely mystified me. She
kept going on overnight and weekend hunting trips with
her parents, during which they forced her to do something she hated. She called it being a "finder" but never
explained what that meant.

*I can't come by tonight. My parents are taking
me away on a hunting trip for the whole weekend.
I told my mother I don't want to be a finder but she
says it's our heritage and my duty to the family. My
father isn't taking his dogs this time so it shouldn't
be too bad, but I still hate it. I can never focus and
then my father gets angry with me. I expect this
weekend will be no different than the rest.*

I thought I was misreading her handwriting until
she mentioned it again in another letter that sounded far
more glum:

*Father said being a finder is essential, but Thomas,
I can't stand it. It's supposed to make me feel better;
mother promised it would, but it never does. It makes
me want to scream. One night I'm afraid I will, and
then Father will never forgive me for ruining the
search.*

Rose also never said what she and her parents hunted, but by the middle of the bundle she stopped talking about them. That was when I could tell that she had fallen in love with my father. She wrote about him, and being with him, and thinking about him to the exclusion of everything else. In her fourteenth letter she confessed her feelings outright:

> *I know you said that we can't be together, that I'm too young and you're too old. But Thomas, I know what I see when I look in your eyes. I hear it in your voice. You love me as much as I love you. That is the truth. That is our truth.*
>
> *Nothing can change how I feel about you. No one else will ever take your place. If you go away, and I never see you again, I'll be lonely for the rest of my life. But Thomas, so will you.*

I hurried to open the next envelope, but found only a short, hurriedly scrawled note inside:

> *I don't know what to do. After last night I'm so miserable, all I can do is cry.*
>
> *It's not your fault. I'm the finder, aren't I? I don't want to lose you, not ever, but it's too dangerous now.*
>
> *I'm so sorry, Thomas.*

I knew my parents hadn't broken up, because Trick and Gray and I wouldn't be here if they had. Plus there were fourteen more letters. But what had made her write such a sad, frightened note? Had my grandfather caught her with my Dad? Had someone seen them together?

I almost tore the flap off as I opened the next envelope. Some thin, dark ovals fell out into my lap like oversize confetti, and I carefully picked up one, which turned out to be a dried, pressed rose petal. More of the same filled the envelope, along with another short note.

> *You are absolutely insane, Thomas. How did you get into the house? Where did you find all these flowers? Do you know what my father would have done if he caught you decorating my bedroom with every rose in Fanelsen county? Lucky for you I have a big closet and I always wear rose perfume, or I think my mother would have called the police.*
>
> *You make me wish for things that are not possible… or maybe they are. Meet me in the meadow tonight.*

I let out a breath I didn't know I'd been holding. I didn't my father had been such a wild romantic, or that he'd used flowers (along with breaking and entering) to patch things up with my mother. I knew why she'd saved some of the rose petals; so that she'd always remember what he did.

No boy had ever given me so much as a daisy… until Jesse Raven. I touched my hair in the spot where he had tucked the moonflower, and a funny ache twisted in my chest.

I'm not going to see him again, I reminded myself. It would be easier if I could stop seeing his face and hearing his voice. I needed to reduce Jesse Raven to something unimportant and finished, something I could forget, like an algebra problem I'd solved: $X = dark\ boy$.

I didn't feel like reading any more of my mother's letters, so I gathered them up, tied them together with the ribbon and wedged the bundle back under my mattress. When I turned off the light and climbed under the covers, I felt the little lump the letters made under the mattress, next to my hip, like the pea that kept the thin-skinned princess awake all night.

Life would be a lot easier if everything worked out the way they did in fairytales. But my mother and father were gone, my brothers had been lying to me, and I had to forget about (X = dark boy). No prince would ever come and take me away to live happily ever after. All I had were some old letters I'd stolen and this nagging emptiness in my heart from wishing for things that I knew would never be.

$X = dark\ boy$. $Y = nothing$.

I rolled away from the lump, buried my face in my pillow, and cried myself to sleep.

After the dismal events of the weekend I was glad to go back to school, so I was the only one who didn't groan out loud when Mrs. Newsom passed around an outline handout and assigned us to write our first research paper of the year.

"All right, settle down," she said, frowning until the sounds stopped. "Since last year's freshman class had difficulty with appropriate research subjects for their papers, I've assigned them this time. You'll find them noted at the top of your handout."

I glanced at mine, which read "Lost Lake town history." Not the most riveting of subjects, but at least I might actually learn something about the town.

"We'll be spending the rest of the period in the media center," Mrs. Newsom continued, "so gather up your things, and pick a study partner so you can share a computer." She stared straight past me. "In the event some of you are thinking of getting lost on the way there, Mr. Boone, Mr. Chatham, Mr. Crowley, be advised that I will be performing a head count once we've arrived."

Barb joined me out in the hall and showed me her handout. "I got 'Central Florida indigenous wildlife,' if you can believe it. I hate Nature more than therapy sessions. And wildlife in Central Florida, come on. That's like a contradiction or something, isn't it?"

"An oxymoron." I felt someone following me so close I could feel their breath against the top of my head, and quickened my step. "She gave me town history."

"Good luck with that." She glanced over her shoulder

and then leaned close to whisper. "Oh. Em. Gee. Aaron is right behind us."

I should have guessed that Boone was the heavy breather. "Good, then he shouldn't get lost."

Three old classrooms had been converted into Tanglewood's media center, with fiction and nonfiction sections separated by the center study area which contained a dozen old cafeteria tables surrounded by chairs. Barb and I left our backpacks in two seats at the end of one table before we went over to the long row of computer terminals set up by the windows.

I let Barb run her search of the library's digital catalog first while I thought of how I wanted to write my paper. Reciting important historic events seemed boring; I was much more interested in people. Like the circus people who had founded the town.

$X = dark boy.$

Barb jotted down some references before she got up from the chair. "All yours."

I sat down, typed in *Lost Lake* in the keyword search box, and waited. After a few seconds, the library catalog returned zero results. I tried narrowing the search with a few other phrases—*town history, important local figures*, and *timeline*—but still came up with no results.

"How can you have a town with no recorded history?" I muttered as I broadened the search to books on the history of Central Florida and picked up a few titles. I wrote down the list and went back to the nonfiction section, but after I checked the index of each one I found that Lost Lake wasn't listed in any of them.

"Great." I only had thirty minutes left before we had to change classes, so I went back to the computer terminals for another try. This time I accessed the remote internet link and tried a few search engines, but I didn't have any more luck than I'd had back at the library in Chicago.

On impulse I switched to an image search to see if there were any online archives with historic photographs of the town, hoping they'd also have some information or reference links. I got one old, sepia-tinted shot of a man hand standing on the back of a white horse, but the photo was too small to make out any details. I clicked on the link and waited for the website to load.

Step Right Up!
Welcome to the largest online archive devoted to the history of nineteenth-century circuses in America and Europe! From facts to artifacts, playbills to photographs, if it happened under the big top, you'll find it here.

I smiled at some of the old but still-colorful images adorning the home page before I scrolled down and found a line of links: *Essays ~ Maps ~ Timelines ~ Images*. I clicked on the last link, which took me to a searchable archive of all the images on the site, where I typed in *Lost Lake*.

A page titled *Circus History's Mysteries* appeared on the screen, along with some odd photographs and several dense paragraphs on unexpected calamities and other weird things that had happened to the circus performers and their audiences. The first section covered bizarre tragedies, but I skipped past the sensational parts until I found the photo of the trick rider on the white horse.

The caption under the photo read, *Geza Ravenov in performance, 1873.*

I sat back in my seat. The rider was a boy, not a man, and he looked exactly like Jesse Raven. It wasn't Jesse, of course; Geza Ravenov must have been his great-great-grandfather. I scrolled down to the paragraph under the photo and began to read.

Individual circus performers frequently immigrated from Europe to America, but one of the first shows to cross the Atlantic was The Ravenov Circus. A small but influential traveling show that originated in Brasov, Romania, the Ravenovs were a tightly knit group of acrobats, clowns and trick riders who performed exclusively on horseback. At the peak of the circus's popularity, the Ravenovs' snow-white horses were among the most highly prized in Europe, but the leader of the troop refused to sell or breed any of their stock. Escaping harassment from avaricious military leaders, local officials and other high-ranking horse enthusiasts is thought to be what drove the Ravenovs to cut short their performances during their last season.

While making a mountain crossing into Romania, the circus caravan was attacked by outlaws, who stole their horses and killed most of the performers during the night. This tragedy forced the survivors to finally disband their show. Shortly after the surviving members of the Ravenov family left Romania for America and disappeared into the far south, where they bought land to breed horses and cattle, and establish a community for other retired circus performers.

The snow-white horses and stunning performances of the Ravenov Circus now exist only in the memories captured by a few precious photographs, most residing in the private archives of circus memorabilia collectors. All that survives of the Ravenov family today is Lost Lake, the town they founded, which still exists in a remote area of Central Florida.

I forgot about my research paper as I scrolled back up to look once more at the photo of Geza Ravenov. He had dark eyes like Jesse, but because the photo was black-and-white I couldn't tell what color they were. They could be brown or even dark blue. I squinted at a tiny dark spot on the rider's right hand. The smudge lay at the base of the ring finger of his right hand.

Was he wearing the same ring?

Stop it. I made myself get up and walk toward the front desk. I'd ask the librarian to help me with finding my references, and get back to work on my paper, and stop thinking about him.

"Mrs. Newsom? *Mrs. Newsom.*"

Tiffany Beck's shrill voice made me glance back, and what I saw made me freeze in my tracks. The cheerleader was standing next to the computer terminal I'd just used, and the edge of the table under it was dripping. A can of soda lay on its side, still dribbling its contents directly onto the keyboard.

My English teacher marched over to the terminal. "Do you want to explain what happened here, Ms. Beck?"

"I didn't do it," Tiffany said quickly. "It was her. That new girl." She gave me an ugly look. "She's always spilling things."

The librarian hurried past me, a roll of paper towels in her hands. "This is exactly why students are not permitted to bring beverages inside the media center," she snapped at Mrs. Newsom.

"Ms. Youngblood," my teacher said. "Come over here. Now." When I went to her, she pointed at the keyboard. "How could you be so careless?"

"It's not my soda, Mrs. Newsom, and I didn't knock it over." I knew who had, judging by Tiffany's satisfied smirk, but I hadn't seen her do it so I couldn't accuse her of anything.

As the librarian blotted up the spilled soda, Mrs. Newsom looked around at the rest of the class, who were watching from a safe, I'm-not-involved distance. "Did any of you see who was responsible for this mess?"

No one was going to contradict the most popular girl in school, not in front of her face. I saw Boone take a step forward and, after glancing at me, raise his hand. That's when I knew I was headed for the dean's office; naturally Boone would back up Tiffany's lie.

"Mrs. Newsom?" When she turned toward him, Boone dropped his hand. "I bought that soda for Tiffany.

She brought it in here, and she knocked it over after Cat left the computer."

No one moved, or made a sound. Everyone stared at Boone as if he'd gone crazy, including me.

"Aaron." His girlfriend's eyes went as wide as her mouth hung open before she turned to the teacher and started sputtering. "He's—he's lying, Mrs. Newsom. I didn't have a soda. I wouldn't—I mean, I'd never—"

The bell rang, making all of us jump.

"All right, class. Get your things and go to your next period," Mrs. Newsom said. "Not you, Ms. Beck." When Tiffany began to protest, she added, "You and I have some detentions to discuss." She didn't give the cheerleader a chance to say anything more as she gestured at Boone. "Aaron, I'd like a word with you as well."

Boone caught my eye and gave me a nod, as if he were trying to reassure me.

I grabbed my backpack and kept my head down as I followed everyone else out. Whispers hissed around me as if I were walking through a nest of snakes. Barb caught up with me halfway down the hall.

"I can't believe Boone just did that. I wouldn't, if I hadn't seen it with my own eyes. Unbelievable." When I didn't say anything, she bumped my arm with hers. "Cat? Are you in shock, or what? Aaron just totally trashed his girlfriend for you."

"I didn't ask him to do anything." Nor did I understand why he'd done it. Nor did I want to.

"Well, he did. That was … whew." She fanned her face

with her hand as if she were hot. "The way he charged to your rescue was so romantic. God, every girl in this school will want to be you now, especially when you go to thank him." She wiggled her eyebrows up and down. "Have any particular reward in mind?"

I stopped outside the door to my next class. "I'm not going to thank him, or reward him. He told the truth. That's all."

"Whatever you say." Barb's braces glinted. "But after this, Cat, you're going to be legendary. The girl who broke up Boone and Tiffany."

"I didn't do that." I saw some kids hovering near us, trying to eavesdrop, and lowered my voice. "I am not interested in Aaron Boone. Not now, not ever." Before she could start gushing over him again I stalked into class.

Boone arrived at class a few minutes late, but handed a pass slip to the teacher before walking back to his seat. I pretended to read my textbook so I didn't have to look at him, and focused my attention on the teacher to block out the murmurs and snickers all around me.

When the lunch bell rang I had to move fast to get out of the classroom ahead of Boone. Instead of going directly to the cafeteria, the way I always did, I went in the opposite direction toward my locker. I was too upset to eat, and I didn't want to sit and give myself a headache listening to Barb gush over her hero. I didn't want to risk running into Tiffany and her cheerleader posse, either. I'd drop off my books and go spend lunch period in Guidance, getting my classes changed.

When I got to the hall where my locker was, I saw something wet and dark on the door, and slowed my step as I smelled aerosol paint. Since everyone was at lunch the hall was completely empty, but someone had sprayed the front of my locker with black paint in a diagonal row of splotches that ran from the top to bottom vents. I unlocked the padlock and opened the door to find everything inside my locker wet and spattered with the black paint that had been sprayed into the vents. Nothing had escaped; all my paper, pens, and textbooks were ruined.

I slowly closed the door and realized that the splotches of paint on the outside formed a word.

SLUT.

Tiffany had gotten the last word after all.

Nine

The spray paint on my locker had dried so it couldn't be wiped off, and I wasn't sure what to do about the ruined books. I couldn't carry them around school with black paint all over them. The thought of spending the rest of the day imagining all the kids walking by my locker and stopping to snicker at the ugly word Tiffany had painted on it made me feel nauseated. I couldn't go to the front office and complain, either. I hadn't seen her do it, so I couldn't accuse her of being responsible.

But how could I cover it up? Not like I could go to the maintenance office and ask for a can of paint thinner…

I turned around to look in the door window of the art class. It was empty, and when I tried the knob I found it was open. I went inside and headed for the big supply cabinet at the back of the class. I didn't see any paint thinner, but there was a long shelf stacked with spray-paint cans. Among them I found one with the same drab brown color as my locker.

I read the label, which said the contents were quick-drying and covered with one coat. "Maybe I don't have to take the paint off."

I stuck my head out the door to see if anyone was in the hall, and then took the can of paint over to my locker. Stepping back and holding my hand over my nose to block the fumes, I sprayed the brown paint in short spurts over the black letters, coating it several times until the new paint covered it. A few more sprays disguised the splotches over the vents. By the time I returned the spray paint to the supply cabinet and came back out, the brown paint had almost dried. As I'd guessed it matched the color of the lockers almost exactly. Because I knew it was there I could still see the outlines of the word, but anyone walking by would have to look closely to make it out.

I'd have to buy new textbooks and school supplies, but I had a little money left over from my last school clothes shopping trip. As long as Tiffany didn't try vandalizing my locker again, no one had to know about it.

Maybe she won't go for your locker next time. Maybe she'll spray paint something nasty on Gray's truck.

Repainting my locker had taken up most of the time I had planned to spend changing my classes in Guidance, but the thought of switching my schedule so I could avoid Boone and his girlfriend no longer seemed like such a great idea. Acting as if I were scared of them would only make things worse.

I wasn't afraid or humiliated, I realized as I walked to my next class. I was furious. With every step I took resentment built inside me, so cold and strong that it squashed all of my doubts. If Tiffany thought she could terrorize me, she had another thing coming.

I held onto my temper and got through the rest of the school day without another incident. Thanks to the anger, I didn't rush through halls or avoid the stares. I didn't see Boone or Tiffany in the rest of my classes, which was fine with me. I felt tall and terrible, immovable and dangerous, a statue filled with explosives, a huge dark storm blotting out the sun.

As they had on the day I'd spilled my drink on Tiffany's uniform, the other kids kept their distance. Barb must have sensed how upset I was, for all she did was follow me in silence to and from the rest of our classes. After the last bell she finally said something.

"Cat." When I looked at her, she made a face. "You could call me at home later. You know, if you want to talk about Boone."

"Thanks." If I never heard the name Aaron Boone again, it would be too soon. "See you tomorrow."

Gray met me at his truck (which I saw was spray-paint free) and, once we were on the road, asked me if I was okay.

"Just peachy." I wasn't surprised that he already knew

about what happened; Gray could be very nosy. Besides, the whole school had to be talking about it. "Can we go home now?"

"Yeah." He hesitated, and then said, "Tiffany got two Saturday detentions, and she has to pay to replace the keyboard."

I stared out the passenger window. "Good."

"She didn't spill that soda."

I turned my head to stare at him. "*What* did you say?"

"It wasn't her," he said. "She left the can there by the computer, but she didn't knock it over. Someone else did."

He was defending the witch. To my face. "And you know this how?"

"I talked to her." He frowned. "Cat, don't you get it? Boone lied."

My brother, who barely spoke to me on a good day, was now chatting up evil, locker-destroying cheerleaders. "Gray, I don't care."

Wisely he shut up while I put my head back and closed my eyes. Of all the places we could have settled down in, Lost Lake was the worst. I hadn't had any friends at my last school in Chicago, but being ignored was a lot better than being blamed for breaking up the most popular couple at Tanglewood High.

It isn't fair. I didn't do anything.

Fair or not, the damage was done. Tiffany was already turning my own brother against me by filling his head with more of her lies. I didn't want to go back to that school, not tomorrow, not ever. I'd talk to Trick again about homeschooling, and this time I'd convince him it was better for me. Or I'd just quit school and get a job. He couldn't stop me from doing that.

As soon as we got home I went to my room, where I shut the door and flopped down on my bed. Now I'd probably get one of my killer headaches, I thought, and considered taking some aspirin before my head started to pound. Even through the pillow I pulled over my face I could hear Gray talking to Trick in the kitchen, and braced myself for a big-brother visit.

Sure enough, five minutes later he knocked on my door. "Hey? Can I come in?"

All at once I couldn't bear the thought of listening to another pep talk from my big brother. I lifted the pillow and lied. "I'm trying to study."

He didn't say anything for a minute. "How about I make dinner tonight?"

Trick could make exactly three dinners: overcooked ziti, overcooked meatloaf and overcooked goulash. But letting him cook would give me the time I needed to pull myself together. "If you want."

I got my backpack and pulled out my homework, which consisted of one worksheet from Calculus and my blank research paper outline. I finished the math in no time, but I had nothing for my English paper. What could I put down? *Lost Lake was founded by a family of runaway circus trick riders whose descendents currently live on a private, no-trespassing island. P.S., the youngest sneaks out to ride around at night, smash through fences, and leave unconscious teenage girls under trees.*

I wished I could talk to Jesse again. I knew he'd understand how awful things were for me. He was stuck on that island with no friends, no life. Being rich and living in a mansion might be cool, but not if you couldn't go anywhere or do anything. Not if you spent all your time alone, like him.

Like me.

I shoved myself off the bed and went out to the kitchen, where Trick was frowning at a page in my cookbook. I went to stand beside him and saw he was studying a recipe for chicken and rice.

Knowing how hard it was to eat burnt rice, much less scrub it off the bottom of a scorched pot, I took the cookbook and closed it. "Step away from the cooking utensils, sir, and keep your hands where I can see them."

He didn't laugh. "Gray told me what happened at school today."

"Lots of things happened." I went to the fridge and hunted through the shelves, collecting things and stacking them in my arm. "But I didn't get in any trouble."

"What about this boy, Aaron?" Trick asked.

"Boone?" I shrugged. "He's NMP."

"NMP." Now he frowned. "Net Material Product?"

"Not my problem." I shut the fridge and carried the pile of food over to the counter. I felt him reach out to put a comforting arm around my shoulders, and I stepped aside. "Trick, don't. Okay? I'm fine, really."

"You keep saying that." He dropped his arm. "I could go to the school tomorrow and talk to someone. See if they can do something about this situation."

"Oh, yes, that will make things *so* much better for me." I unwrapped a rotisserie chicken and started carving away thin slices. "Don't you remember anything about how it is in high school?"

He shrugged. "I never had a problem with bullies."

"That's because you were always bigger and meaner-looking than them. Two things I, regrettably, am not." I shook my head. "I have to go to Tanglewood until I graduate, which unfortunately is not tomorrow morning. So unless you want me to be treated like a communicable disease for the next three years, you should maybe stay out of this."

"You don't have to graduate from Tanglewood," he said quietly. "We can move."

I stopped slicing and eyed him. "Excuse me?"

"I would like to stay and make a go of the farm," he said, "but not if it has you this unhappy."

I knew exactly why my brother wanted to stay: the farm that had belonged to our father. I couldn't talk to him about that because I wasn't supposed to know. I wondered how he'd react if I told him I'd seen the deed. Would he lie about it, or say it had slipped his mind?

"Cat?"

I didn't know what to say to him. I *was* unhappy. Part of me relished the idea of packing up and moving again. Trick would take us somewhere far from Lost

Lake, somewhere I could start over and not have to worry about Gray or school or cheerleaders who hated me or—

Jesse.

I couldn't move away. Not from him. Even if he didn't want to see me again, I had to stay. There was always a chance that he'd change his mind, or that we'd meet again one night and he'd like me better. He needed to know I was here, that I was waiting for him.

I know you are.

That thought came out of nowhere, and it wasn't mine. It sounded like Jesse was inside my head. Great. I'd obsessed over him so much that now I was pretending to hear him in my thoughts. Then everything around me dimmed as I felt another heartbeat join the throb of my own.

Does this feel like a pretense to you, Catlyn?

Dimly I heard the knife fall out of my hand and skitter over the edge of the counter.

Trick caught before it hit the floor. "Cat?"

The sharpness of his voice snapped me back to reality, where for a second everything seemed too bright and crowded.

"Sorry," I said quickly. "I guess the thought of packing up my room again made my brain freeze." I composed my expression before I faced him. "Trick, we *don't* have to move whenever I have a bad day. My life is not exactly charmed. We'd have to live on a houseboat."

His mouth hitched. "It must not be as bad as I thought if you're already joking about it."

"I'm serious," I assured him. "A houseboat with no anchor. And really big, souped-up engines. Like a house speedboat." I paused before I added, "Let me handle this, okay? Please?"

"All right." He handed me the knife before he peered at the pile of chicken I'd sliced. "So how do you heat that up? In the oven, or in a skillet?"

"If *you're* cooking? Neither of them." I gave his shoulder a comforting pat. "Let me introduce you to this marvelous, cooking time-programmable appliance called the microwave."

———

Teaching my big brother how to rewarm chicken without turning it into jerky made dinner edible and helped avoid any further discussion of my awful day at school. While we ate I could feel Gray looking at me now and then, but I pretended he was invisible. I was still mad about him taking Tiffany's side and telling Trick about Boone.

I left my brothers to clean up and took a shower before I went to bed. I meant to read a few more of my mother's love letters, and took out the bundle, but as soon as I lay down on my bed I felt exhausted. I closed my eyes to rest them for a minute, and drifted off.

Sometime during the middle of the night a tapping sound woke me, and I sat up feeling grumpy and disoriented.

"Unless the house is burning down," I told my door, "go away."

"Catlyn."

The voice wasn't coming from outside my door. I turned around and saw a shadow move across the glass panes. "Gray?"

"Catlyn, open the window."

Was he locked out of the house? Had he climbed up the pine tree outside my window? As big as he was, the branches would never hold his weight.

I grabbed my robe and yanked it on before I went to unlock the window latch and pull up the bottom slider. "What are you..." I stopped as I looked down twenty feet at a boy standing next to the pine tree. A boy who was definitely *not* my brother. "Jesse?"

He bent down, and when he straightened he soared straight up and caught my windowsill with his hands. When I stumbled back, my hand over my mouth to smother a yelp, he swung himself over and into my room.

"Catlyn." He straightened, glancing all around before he met my gaze. In the light from my lamp his eyes looked lighter, like the chrome on Trick's Harley. "I thought this might be your room."

I couldn't believe it. He'd jumped two stories and vaulted into my room. As if gravity didn't affect him at all. "How did you do that?"

"I had to see you." He stepped toward me. "I know I said I wouldn't, but I can't stop thinking about you."

When he saw that I was backing away, he stopped. "It's the same for you, isn't it?"

"Yes. No." The back of my legs hit my bed and I sat down on it. "Jesse, for God's sake, it's the middle of the night. If my brother heard you out there—"

"He didn't." He came and knelt down in front of me. "Catlyn, your face is so pale, and your eyes look bruised." He reached out to touch my face and I pulled back. "Why are you frightened of me?"

"Aside from you pole-vaulting in here without a pole, I'm alone with you in my bedroom at one a.m." I glanced down as he took my hand in his. "Jesse, you can't come into someone's house like this. Not when she has two large brothers who could very easily beat you to a pulp and will if they find you here."

"I've never done this before tonight," he admitted, and curled his strong fingers around mine. "Do you really want me to go? I will."

"No." I breathed in his scent, like a spice garden in the moonlight, and felt it warm me from the inside out. "You made that jump; you've earned a few minutes."

Instead of the weirdly formal riding clothes I'd seen him in the last two times, Jesse wore a pair of jeans and a long-sleeved shirt. Both had been black once but had faded to gray, and the jeans had ladders of small, frayed rips. His silky black hair hung in a wind-blown mane around his face, as if he'd been out riding with it loose.

I didn't look half so good. I wished I was wearing the new navy blue robe Gray had given me for my birthday, which looked like silk, instead of the ratty old pink terry cloth from four Christmases back. No way I was going to take it off and show Jesse my candy-striped pajamas, which were even more ancient and so threadbare they were practically transparent in the most embarrassing places.

"You look cute." He tugged on the lapel of my robe. "I like you in pink."

"I despise pink, but it was a Christmas gift. Quit reading my mind." I gave him an uneasy look. "How did you know what I was thinking?"

"I don't know." He stood up and drew me to my feet. "But you *have* been thinking about me."

If he were psychic, he would know. "Sometimes. You're kind of mysterious."

"So are you." He inspected my face. "I've been feeling your thoughts in my mind, as if you were calling my name out loud. Wherever I was, I could hear your voice inside my head. Even when I watched you from the hayloft."

"The hayloft?" I echoed blankly.

His mouth hitched. "You don't know how many times I've sat up there on that old trunk so I could watch you groom your mare. You were brushing out her mane and wishing your hair had the same tinge of red as hers."

"Reading someone's thoughts is impossible." So was his jumping up into my room, and the way he was looking down at me now, as if I were as beautiful as he was, and being with me was the only thing in the world that mattered to him. "Jesse, why did you really come here?"

"I couldn't stay away another night." He slid his arm around my waist and used it to pull me a little closer. "I wanted to be with you."

I would not blush. I would not stutter. I would start breathing again, any moment now. "You don't even know me."

He smiled. "You love reading poetry and listening to music and riding at night. You love your horse and your brothers. You would help a stranger in trouble, even if it meant getting hurt yourself. You're not afraid of the dark."

I turned my head to look at the open window, and his hair brushed across my cheek. It was so soft it felt like a cool breeze against my skin. "This isn't real. Things like this don't happen to me."

"Or me," he murmured, stroking one hand over my rumpled hair. "Catlyn, listen. All that matters now is this. I need you with me. I want you to come away with me tonight."

I could feel his heartbeat against mine, racing as fast as my own, and shivered. "Why?"

"It's the only way we can be together." He put his fingers under my chin and tipped up my face. "We belong to each other. You can feel it just as I do. You've known it since the moment we met."

I did feel connected to him, more than I'd felt to anyone, even my brothers, but I wasn't so sure it was love at first sight. How could I love someone I barely knew? "What if you're wrong? What if this is a big mistake?"

He smiled down at me. "Nothing about us is wrong."

I went still as he bent his head to mine, and his hair fell like a curtain around our faces. He was going to kiss me, and in that moment I thought my heart would stop. I closed my eyes and waited for the touch of his mouth against mine.

Something yowled, and I opened my eyes to find myself standing alone in the middle of my dark room. I whirled around. "Jesse?"

He was gone.

No, I thought as I pressed my hands over my eyes. He'd never been there. I'd been dreaming.

Damp air washed over me, and I looked at the window, which was sitting wide open. When I went over to shut it, I stepped on something made of paper that made my foot slide. I changed direction and reached for the lamp next to my bed, and then it struck me. I didn't remember turning off the lamp, or opening the window. I flipped on the switch and turned slowly around.

My mother's letters lay scattered all over the floor.

Maybe the wind blew them off the bed. I hurried to pick them up and put the stack on my nightstand. There I found the old ribbon that had been tied around them draped around the base of my lamp. The ends of the ribbon had been tied in a bow.

I'd fallen asleep before I'd started reading the letters, I was sure of it. I might have untied the ribbon first, which would explain why they were scattered all over the floor, but no wind in the world could re-tie a ribbon around something else.

I walked over to the window and looked out, expecting to see Jesse standing on the ground beneath. A dozen eyes glinted up at me, making me catch my breath until I made out a little patch of white, and heard the plaintive meows that had woken me up. Soul Patch and a small group of stray cats—I counted seven of them—sat in a little group directly beneath my window.

As if they were guarding it.

Ten

After putting away my mother's letters I lay staring at the ceiling and wondering what was happening to me. Had I been sleepwalking again? Could I have done everything myself, and just not remembered doing it? Was I imagining the whole thing?

Each time I'd almost convinced myself that it had all been a dream, I'd take a deep breath and pick up the faintest trace of herbs and spices and honey. I could imagine plenty things, but not how someone smelled.

Jesse had been in my room. I was sure of it.

My alarm went off just as I was starting to feel drowsy, and then I had to get up. Trick had to leave before me and Gray to meet with the local equine vet to examine some brood mares before he bought them. I ate the lukewarm, lumpy oatmeal he'd made for us without even tasting it.

If Jesse had come to the house last night, then everything in my dream might have happened, too: What he'd said to me, how he'd held me in his arms, how close I'd come to having my first kiss. But that part of it seemed completely unreal. Why would someone like Jesse ask a girl he'd met exactly two times to run away with him?

It's the only way we can be together.

As I rinsed the breakfast dishes I tried to imagine us just being together without running away. Because of his condition he couldn't go out in the sunlight, so we'd never be able to do normal things like have picnics or go for walks (unless we did them after sunset).

We had almost nothing in common. He lived in a mansion on an island; I lived in an old farmhouse on a horse ranch. His family had built this town; mine just got here. The Ravens were rich and probably gave their son everything he wanted. Trick had always taken care of me and Gray, but we didn't really have anything except the farm and the horses.

Then there were the differences between our personalities. Jesse was confident and did what he wanted; I was shy and did what I was told. He was incredibly good-looking; I wasn't even that pretty. He could have any girl he liked. I'd never been kissed.

No, it had to be a dream.

Gray didn't try to talk to me again about Tiffany or Boone, but I knew he wanted to, especially with the way he kept glancing over at me on the way to school. I got out of the truck as soon as he pulled into his space in the student parking lot, not waiting for him to shut off the engine. He called after me, but I strode off to my first class.

Over the next couple hours it took all my energy not to nod off or think about last night. By the time I went to lunch I began feeling achy and slightly feverish, as if I were coming down with a cold. That combined with my physical and mental exhaustion was turning me into a zombie.

If Jesse saw me now, I thought as I found an empty table and sat down, *he'd run the other way.*

"Hey, Cat." Barb put down her tray next to mine and looked at the other empty chairs at our lunch table. "Geez. I guess everyone heard."

"Everyone heard yesterday." I took a bite of the sandwich I'd made at home, which had mayo and lettuce on it; I'd forgotten to add turkey. "Today they're waiting for the big breakup scene."

"Jamie Maloney told me that Boone called Tiffany last night to break up with her," Barb said. "That's probably why she's ... never mind."

I propped my cheek against my fist. "Why she's what?"

My friend took a big drink of her soda and cleared her throat. "Tiffany thinks Boone did this whole thing because he's, um ... " When I rolled my hand, she rushed out with, "Because he's been secretly cheating on her."

I dropped my sandwich bag into my lunch bag. "He probably has."

"With you."

I stared at her.

"At least, that's what she's telling everyone," Barb said quickly. "She thinks you two have been seeing each other behind her back for a while. Like since summer."

I almost told her that I had been seeing Jesse Raven, but then I'd have to admit that we'd only met twice while out riding and he didn't want to see me again. Not exactly the best alibi in the world.

"She can't be serious." I grabbed my lunch bag and crumpled it into a ball. "I just moved here three months ago. I didn't know Boone until after I started school. The only time I see him is at school. What does she think, we're making out in the back of the classroom?"

"Only if you're doing it under the desks," Ego said as he dropped into the chair next to mine. "But I would have noticed if you were. All I've seen you do is dodge the big baboon."

"Ego, don't call him that." Barb glowered at him before she turned to me, her expression concerned. "Jamie told me that Tiffany's pretty mad at you. Not just for the library thing, but for stealing her boyfriend. She told Jamie that she's going to do whatever it takes to get even with you."

"For the last time, I did *not* steal Boone from his girlfriend. I don't want Boone." I saw kids sitting at the tables around us turn to look at me and lowered my voice. "This is crazy. I don't even like him. She's making this all up so she can blame me for what he did to her."

"Classic denial and competitive devaluation," Ego said after guzzling down some milk. "Tiffany can't blame Boone for what he does because he's her boyfriend, so she transfers the blame onto Cat, the new girl no one knows."

"She wouldn't do that," Barb protested.

"Sure she would." He wiped his white mustache off on the back of his sleeve and grinned at me. "She also makes you look like a conniving boyfriend thief by holding you responsible for Boone's actions, which makes her feel better about the situation and herself. It also gives her hope that once her rumors destroy your rep, Boone won't want you anymore. Talk about deluding yourself." He looked us, puzzled. "What? I'm taking psychology this semester."

"Great, just what I need in my life," Barb snapped. "Another shrink."

I pressed my hands to the sides of my head. "What will Tiffany do if my head explodes?"

Ego snickered. "You mean, besides throw a huge party and invite Boone to be her date?"

"Will you stop?" Barb gave him a dirty look. "Cat, you don't have to let her intimidate you."

"She doesn't."

Ego scoffed. "What you have to do is be proactive. Make the first strike and show her what will happen if she messes with you. Sprinkle some pepper on her pom-poms. Hide a couple of roaches in her desk. Girls really hate bugs."

"He's right," Barb agreed. "I could help. I know plenty

of ways to get to Tiffany. You could snitch a bag of fertilizer from the agricultural club and empty it into her gas tank."

Ego choked back a laugh. "Uh, Barb, I'm pretty sure that's the same way you blow up a federal building."

"No homemade manure bombs, please." I saw my brother walking through the tables and looking around. "Gray?"

He heard me and changed direction. "Hey."

"My brother, Gray," I told my friends. "Gray, this is Barb and Ego. Gray." He was looking around again, and I had to poke him to get his attention. "What are you doing here? Are you lost or something?"

"No. Hi." He spared Barb and Ego a glance before he looked past me again. "I have to stay after school today."

I certainly didn't feel like doing the same. "How long?"

"An hour or two. You can wait for me or take the bus home. I already checked with the front office, and they gave me a pass for you. It's number seventeen." He handed me a bus pass.

I felt a little hurt, but I took the bus pass and stuck it in my shirt pocket. "Why are you staying after?" He couldn't have gotten a detention; Gray never got into trouble.

"Tryouts." His eyes shifted past me. "They start today."

So he was really going to do it. "Do you want me to stay and watch?"

He lifted a shoulder. "It would be okay if you were there."

"I wish I could stay after with you, Cat," Barb said, "but I have a doctor's appointment, and my mom will kill me if I miss another one."

Ego shook his head. "Don't look at me. I'm allergic to jocks. They make me break out in uncontrollable laughter."

"I'm really tired, Gray, and I think I'm getting a cold, too. Would you mind if I went home?" When he didn't answer me, I followed the direction of his gaze and saw he was looking at Tiffany and the cheerleaders. "Gray. *Gray.*" I nudged my brother until he looked at me. "Do you mind if I go home instead?"

"Do what you want. I gotta go." With that he walked off.

"Why is your brother even bothering to try out?" Ego sounded amused. "He just has to show up. The minute the coach sees him, he'll hand him a uniform. Then he'll get busy kissing the ground your brother smears everyone into."

"Gray might make the team," I said, looking over at the cheerleaders' table, "but I doubt he'll stay on it for long."

Ego laughed. "Cat, if you haven't noticed, your brother is built like a tank. All he has to do is stand on the field, and the other team will either faint or run home whimpering for their mommies."

I knew that. What I didn't know was why Gray had been looking at the cheerleaders. Was it Tiffany? Was she pretending to be his friend so she could fill his head with more lies? Was that how she intended to get back at me, by using my own brother?

I hated this not knowing. The only time I felt like I knew anything for sure was when I was back at the farm or out riding Sali. I could wait until dark and take her along the boundary fence, and maybe catch a glimpse of Jesse. Even if he didn't want to see me again, I was sure he was still out riding after midnight.

I looked over at Tiffany, who glared back at me. *Give me all the dirty looks you want,* I thought. *I've walked in the moonlight with the most beautiful boy in this town, and he held my hand and compared me to a flower.*

"I love football season," Barb said dreamily. "Boone makes every game so exciting. He's the best quarterback in the county." She saw how Ego and I were looking at her and sighed. "Well, he is."

"I'll see you guys later." I carried my trash over to the garbage cans in the corner, but when I turned around a brown and white varsity jacket was in my face. I looked up into the cold green eyes of the last person I wanted anywhere near me. "What?"

Boone's smile dimmed. "Well, hello to you, too." He sounded faintly resentful, as if he'd expected a nicer reception.

"Hello. Good-bye." When I tried to go around him, he shifted to block me. "I have to go."

"Remember the library, yesterday?" When I didn't reply, the last of his smile disappeared. "Don't thank me for what I did."

"Okay, I won't." He wouldn't budge, and I let out an exasperated breath. "I don't want to be late for next period. Please move."

"I saw your brother signed up to try out for the team," he said. "I could put in a good word with the coach for him." He reached out and ran his finger across the collar band of my T-shirt before I could move out of reach. "I will, if you'll do something for me."

What I wanted to do in that moment was find a baseball bat, and convince someone to hold Boone down for me. "My brother doesn't need any favors from you, and neither do I."

"But everyone needs friends." Boone chucked me under my chin. "Look, all I need you to do is go out with me once, and I'll let your brother join the team."

"I'm not allowed to date." I got an idea and smiled past him as if a teacher were there. "Hello, Mrs. Newsom." When Boone turned around to look, I finally got past him and deliberately joined a group of kids I didn't know who were leaving the cafeteria.

"You're Cat Youngblood, right?" one of the girls who was walking beside me asked.

"That's me." I was not going to look back to see if Boone was stalking me, so I focused on her. "Aren't you in my Calculus class?"

"Yeah, I am." She uttered a nervous giggle. "Um, do you mind if I ask you something?"

"Sure."

"Are you, like, going steady with Aaron Boone now?"

"No." I gritted my teeth, until I realized what an excellent opportunity this was to spread some of my own gossip. "I already have a boyfriend. A big, mean, extremely jealous boyfriend, who adores me and hates football players. His nickname is Killer."

"Really? Wow." Her eyes widened. "Does he know about you and Boone?"

———

As soon as the dismissal bell rang I took the bus pass out of my pocket and started walking to the loop behind the school where the buses were parked and waiting. I was so tired now it was making me sick; I desperately needed to go home, pop some aspirin, fall on my bed and not move for at least twelve hours. I didn't want to see Boone again, and Grim could obviously take care of himself. He hadn't asked me to watch him at the tryouts. He wouldn't care one way or another.

It would be okay if you were there, he'd said.

Anyone listening would agree with me. Except I knew my brother, and while Gray would walk barefoot through a dead sticker-burr patch before he'd admit it, he wanted someone there who cared about him.

I hated myself as I turned around and started walking toward the east side of campus, where the gymnasium and the football field were. I saw a bunch of boys standing along the sidelines and putting on shoulder pads and unmarked brown jerseys, but I stopped in the shadow of the stands so no one would see me.

Gray had already put on the gear and stood slightly apart from the others. He turned and looked in my direction, and I stepped out into the sunlight for a minute to give him a wave. He flashed me a grin before he pulled on the brown and white tiger-striped helmet in his hands.

An older man in a brown polo shirt and white baseball cap who was carrying a clipboard walked out to the sidelines. He must have been the coach, because Gray and the other boys gathered around him.

"I could home by now," I grumbled as I sat down on the end of the very bottom row of the stands. "Sleeping."

A couple other students and a half-dozen parents came to sit in the stands, but all of them sat at close to the fifty-yard line, which was where the coach was dividing the boys into small groups. Boone was the last to arrive, and unlike the others he was wearing an official team jersey with the number eight and his last name printed across the shoulder yoke. The coach waved him over to the group Gray was in before he blew his whistle and the groups lined up.

"Hi." A middle-aged woman with graying red hair

sat down next to me, and tucked her purse under the bench seat. "Is your boyfriend out there?"

"No, my brother." I glanced at her. "Are you here to see your son try out?"

"My nephew. His mom had to work today, so I told her I'd drop by." She scanned the field. "We should have a good team this year." She pointed to one boy with red hair like hers. "That's him. Peter Norris, do you know him?"

I shook my head. "I don't know many kids at this school. My family just moved here this summer."

"Really." She gave me a longer look. "I haven't seen you in town."

"I live out on a farm with my brothers," I explained.

Her expression changed in a flash from curious to disapproving. "Oh. My husband Jim told me about you." She reached for her purse and got up. "Excuse me, I see some of my friends." She walked to the opposite side of the stands to sit with the other moms.

"Nice to meet you, too." Peter's aunt must have also been the sheriff's wife, since he was the only Jim we'd met. Judging by her reaction, we hadn't impressed him much. Anger erased my exhaustion, and I sat up a little straighter. I could sleep any time; this was the only chance I'd likely ever have to see Gray play football.

As the sun dropped low and made me shade my eyes with my hand, I wondered if Jesse had ever wanted to do something like this. He didn't seem like the jock type, but that didn't mean anything. He had to be pretty strong to control Prince as easily as he did. Then I realized he could never try out for any team because it would mean coming outside in the sun. *How much of life has he missed because he can't go out in the daylight?*

After the players went through a series of what looked like warm-up exercises, the coach went down the lines and marked X's in chalk on the front and back of every other boy's jersey. Gray got an X and when the next whistle blew he ran across the field to the opposite sideline with all the other X's. They turned around and ran back, and repeated that six times before the coach blew his whistle. At that point all the boys with unmarked jerseys did the same thing while the X's trotted toward one end of the field.

X = dark boy, I thought, and jumped a little as I felt someone behind me. I glanced back to see a girl dressed in baggy black parachute pants and an oversize black T-shirt climbing up onto the seat behind mine. Her baby-blonde hair had been cropped like a boy's, and she wore thick, heavy dark makeup including dark blue lip tint that made her fair skin look even paler. I smiled and tried not to stare at the silver stud gleaming in the crease of her nose or the matching ring piercing her left eyebrow.

"You mind if I sit here?" she asked gruffly, half-rising as if she already knew the answer.

I shook my head and turned back to watch the field.

I could feel the tension growing. However these boys performed today would decide if they made the team, so every one of them must be determined to play their best. I also guessed that most of them had been on teams before or had at least practiced with their dads and friends.

Gray, who had never once played football, didn't really stand a chance.

I noticed that Boone didn't put on his helmet or run with either group, but stayed on the sidelines tossing a football back and forth with one of his friends. I wondered if being the best quarterback in the county meant that he didn't have to do what the other players did. It didn't seem fair, and I caught a couple of the other boys giving him disgusted looks.

"You're Catlyn Youngblood." The Goth girl who had been sitting behind me dropped her backpack by my feet and sat down next to me. "Aren't you?" When I nodded, she said, "I'm Karise Carson. Call me Kari, or *hey, you.*"

"I'm Cat. Hey, you." I glanced at the front of her T-shirt, which had Asian characters all over it. "Have we met before and I've been rude and forgotten it?"

"Unless I did the same, no. I'm the junior editor for the school newsletter." She looked out onto the field. "Want to give me an exclusive about how it feels to be harassed by a jerk, excuse me, jock like Aaron Boone? Not that it would get printed, because our teacher sponsor isn't interested in the truth per se, but I'd save it for the high school expose I'm writing."

Her attitude was as unsympathetic as her appearance was bizarre, but I found it refreshing. "Did you come here just to talk to me?"

She shook her head. "Today I'm stalking someone else." She pointed toward the boys on the field. "I'm hoping one of them gets hurt. Aside from the sheer delight it would give me to write up the eyewitness account, I want his job as senior editor."

"You're ambitious. And bloodthirsty." I grinned. "I like that in a Goth girl."

"Please. We prefer to think of ourselves as displaced tragedy addicts," she informed me in a lofty tone. "Or we would, if I wasn't the only one residing in this Podunk sinkhole of a town."

The coach tossed a football out to Gray's group, and to my surprise Gray caught it. He then stood in a huddle with the other players while the boys in the unmarked jerseys finished their runs and got into formation facing them.

"Here we go." Kari openly crossed her fingers on both hands. "Is it too much to hope for two broken arms on the first play?"

"Probably," I told her.

Boone looked across the field and then strode over to the coach. They both got into a heated discussion until the coach jabbed his finger at the group with unmarked jerseys. From the way Boone stalked off onto the field, he wasn't happy about being on that side. The coach called out some numbers, and the boys got into position, some crouching, others leaning forward as if getting ready to run.

I knew enough about football to realize what position Gray was playing: quarterback.

I tried not to cringe. "This is going to be bad."

"Stop teasing me," Kari said.

Eleven

Gray moved back into position, called out something, and caught the snapped ball. My vantage point allowed me to see right down the middle of the two teams, and I saw Boone barreling toward my brother. Gray held onto the ball until a second before Boone reached him, then threw a quick pass and side-stepped Boone, who fell on his face. The boy who caught the ball ran it in for a touchdown.

I wanted to stand up and applaud like everyone else in the stands, but I was too astonished. My brother had just thrown his first pass. For a touchdown.

"Dude, close your mouth before you catch a bug," Kari said. She studied my face. "You have a thing for the new QB? Please say yes."

"No." I laughed a little. "He's my brother, Grayson."

"Oh. So the brother of the girl Boone used as an excuse to break up with Tiffany Beck is trying out for Boone's position on the football team." She made a *hmmm*ing sound as she jotted down some notes. "This is getting really complicated. And interesting." She pretended to hold a mike out in front of my face. "So tell our audience, Ms. Youngblood, who *do* you want to make the team? Big bro, or the not-so-secret heartthrob?"

I pushed her imaginary mike away. "No comment."

Kari sighed heavily. "The good ones always say that."

Boone finally got up, shook himself off and went directly over to Gray to shove him, which made me grab the edge of my seat with my hands. Instead of shoving back, Gray just stood there while he and Boone were quickly surrounded by Boone's friends. The coach blew his whistle and then threw down his clipboard as he strode onto the field. A few minutes later Gray trotted off and Boone switched sides.

"Hey." I watched my brother take off his helmet and go down on one knee on the sidelines while Boone took his place. "That's not fair."

Kari patted my shoulder. "Welcome to the Matrix."

I looked over and saw Mrs. Yamah and the other moms staring at me and the Goth girl, and suddenly I didn't care. My brothers and I might be outsiders in this town, but Gray deserved the same chance as everyone else at the tryouts.

The coach had the divided team run several more plays, and my resentment grew as I watched Boone taking my brother's place. He threw passes around like they meant nothing, and half the time they were too short or too long. Then he and his friends began goofing around, disrupting the game by playing hot potato with the football while the other boys stood around waiting. The coach blew his whistle so often and loudly that my ears started to ring.

Finally the coach waved at Boone, who ignored him and called out his own play. I saw one of the boys on the other team take off, rushing at Boone who had turned to toss the ball to one of his friends. He tackled Boone so hard his helmet came off and bounced away like it was made of rubber.

"Yes." Kari shot up and whooped. Then she peered at Boone and dropped back down in a huff. "Rats. Wrong guy."

The coach hurried out onto the field as Boone sat up and grabbed his leg. He crouched beside him to check his ankle, then put an arm around him and helped him up. Boone leaned heavily on the coach as he limped off the field, followed by the friends he'd been goofing off with.

The coach called out to Gray, who got up and trotted out to the field. I heard Boone protesting even as the coach helped him to the bench and knelt down to take off his shoe and sock.

I looked out at Gray, who had already gathered his players into a huddle. By the time the coach stood up both sides were in position, and started the play as soon as the coach's whistle blew.

Just as he had before, Gray threw a perfect pass to one of the receivers, who ran for thirty yards before one of the other boys caught up and tackled him. Gray and the others moved down the field, and his third pass resulted in another touchdown.

The coach gestured for the boys to move back to center field. They lined up and waited while Gray watched the coach for the next play.

"Come on, Grim," I said under my breath. "Show him what you can do."

The coach ran six more plays. Gray threw the ball for four of them, passed it to another player on the fifth, and ran with the ball himself on the last. By the time they were finished the X's had racked up another three touchdowns, one of them made by my brother himself.

"I hope you like living with a god," Kari said. "Because I think your brother just turned into one."

"He's never played football before today." I saw her skeptical expression. "I'm serious. We don't even own a football."

"Then he's either an indestructible cyborg created to ultimately destroy humanity, or a natural." She gave me a shrewd look. "If he turns out to be the robot, I should get an exclusive. Just saying."

The coach called the boys off the field, and I moved down to where I could hear what he was saying. Kari followed me. He read positions from a clipboard and then said a name. When he got to quarterback, the coach glanced back at Boone, who was pale and frowning, before he said, "Youngblood."

"Coach." Boone shot to his feet, stumbled, and grabbed the shoulder of one of his hovering friends. "I play quarterback for the team."

"Not with an injury," the coach told him. "If that ankle is broken, you're out for the season."

"God, this is so great," Kari murmured, looking completely riveted now. "Boone looks like he's gonna cry. Do you think he will? I knew I should have brought my camera."

Boone scowled at the coach. "It's just a sprain."

"We'll see what the doctor says, son," the coach told him. He looked over as Sheriff Yamah walked out to the sidelines. "Jim."

Kari quietly hummed a couple bars of a funeral dirge.

"Frank." The sheriff's mirrored sunglasses flashed as he looked over the boys. "I think you're making a mistake here. Don't throw the season away on a rookie with beginner's luck and no experience."

Gray took off his helmet and looked at the sheriff but didn't say anything.

"Youngblood's completed every pass he's made," the coach pointed out. "If Aaron's not in a cast by the end of the day, he'll be out of commission for at least three games."

"Cat, I was wondering, do you know a big muscular bald guy who wears my favorite color and rides a Harley?" Kari asked.

I nodded, still focused on the sheriff and the coach. "My oldest brother, Patrick. Why?"

"He's standing right behind you."

I turned around to see my brother also watching the argument between the coach and Jim Yamah. His sunglasses kept me from seeing his eyes, but his shoulders were rigid and his hands had curled into fists. "Trick."

"Great nickname," Kari murmured as she watched both of us.

"It's not what you think," I told my brother. "Gray was just trying out. For fun. That's all."

"For fun." Trick turned his head toward me. "Is that what you think?" He walked over to the sidelines.

"Suddenly I'm very grateful that I'm an only child." Kari shouldered her backpack. "Now I've got to go and write up five hundred nauseatingly PC words to describe this event. I'll probably have to puke at least once." She gave me a sympathetic squint. "You okay, Youngblood?"

"I'm fine," I lied. "Thanks for talking to me. It was nice to meet you."

She grinned, making her nose stud twinkle. "No, it wasn't."

After Kari left I thought about going over to join my brothers and provide some moral support for Gray, but I didn't want to make Trick angrier than he already was. I couldn't hear what they were saying, but my older brother stood very still and didn't say much, which meant he was furious. For once Gray seemed to be doing most of the talking, and the coach nodded as if agreeing with every word. Trick finally said something that made Gray shut up and hang his head. After that the coach shook my brothers' hands while the sheriff glared at them. I grabbed my backpack as my brothers walked off the field, and met them halfway.

"Hey," I said to Gray. "You were terrific out there. Really. My goose bumps got goose bumps."

"Thanks." He glanced at Trick before he added, "I made the team. Starting quarterback."

"I heard the coach call your name." I saw Sheriff Yamah walking toward us. "We'll talk about it at home."

"Youngblood." The sheriff joined us like one of the family. "If you have a minute, I'd like a private word with you."

"Whatever you have to say," Trick told him, "you can tell me in front of my family."

"Fair enough." Yamah hitched a thumb in his belt loop. "Lost Lake is a small community. We all know and look out for each other, and we don't appreciate outsiders thinking they can come here and do as they please." When Trick didn't say anything, he added, "You three in particular strike me as nothing but trouble waiting to happen."

Trick didn't twitch a muscle. "Is that right."

"You've got a nice piece of land, so you shouldn't have a problem selling it," Yamah continued. "I'll wager if you put it on the market this week, you'll make a good profit. Enough to start over somewhere else, and then some."

Gray started to say something, but Trick gave him a

small shake of his head. To Yamah, Trick said, "I'm not interested in selling the farm, Sheriff."

"You want me to be plain about it? All right, then." Yamah's mustache bristled. "You three aren't welcome here. I suggest for your sake that you pack up and head out. Find another place where folks don't care who lives in their backyard." He turned and went to where his wife was waiting for him, and the two walked away.

I watched them go. "Okay. What was that all about?" I glanced at Trick. "Why are we trouble? We haven't done anything."

"Let's go," was all Trick said.

———

I expected all hell to break loose between my brothers as soon as we got home, but Gray just headed for the shower while Trick went out to the barn. I went upstairs and hid in my bedroom for a while until it was time to make dinner. When I went down, I decided to make a peace offering of homemade deep dish pizza and a Caesar salad, Trick's favorite meal.

Gray came out to set the table, but when dinner was ready at the usual time Trick didn't show up to join us.

"Maybe we should wait for him," I told my brother as he sat down.

"He's not coming in yet," Gray told me as he reached for the salad. "He's too mad."

I sat down and sipped some milk to ease my dry throat. "Did he say anything to you?"

Gray glanced at Trick's empty place setting. "He didn't have to."

Neither Gray or I had much appetite, so there were plenty of leftovers for Trick. I put them away in the fridge while my brother did the dishes, and then I went out and sat on the back porch. From the hammering sounds coming from inside the barn I could tell that Trick was working on fixing the stalls. That went on for two hours, during which time Soul Patch, Princess and Terrible came to keep me company.

"It's too bad you guys can't talk," I told Princess as she delicately leapt up and turned herself into a fuzzy collar. "You'd probably be able to explain the whole thing a lot better than me."

I knew I'd have to be the one to talk to Trick. Gray never spoke up for himself, not even when he should have. I also understood—kind of—both sides of the argument. Gray secretly wanted to be a normal kid, which he wasn't. Trick didn't want him to hurt himself or anyone else.

There was probably more to it than that that I didn't know. Seeing how my brothers always kept things from me, maybe it was time I talked to Trick about that, too. I wasn't proud of what I'd done to help Gray, but maybe if I were honest and accepted to consequences without making a fuss, Trick would tell me why he'd lied to me about the farm.

I finally got up and fed my stray companions before I went inside to take a shower. While I was dressing I heard someone moving around in the kitchen under my bedroom and went downstairs to find Trick warming up the pizza. He looked tired now, as if he'd worn himself out.

"There's salad in the fridge," I told him. "Caesar, with garlic croutons."

"I recognize a bribe when I see one, Catlyn," he said drily, and brought his plate over to the table. "Sit down."

I sat across from him and decided to attack him straight on. "Military school is really expensive. You'd probably have to work like three jobs to cover the tuition and boarding fees. I admit, the uniforms are kind of cute, but all they'd teach us would be how to march and dig foxholes and use things like bayonets and grenades and rocket launchers."

"You've researched this," he said, eyeing me.

"Oh, extensively. Then after graduation we'd have to join the military and occupy third world countries and walk through a lot of minefields. Which, when you think about it, is kind of like repeating high school." I tried out a tentative smile on him. "So, what if I just admit how truly and deeply sorry I am? Gray is, too. He would tell you himself but he lacks the necessary verbal skills. Say something."

"How involved were you in this fiasco?" he asked.

"I knew he was going to do it." I ducked my head. "I also sort of stole something out of your desk." When he put down his fork, I added, "Gray's last physical. He needed it to be cleared for tryouts."

My brother sat back and rubbed his eyelids with his fingers. When he looked at me again, I could see the disappointment in his eyes.

"Catlyn, I don't often say no to you or Gray," he said slowly. "When I do, there is always a very good reason. I assumed the two of you respected that."

"We do, it's just..." I made a face. "Wherever we go, I've always been able to blend in with the other kids. No one hardly notices me. Gray hasn't been able to do that since the fifth grade."

"Your brother's size is hardly an excuse to defy me," Trick pointed out.

"Don't you ever wonder why he's so hostile and antisocial? It's because he *can't* fit in. He scares other kids, and they avoid him, and he knows it." I leaned forward. "Trick, I think Gray is lonely. He wants to be accepted, to be part of something. I don't know why he picked football—he's never been into sports—but I think he sees this as his chance to be more like other kids. That for once his size will be a *good* thing."

"If he doesn't put someone in the hospital," my brother said flatly. "What will happen to Gray after he hurts someone on the field? Do you think the other kids will admire him for it?"

"He won't hurt anyone." His expression made it clear he didn't believe me, and then I thought of Gray's truck.

"You let him get a driver's license. He takes the truck to school every day."

"So?"

"So it's a big truck. A big, powerful truck, right?" I spread my hands. "Why don't you worry that he'll run down someone in the street? You don't because you know Gray is a good driver. He's careful. He doesn't speed or drag race or do anything stupid. You can depend on him to drive safely."

Doubt clouded his eyes. "You think playing football is the same as driving a truck?"

"They're both a matter of trust." I folded my arms. "Gray knows exactly how big and strong he is. He's not a hothead. He'd never hurt a fly and you know it. So either you trust him, Trick, or you don't. Your choice."

He pushed his plate with the half-eaten pizza away. "Is there anything else I need to know?"

Might as well tell him everything now, so he'd get angry all at once instead of in stages.

"While I was poking around in your desk looking for the physical I found the old deed to the farm. I know this place used to belong to Dad. I also took some letters mom wrote. I've been reading them." I thought of Jesse, but I felt sure now that I'd only been obsessing and dreaming about him. It was over; I'd never see him again, and in a few weeks I'd forget all about him. "That's all."

He didn't say anything for a long time. "And you want me to trust you."

I winced a little. "It was wrong of me, I admit it. But

I wasn't looking for them, and I didn't have to tell you that I'd found them." I needed to go carefully from here. "I've known for a long time that you and Gray have been keeping certain things from me. I'm almost sixteen, Trick. Isn't that old enough to know the top secret stuff?"

He looked uncomfortable now. "What do you think we're hiding from you?"

"In that box with Mom's letter was the key to that old trunk; the one you said got lost when we moved." A jittery feeling came over me as I thought of the trunk, and my hand shook a little as I gestured toward the barn "If that's true, why is it up in the hayloft covered with a horse blanket?"

"I wasn't hiding it. Gray and I found it with some boxes we hadn't bothered to unpack after we got here," he said. "The house attic is packed, so I put it up in the hayloft until I have some time to go through it." He put his hand over mine. "You should forget about the trunk; it's probably full of bugs. What else?"

I felt a little dizzy, but after a moment the sensation passed. "I'd like to know the real reason why Sheriff Yamah hates us," I said. "And don't give me the *we're the outsiders here* speech again. He said we're trouble, and he sounded pretty serious. Why would he think that?"

"He knew our father," Trick said slowly. "Dad told me that he and the sheriff had a fight over our mother, and Yamah lost. So he had Dad arrested for assaulting a police officer, and almost got him sent to prison for it. After the charges were dropped, Yamah made life so unpleasant for our parents that they chose to leave town. The sheriff has been holding a grudge against the Young-bloods ever since."

I exhaled slowly. "I didn't know mom had lived at this farm."

"Our parents came to Lost Lake right after they were married." Trick picked up his dishes and carried them over to the sink. "I lived here, too. I was born here."

No wonder the farm meant so much to him. "But that's like nothing. Why keep it from me?"

"I guess I'm old-fashioned. I didn't want you to think of our father in jail. He was only defending me and Mom." He finished rinsing his dishes and came back to the table. "I don't look much like Dad, and neither does Gray, but you're the image of him, Cat. That's why it's important that you stay clear of the sheriff."

"Now that I know what happened with him and Dad," I chided, "I will. Is the sheriff the reason you hid Mom's letters? Does she talk about him in them?" When he gave me a surprised look, I said, "I haven't read all of them yet."

"Does Gray know you have them?" When I shook my head, he said, "I have to check on the horses. Walk with me out to the barn."

I suspected that he'd already gotten the horses settled for the night, but he obviously didn't want to answer my question, so I followed him out anyway. Sali whickered to me as soon as she saw me, and shuffled forward, obviously expecting to be saddled. As Trick went to Jupiter's stall I glared at her and shook my head. Sali snorted in disgust but drew her head back inside.

I glanced in at Flash, who ignored me because I wasn't Gray, before I went to Jupe's stall, where the big white stood blinking sleepily as Trick rubbed his neck. "Gray doesn't know about Mom's letters, does he?" I asked.

"No." Trick walked over to the hay bales stacked inside the feed bin and hefted one over, carrying and dropping it outside Jupe's stall. "I didn't want either of you to know anything about our grandparents."

"The Fanelsens," I said, and he nodded as he sat down on the bale. I sat beside him. "Why not?"

He sighed. "I was afraid you or Gray might try to contact them."

"But how could we? They're dead." Then I got it. "Oh. They're not dead."

"No, they're not." He hesitated, and then said, "After Mom and Dad died, the Fanelsens took me to court. They disputed the terms of our parents' wills, and sued for full custody of you and Gray."

"You're kidding."

He shook his head. "Mom's family has a lot of money and influence, and their lawyer was very convincing about quality of life you would have with them." His mouth flattened. "But I knew how they'd treat you. The same way they treated Mom: badly."

I thought of how unhappy my mother had sounded

in her letters. "So that's why Mom and Dad dumped us on you."

"Our parents wanted me to be your guardian because they knew I loved you both, and that I'd work hard to provide you with a good home," he said, his gaze growing softer and a little sadder. "But when they died, I was still pretty young myself. At the time the only thing I owned was a motorcycle. I worked in an entry position in my company and I lived in a one-room apartment. My lawyer told me upfront that it was hopeless."

I felt appalled. "How did we end up with you?"

"Our grandparents never came to court, even after they were ordered by the judge to appear." Trick's expression turned contemptuous. "Their lawyer kept making excuses, saying they were traveling in Europe and couldn't be reached, but after he was given two extensions and they still didn't show, the judge finally lost his patience. He upheld the terms of the wills and awarded me full custody."

"Good." I blew out a breath. "I don't get why they wanted custody of us anyway. I mean, I don't remember ever meeting them."

"You never have," Trick said flatly. "After our parents got married, the Fanelsens immediately disowned our mother. They cut her out of their will, refused to speak to her and wouldn't even let her on their property."

I felt a little shocked. "They really didn't like Dad. Okay, so if they hated Mom for marrying him, why sue for custody of us?"

"A few years after Mom married Dad, her brothers were killed in an accident," he told me. "Our grandparents didn't have any other living family except her. When she died, you and Gray and I became the last of the Fanelsens." He said their name like it was a swear word, then sighed and checked his watch. "It's getting late. We'll talk more about this later."

After that we walked back to the house I offered to get my mother's letters, but Trick told me I could keep them. He also promised to talk to Gray about our grandparents.

"I do have to ask one more thing," I said before I went upstairs. "Are Gray and I grounded forever?"

"No." He looked in the direction of my brother's room. "He has football practice, and I'm not going to his games by myself." He kissed my cheek. "Now go to bed. You look ready to collapse."

I went up to my room feeling relieved and satisfied. I was happy for Gray and glad that Trick had fought our grandparents for custody of us. I couldn't imagine growing up in the Fanelsen's house the way my mother had, with private tutors and servants and mandatory hunting trips. I'd have hated that life as much as she had. I was too tired to read any more of the letters, but I didn't feel the need to hurry anymore. Whatever she wrote, I knew the truth about my grandparents now. They'd tried to split up our family, probably just to get back at our mother for defying them.

As I pulled back the covers, I looked over at the window, which was closed. Hopefully I was too tired to have another weird dream about the dark boy, because I really didn't want to. I'd coped with enough stressful situations in one day to last me a couple of years.

Twelve

That night I didn't dream or wake up to find my room in shambles; I fell on my bed and didn't move again until my alarm clock went off the next morning. My brothers were in the kitchen by the time I went downstairs, and from their normal expressions I assumed they'd already talked, too.

Peace. It was a beautiful thing.

I was grateful that things at home were okay now because I still had to deal with the problems at school. Problems I expect would be made worse by Gray being picked as first-string quarterback. Then there was the dark boy, and trying to forget about him.

Although I was happy for Gray, and glad that Trick wasn't angry anymore, I didn't feel so great. I couldn't stop thinking about Jesse Raven. Before, every time I saw a tall boy, or one with black hair, I'd thought of him. Now I didn't even need reminders. I looked at the rising sun, and thought of his face in the moonlight. I gathered up my books, and remembered how gently he'd handled a flower. I brushed my hair, and my fingers tingled with the memory of the liquid silkiness of his. I breathed in, and my nose expected to smell dark, sweet spices.

I had to get over him. He'd become the shadow of all my thoughts, a ghost who haunted my heart. Maybe I needed to treat him like an addiction: see if I could go one day without thinking of him, and then go another, and another. It would have helped if there had been a twelve-step program to follow: Dark Boys Anonymous. Raven Recovery. Freedom from Jesse.

Would I ever be free of him?

When I walked into my first class I couldn't help looking for Boone, but his seat was empty and stayed that way for the whole period. The other kids still whispered and looked at me, but a couple of them already knew about Gray making the team, and offered me some odd forms of congratulations.

"I heard your brother's our new quarterback," one guy who sat in the row next to mine murmured. "Hope he's insured."

"My boyfriend told me Grayson made the team," another girl said to me in the hall between classes. "I mean it's great, but when Boone comes back ... " She tried to smile. "Maybe you should talk your brother into playing another position."

Even the teachers seemed more anxious than happy about Gray. "Your brother put on a quite a show at tryouts," Mrs. Kelsey said. "But football isn't the only team sport at our school, you know. There's baseball in the spring, soccer, tennis... maybe one of those might appeal more to him."

"I think he's only interested in football, ma'am," I said politely.

She looked pained. "Well, do give him my best wishes for a successful, ah, season."

By the time I got to lunch I was fed up with everyone's gloomy predictions. Barb didn't show up, but Ego came to the table and bent over three times before sitting next to me.

"What are you doing?" I asked him.

"I bow to you, oh sister of the mighty Grayson Youngblood," he replied. "Strong of arm, clear of eye, damaged of brain."

"My brain is damage-free, thanks." I handed him the extra apple I'd packed for him. "Unless you're talking about my brother, of whom I am extremely fond."

"I meant him," Ego said. "If I were you I'd spend as much time with him as you can before Boone's ankle heals enough for him to come back to school. That way you'll have some good memories."

"Boone isn't going to do anything to Gray." I heard the sound he made and turned on him. "All right, what have you heard?"

"Nothing, nothing." He held up his hands. "I just

know Boone. Unfortunately, since third grade. That was when I scored the final run and beat his team at kickball. He and his buddies jumped me after school. Don't make me describe how badly they kicked my butt. It'll ruin your lunch."

I sighed. "He's not going to go after Gray, not when he's limping around in a cast."

"His ankle was sprained, not broken," Ego said, and polished the apple on his sleeve. "Barb called me last night with an update. She's skipping school today because she's not feeling well. She's not sick enough to miss getting her daily dose of Aaron news, of course."

Knowing Boone wouldn't be in a cast made me uneasy. "Still, even with a sprain, he'll be on crutches for a while, right?"

"On crutches and surrounded by a dozen of his jock friends. You know, the guys who would do anything for him." Ego took a bite of the apple and then shook it at me. "The baboon, he does not like to lose. Remember this, *chica*."

I shrugged off Ego's unsubtle warning, or thought I did until I caught myself looking for my brother in the halls. Boone might've been absent, but his friends weren't. What if he'd asked them to ambush my brother? I hardly ever saw Gray during school, and I couldn't remember his schedule. I couldn't go to the school nurse and ask if my brother had come in to be treated for a beating.

My last two classes seemed to go on forever until the

bell finally rang. A teacher yelled at me for running down the hall, but I didn't stop until I got to Gray's truck.

I stood waiting and watching for him, but he didn't show. I started checking my watch and counting minutes, first ten, then fifteen. Where was he?

"Cat."

I shrieked and whirled around to see Gray standing on the other side of the truck. His clothes weren't torn. His face wasn't bruised. His hair wasn't even messed up. I could have killed him.

"Where have you been?" I demanded.

"I had to go to the gym to pick out my number." He unlocked his door. "I told you this morning."

"No, you didn't. You didn't say a word." When he reached across to unlock my door, I yanked it open. "Are you going to be late like this every day?" I didn't wait for him to answer. "Because next time I'm just taking the bus home, and *you* can stand here and wait forever."

"I thought I told you." He gave me a wary look. "Sorry."

I didn't accept his lousy apology or speak to him again until we got close to home. "Boone doesn't like to lose," I said. "Everyone at school says he's going to come after you for this."

"Let him." Gray sounded totally unconcerned.

"His friends will help," I snapped. "You know, all the friends he has on the football team. That's what, like ten or twenty jocks? Some as big as you?"

"Two," my brother said. "Neither of them are my

size. The rest of the guys on the team are tired of Boone's ego. They don't want him back."

I huffed out some air. "I suppose they told you that."

"Couple of them did." He made the turn onto our driveway. "I have practice two days a week after school, and the team doesn't go home on Friday until after the game. If you don't want to ride the bus, Trick can probably pick you up."

I didn't care if I had to walk home every day. "Are you really sure this is worth it?"

"Yeah." He put the truck in park and turned to me. "Trick said you talked to him about it last night. You told him to trust me. So why can't you do the same?"

"I trust you," I muttered. "It's Boone. And everyone else." I glanced at him. "So what number did you pick?"

"Three."

"Went with your I.Q. huh?" I nodded. "Good idea. But are you sure you can count that high?"

"Brat." He made a rusty, rumbling sound that might have been a laugh. "It's for the three of us."

He'd picked out his number to remind him of his family. It was touching, and the kind of sneaky thing Gray liked to do, and I couldn't resist needling him a bit as we got out of the truck. "Aw, that's so sweet. Can I draw three little hearts in hot pink marker on your jersey?"

"Only if you want me to hurt you," he said as he followed me inside.

———

After dinner I resisted thoughts of the dark boy by trying to call Barb and see how she was feeling. Her mother answered the phone, but after I asked for her she told me that Barb had already taken some medicine and gone to bed.

"I'm sorry to hear that," I said. "Will she be able to come to school tomorrow, Mrs. Riley?"

"I don't know." Her mother's voice sounded strained. "I'll have to see how she's feeling in the morning. Thank you for calling." She hung up before I could say anything else.

Barb's mother didn't sound very friendly, but she was probably worried about her daughter. I jotted down a note to pick up Barb's schoolwork if she were absent tomorrow; Gray could drive me over to her house after school to drop it off.

Before I took my shower I went out to the barn to muck out Sali's stall and spread some fresh straw for her. As chores went this was one of the nastiest, and the smell of horse manure and urine grew stronger every time I pitched another layer of dirty straw into the barrow. But once, when I'd griped about it, Trick had asked me how I'd feel if I had to stand in a dirty toilet all day. I'd never complained about it since.

My mare seemed impatient, and nudged my back a few times while I finished spreading out the fresh straw.

"Stop tempting me," I told her, knowing she wanted to go for a ride. "I'm trying not to think about that, much less do it."

I saw something white sticking up behind one of the boards at the back of the stall and took off my work gloves to pull it out. It was an envelope, and I wondered if it was some mail Trick had picked up and then stuck there while he was working on the stall. But Sali's stall didn't need any repairs, and I usually did everything else for her. I opened the envelope.

There was something inside, and it wasn't a bill.

I knew my horse wasn't leaving notes for me, and my brothers wouldn't bother. I took out a square piece of stiff, semi-transparent paper with dark, bold writing on it.

Meet me tonight by the moonflowers.

"Cat?"

Quickly I stuffed the note back in the envelope and shoved it into my back pocket before I came out of the stall. "Over here."

Trick walked in with a sack of feed balanced on each shoulder, which he carried over to the plastic bins where we stored it. "Have you seen my cutter?"

I glanced around and spotted it sitting on the work bench. "Got it." I brought it to him, and he dropped the sacks by the bin.

"Thanks." He cut open the end of one sack and emptied the feed into the bin, which was almost full. It had been nearly empty the day before, so he must have been emptying sacks into it all day. "You've got straw in your hair." He glanced past me. "You haven't been up in the hayloft, have you?"

Since there was nothing up in the hayloft except hay, it surprised me that he would ask that. "No, I've just been working in Sali's stall." I glanced inside the bin, which was close to overflowing now. "Do we need all this feed?"

"We will next week," he said. "The vet didn't find any trouble with those mares, so I'm going to buy them. I'll need you and Gray to help me bring them over on Saturday. Did I tell you one of them is an Arabian?"

I listened as he described our new horses, and tried not to move too much. Every time I did the note in my pocket crackled a little.

What had Jesse written the note on, parchment? When had he written it? Why? He'd been smart enough not to write my name on it or sign it, but he'd still taken a big risk leaving it in Sali's stall for me. If one of my brothers had found it, they wouldn't think it had been left for them.

Trick was saying something and I shook my head a little. "I'm sorry, what?"

"I said, leave your boots by the door outside and I'll clean them for you." He closed the bin and latched it.

If he was working in the barn tonight I'd never get away to meet Jesse. "You aren't going to stay up all night again, I hope. You know you'll feel terrible in the morning."

He shook his head and rubbed one shoulder. "I'm too sore for that. I'll do all the boots tomorrow." He sniffed. "Be sure to shower before you go to bed. Not to be crude, but you smell like Sali's rear end."

"Thanks." I tried not to rush until I was out of sight, and then I ran to the house and up the stairs to my room, where I took out the note and tucked it under my mattress next to Mom's letters.

I spent extra time in the shower so I could scrub away the dirt and sweat from working in the barn and wash the smell out of my hair. After I dried off I changed into a fresh pair of jeans and a flannel shirt, and covered them with my robe. I had to use the blow dryer on my hair, but that made it a little smoother than it usually was.

I was too nervous to sit down, but I did shut off the lights so my brothers would think I was asleep. Then while I waited to hear them going to bed I had to torture myself by wondering why Jesse wanted me to meet him.

Had he changed his mind? Why hadn't he tried to call me first? Our number wouldn't be listed in the local phone book yet, I remembered, and Trick might have even had it unlisted. He couldn't have mailed me a letter without his parents finding out, and despite what he'd said about them I had the feeling they didn't know about us.

Us.

Not counting my weird dream, this would be only the third time we'd met, and I was already thinking about me and Jesse as a couple. And I didn't care. He'd left a note for me. In our barn. Exactly where he knew I'd find it.

But *when* had he left the note? What if I'd found it too late? What if he'd been waiting for me last night, or the night before that, and when I didn't show had given up on me?

I couldn't stand waiting another second; I had to get out of the house. Instead of trying to sneak downstairs, I opened my window and looked at the pine tree. The branches seemed sturdy enough to hold my weight, but if they didn't, it was a long way to the ground.

Calm settled over me. *I can do this.*

I took off my robe and draped it on the end of my bed like I always did. After I put one of my pillows under the covers, I scrunched them up around it so it looked like I was huddled under them. Then I went and climbed onto the windowsill, and reached out for the thickest branch.

"Don't break," I whispered just before I swung out and grabbed the branch with my other hand. I heard the wood creak and felt the branch dip and swung my legs over to the trunk. I found footholds on some lower branches and went hand over hand until I could get my arms around the trunk. I stopped for minute, my whole body trembling, before I looked down and saw the next branch I could grab and step down to.

"Next time," I promised myself, "I'm going to wait and use the door."

The trees held me until I had climbed down halfway, but from there the branches looked too thin to support my weight. It was a ten-foot jump to the ground, too far for me to make it without hurting myself, or so I thought until I heard a rushing sound in my ears and without thinking let go of the branch I was holding.

I plummeted straight down and landed on my feet. Quickly I bent my knees to keep from toppling over, and waited to feel horrible pains shoot up my legs, but nothing happened. I slowly straightened, and wanted to laugh out loud at how easy it had been. As if I dropped ten feet on a daily basis.

I heard a little yowl and stepped into the shadow of the house, only to see Soul Patch padding up to me. He rubbed his head against my calf and meowed plaintively before scampering off into the back yard. Princess and Terrible appeared and did the exact same thing. I didn't move until a pure white cat I recognized came and purred while he batted my leg with its paw.

"I don't know what they told you, but I don't feed the homeless in the middle of the night," I said. The white cat yawned before he took off around the corner. I followed him into the backyard, and saw dozens of cats gathered just outside the porch. "Oh, no. Come on, you guys."

"Don't be angry with them," someone said. "They've been waiting with me."

I peered in the direction of the voice, which seemed to be coming from the trees at the back of the yard. "Jesse?" I looked back at the house before I walked toward the trees. "Is that you?"

He stepped out from behind the trunk of a big maple. "I'm here." He held out his hand.

As I walked over the strays came after me, escorting

me like furry bodyguards, but when I reached Jesse they dispersed, taking off in different directions. "Your note said to meet you by the moonflowers."

"I wasn't sure if you would find the note," he said as I came to him and took his hand. "When I saw you leave the barn earlier, I thought you might have missed it. My plan was to wait until all the lights went out and throw some pebbles at your window."

"They only do that in movies." He was leading me past the trees and into the training pasture where Trick worked with the horses. "Where are we going?"

"I left Prince over there." He stopped and looked down at me. "Would you like to take a ride with me?"

"I was planning to," I said, and pointed to the barn, "but my horse is that way." I started to let go of his hand.

He held onto me. "Prince will carry us both."

Oh. He wanted me to take a ride *with* him. "You're not going to jump any fences, are you?"

"No fences." He brought me to Prince and after untying him, handed me the reins. Then he mounted the stallion with one impossibly fluid movement, and held out his hand to me again.

I eyed the back of his saddle. There was enough room for me, but it was too high up. "I'm going to need a step-up."

His hand didn't waver. "I won't let you fall."

I reached up, and a moment after my fingers met his I was straddling Prince's broad back. Flustered by how easily Jesse had boosted me up, I braced a hand against his shoulder and situated my legs. Fortunately we were both slim through the hips, and fit the saddle as if it had been made for us to ride together.

When I took my hand down, Jesse reached back and caught it, drawing my arm around his waist. "Are you ready?"

No. "Yes."

I felt him shift the reins and murmur something, and Prince wheeled around. Then the stallion began to trot along the fence to a gate that stood open.

I wanted to press my cheek against Jesse's back, and hug him with my arm, I felt so relieved. He'd waited for me. He'd come to the house to toss pebbles at my window.

Now all I needed to know the reason for this. "Why did you come back?"

He glanced over his shoulder as he guided Prince through the gate. "You won't believe it."

"Try me."

"I've been dreaming of you." He looked ahead. "I never dream."

I was glad he wasn't looking at my face so he wouldn't see my goofy grin. "Jesse, everyone dreams. They don't always remember it, but it's part of the wiring."

"I did once, but not anymore. Not since I was … I was a boy." He walked Prince across the drive and down to the slope dividing our property from the road. "I thought if I saw you the dreams would stop."

"Oh." I drew back a little. "So this is some kind of sleep disorder therapy."

"No, Catlyn. I wanted to see you again." He sounded a little baffled now. "I didn't know how much until you came out tonight. Life has been very difficult for me. Very complicated."

I understood that only too well. "I'm sorry."

"Don't be." He squeezed my hand. "Seeing you makes me remember what matters."

I had to know. "What's that?"

"I'm going to show you."

Thirteen

*O*nce we left the farm and crossed the road, Jesse guided Prince through a dense section of trees to an old, secluded riding trail. I'd never realized it was there, but it was pretty well-hidden from view. Judging by the overgrown brush and low-hanging branches it hadn't been used for years.

I assumed he was going to head east, down toward an strip of undeveloped land where occasionally I'd seen other people riding, but instead he turned Prince toward the property next to ours.

"Are you going to tell me where you're taking me?" I asked as Prince passed through a gap in another fence, this one covered in a thick layer of fragrant honeysuckle vines.

"I want it to be a surprise," he told me. "Don't worry, you'll like it."

"You keep saying *it*," I teased. "Is it a place, or a thing? Please say it's a brand-new car."

"It is not a car." Jesse looked back at me. "Do you want a car?"

I kept forgetting how rich he was. "Thanks, but I think that would be a little hard to explain to my brothers." Now I was curious. "Do you have a car?"

He shook his head. "My parents think they're too dangerous. We have a chauffeur and limousine for whenever we leave the island. Our housekeeper and estate manager also keep cars at the dock."

I tried to imagine what it must be like, living with servants and having private cars. He probably never had to do things like clean the bathrooms or fold laundry. "It must be great to have other people do all the work."

"I appreciate their efforts, but I would rather do things myself." He hesitated. "Are you going to learn how to drive?"

"Trick let me drive Gray's truck a few times around the farm during the summer while I was helping him with the fencing, so I already know how. I just need to get my learner's permit to be legal. My older brother promised I could, if I get good grades this semester." I saw lights flickering ahead of us, and frowned. "What's that?"

"My surprise."

As Prince reached the end of the trail the trees on

either side thinned out and the ground became paved with cobblestones. They surrounded a two-story white house, but it wasn't a farmhouse like ours. I knew that the moment I saw the square-sided tower rising to the side of the low, rounded stone stairs leading up to the front door.

Glowing lights in the windows showed off short, scrolled wrought iron bars surrounding little terraces outside the long, narrow windows on the second floor. The glass in the windows had a crackled texture that caught the glow from inside and turned it into golden cobwebs of light. I saw some funny stone carvings here and there that resembled the heads of different wild animals. This wasn't a country house; it was a country mansion.

"What is this place?" I asked him.

"It's called Conac Ravenov," Jesse said as he tugged Prince to a stop. "It's my family's ancestral home."

"You have *another* mansion?" I asked blankly. "In the middle of the woods?"

He chuckled as he swung off Prince and reached up to whisk me down. "It's not really a mansion. It's too small."

"Small." I was pretty sure our entire farmhouse might fit comfortably into one corner on the ground floor. "Right." I glanced up at him. "Do you live here?"

"Not since my parents bought the island." He took my hand. "Come inside."

The terraced steps leading up to the front door had once been soft white stone, but now were cracked and grimy with layers of dirt and dead leaves. The front doors, two immense panels of dark, carved wood, had old-fashioned brass handles instead of knobs, and their hinges creaked badly as Jesse pulled them open.

I peered inside and saw filmy, ragged curtains of dusty cobwebs and candlelight. "This place already looks haunted. It would be great for a Halloween party." I expected to see rats or beetles scurrying around the floor, but there was no sign of any critters. "Is it okay if we go inside?"

"Of course." He sounded amused. "It is my house."

"You mean it's your parents' house," I said as I walked into the wide entry hall.

"No, it belongs to me." He pointed to the right. "So does the land."

"But you're just a kid. You can't own things yet." Sometimes I thought about what sort of apartment I'd get when I went to college, but the thought of having a house was only a distant, vague thing I wouldn't have to worry about until I was a lot older. "Can you?"

"I don't think anyone has ever asked that question. Including me." He opened another door. "Someday I want to live here."

"So we'll be neighbors." I ducked under the bottom of an old orb spider's web. "I'll come over whenever we need a cup of sugar." I glanced down at the floor, which was thick with dust. "Maybe I'll bring the vacuum."

There wasn't any furniture to speak of; by one wall I saw a couple of old straight-backed chairs with fancy tapestry seat cushions that looked as if they'd fall to pieces if anyone sat on them. Between them was an old trunk with brass fittings caked with rust. But framed pictures cover the walls, including one gigantic painting hanging over the stone mantel of a dark fireplace.

"Stay here." Jesse went over and picked up something from the floor, and lit it with a match. The flame inside the storm lamp sputtered for a moment before he turned up the wick and set it on the mantel.

The lamp illuminated the hanging pictures, all of which were colorful old circus banners. They were all written in different languages, and illustrated with images of smiling clowns, beautiful women in spangled costumes and bare-chested men lifting weights. In at least half of them I saw the Ravenov trick riders performing on their white horses.

I walked up to one and saw from the visible brush-strokes that they were canvas paintings, not printed pictures as I'd assumed. I grinned as I turned around. "These are incredible. How old are they?"

"Very old." He sounded wry as he shook out a faded quilt and spread it on the floor.

I glanced at the quilt and then at him. Under the circumstances—me and Jesse alone in an empty house in the middle of the night—I should have felt a little alarmed, but oddly enough I didn't. "Are we camping out here?"

"Perhaps another time." He produced a big wicker hamper and set it in the middle of the quilt. "Tonight we are having a midnight feast."

He opened the basket and began unloading it, placing cups, covered plates and stacks of small containers on the blanket.

"You brought a picnic." I inspected the feast he unpacked, which consisted of three loaves of French bread, five packages of sliced meats and cheeses, a dozen containers of fresh veggies and fruit, and a huge tin of homemade cookies and brownies. He even pulled out two slices of cake on little plates covered with plastic wrap. "Where did you get all this stuff? Did you knock over a deli?"

"No, I took it from Sheriff Yamah's refrigerator." He bent to retrieve some napkins from the basket and missed the horrified look I gave him. "Do you like ham and cheese? I believe he does. He keeps several packages of it—"

"Jesse," I said, cutting him off. "You *stole* this food from the sheriff?"

"I borrowed it," he said as he poured a bottle of iced tea into a cup and handed it to me. "He won't mind. James is very good friends with my parents."

"That makes it worse, not better." I looked at enough food to feed me and my brothers for a week. "You couldn't have just walked into his house and helped yourself." When he gave me a blank look, I added, "You're kidding. Wasn't he there? He didn't try to stop you? What about his wife?"

He shrugged. "I would have asked first, but they were sleeping. I didn't want to disturb them." He frowned at me. "I left a note. My parents will pay for everything."

"If the sheriff doesn't stop by the island in the morning to arrest you for burglary." I sank down beside him. "Jesse, you can't just break into people's houses and help yourself to their stuff. It's rude. It's a felony."

"I didn't break in." He showed me a key. "James gave me this and said I could stop in whenever I liked. He won't be angry, Catlyn, I promise."

"Okay." Maybe rich people had a different set of rules than the rest of us. Maybe the sheriff was a much nicer man than I'd thought. Maybe I'd be brought in as an accomplice. "Do you do this a lot? Borrow things?"

"No. In fact, this is my first picnic." He looked around at the food. "Did I forget something? I have napkins."

"You have stolen napkins," I pointed out. "Sheriff Yamah's stolen napkins."

He studied my face. "I'm not a thief, Catlyn. I would have gone to one of the shops in town and bought the food, but none of them are open after sunset."

Now his arrangement with the sheriff made a little more sense. "You're sure this is okay, and he's not going to be mad at you?"

He nodded. "Eat something. Please."

I felt a little self-conscious as I tried the iced tea and picked up a sandwich, so I looked over at the old rusty trunk. For some reason it drew my gaze like a magnet. "My brother used to have a trunk like that. I think it belonged to my parents. It got lost during one of our moves."

"No, it didn't." At my blank look he added, "It's under an old horse blanket in the back of the hayloft in your barn."

My head ached as I recalled my own voice saying almost the exact same words to Trick, and then Jesse saying them to me before. "How do you know what's in our hayloft?"

"I sat up there one night and watched you." He frowned. "I told you about it before, don't you remember?"

I thought I remembered everything that he'd said to me, but nothing like that came back to me but a shaky, startled feeling that I didn't like at all. I shrugged to cover my confusion. "Sometimes I forget things. So what was I doing?"

"That night you were brushing out Sali's mane and tail. This was before we met." He smiled. "I enjoyed how you spoke to your horse. You kept apologizing to her for pulling her hair."

I knew I talked to Sali as if she were a person, but I still felt a little embarrassed. "You shouldn't spy on people when they're grooming their horses. Why didn't you just come by the barn and say hello?"

"I wanted to." He folded one of the napkins into a triangle. "I didn't know if you would welcome me."

"I always have time for guys who bring me food." I admired the feast again. "This is really nice, you know. I haven't been on a picnic in ages. When I was little Trick used to take me and Gray to a park to have cookouts on the Fourth of July, but then he started having them at home."

"What did he cook out?" Jesse asked.

"Oh, anything he could burn," I said as I eyed a pint container of ripe red strawberries. "My brother tries, but he never thinks anything is done, so whatever we get is usually triple well-done. Is your mom a good cook?"

"She was, once." He refilled my glass. "Mother doesn't cook anymore. The servants do."

"Must be nice." I offered him the container of strawberries, but he only shook his head. "I know it takes a lot to keep a mansion tidy, but isn't it a little creepy, having strangers in your house all the time?"

"It was in the beginning, when we came here," he admitted. "I didn't know some of them very well, so I didn't trust them. I thought they might try to take advantage of us."

I frowned. "You mean, like steal from your parents?"

"Steal from them, betray them, hurt them." He handed me a big chocolate chip cookie. "My father is cautious, but my mother still believes that there is good in everyone."

I thought of Boone. "I don't know if I buy that. There are a lot of selfish people in the world. Some of them don't care who they hurt in order to get whatever they want."

"You are not like that," he said.

"Me? I can be just as selfish as the next girl." I looked

around the room. "If I were really a good person, I wouldn't be here with you."

His brows rose. "Why do you say that?"

"Jesse, I had to sneak out of my house to see you," I reminded him. "If my brothers knew I was here, alone with a boy at night…" I stopped as I realized what I was saying. "Not that I think you brought me here for anything but a picnic." I glanced at his empty hands. "Which you are not eating."

"My condition strictly limits my diet," he explained. "But I enjoy watching you eat."

"Yes, my chewing and swallowing being so attractive." I held out the cookie, but he shook his head again. "Come on, you can't even have one bite?"

His expression turned wistful. "I could, but it wouldn't stay down very long."

"That's just not fair." I put down the cookie. "Can't your parents do anything about this? Take you to a specialist or something? Maybe there's something on the internet—"

"No, they've done what they can." He looked at the food. "I did bring far too much, didn't I? Stupid of me." He stood up and went to the window.

I followed him. "You're not stupid. Actually, you're pretty amazing."

His broad shoulders went rigid. "You think that now."

"No, I've thought that from night one." I touched his arm. "I'm not perfect, either, Jesse. This past week, I've felt like the biggest loser on the planet. I found out that after our parents died, my brother Trick had to fight for us in court. I never knew that. He gave up his life to take care of us, to protect us. And what do I do in return? I lie to him, I keep things from him." I looked at our picnic and felt a twinge of regret. "I sneak out of the house at night."

"Would your brother let me see you if I came to your house?" he asked softly.

"I don't know." But I did. I knew if my very overprotective big brother found out about my friendship with Jesse it would be very bad. "I don't think so. He's kind of antisocial."

"Now I should say that I understand, and that I won't try to see you again." He reached out and tucked a piece of my hair behind my ear. "But *I* am too selfish for that." He glanced out the window. "It will be sunrise in a few hours. I'd better take you back home."

"Do you really want to see me again?" I asked.

He nodded. "Tomorrow night. I want to ride with you. I want to talk with you. I want to know everything about you, Catlyn." He smiled. "Will you meet me at midnight?"

"By the moonflowers?" I didn't even hesitate. "Yes."

———

After Jesse brought me back to the house, he insisted on standing under the pine tree while I climbed back up to my bedroom window. As soon as I was safely inside, he put his hand over his heart, and then lifted the palm toward me. I didn't have the nerve to blow him a kiss in return, but I waved back and watched as he disappeared into the shadows.

I never got the headache I was expecting but went to sleep at once, and woke up the next morning feeling so rested and content I practically skipped downstairs.

"Good morning," I said to my brothers as I breezed over to the table. Life was so wonderful that I didn't even mind seeing the bowl of oatmeal waiting for me. "Anyone want some fruit?" I went to look in the fridge. "Do we have any strawberries?"

"No, thank you, and no," Trick said from behind his paper.

Grayson only grunted.

I took out a cup of the mandarin oranges I usually packed in my lunch bag and brought it over to the table. "So what's up with you guys today? Anything interesting in the paper?"

"I can't tell." Trick squinted. "Your glow is blinding me."

"Grump," I chided as I emptied the orange slices into my oatmeal and stirred them around before taking a big spoonful. "Do you have practice today?" I asked Gray after I swallowed. He just stared at my oatmeal. "If you do I'll take the bus home so Trick doesn't have to come pick me up. Unless you're not busy, Trick. I wouldn't mind a ride on the Harley; it's been ages." Neither of them said anything. "What?"

"You just put oranges in your oatmeal," Gray said.

"Yeah, so?" I took another bite.

"Your maple-flavored *raisin* oatmeal."

I stopped chewing for a second and then shrugged. This morning even raisins didn't seem so bad. "The oranges are a strategic addition. They disguise the taste of the evil wrinkled grapes."

Gray eyed Trick. "You ever see her eat a raisin before? Voluntarily?"

He shook his head and peered at me again. "Maybe I should make a doctor's appointment."

Gray nodded. "She probably rolled out of bed last night and cracked her skull."

I sighed. "Can't a girl wake up in a good mood without everyone thinking she has a head injury?"

My brothers looked at each other and then me. "No," they both said at once, making me laugh.

That was the beginning of the happiest three weeks of my life. Seeing Jesse again fixed something inside of me that I hadn't known was broken. I didn't have a single headache, and being with him began to change my attitude, too. All the problems I had worried over so much suddenly seemed so trivial and meaningless. I had more important things to think about now.

After our midnight picnic at Conac Ravenov, I went to school feeling completely different; as if overnight somehow I'd grown taller and stronger and prettier. I felt more alert, too, as if the world had come back into focus after being fuzzy for so long. As the weeks passed and the temperatures gradually grew cooler, everything seemed crisper and more alive. Colors seemed brighter; on cold mornings the air still smelled of sunlight. Even the shabby old shops in town we passed on the way to school acquired a new kind of quaint charm in my eyes.

Jesse and I met every night at the patch of moonflowers. At first we just rode over to the house where we'd sit and talk, but then we started exploring the old riding trails. There seemed to be a million of them, hidden all over his property. We even found one that led to a small lake surrounded by rushes and sea oats. The surface of the lake was so still that it glittered like a mirror in the moonlight.

"How could you not know this was here?" I asked him as we stopped to water the horses.

"I've never ridden down this trail." He looked out over the lake. "It is beautiful. I'm glad I own it."

We were at least four miles from the manor, and I'd been on the lookout for *No Trespassing* signs. "This can't be yours."

He glanced around and nodded. "All of this land is."

I couldn't believe it. "Jesse, just how much property do you own?"

"I don't know. My parents gave me seven or eight hundred acres, I think." He grinned at me. "I have three other lakes, too."

"You *own* four lakes."

He made a casual gesture. "They aren't very big."

"Four *little* lakes. Yes, of course, that makes all the

difference." I rolled my eyes. "Next thing you'll be telling me is that you own the state of Florida."

"No, only a small part of it. The land and buildings in the downtown section of Lost Lake belong to my family. Some of the houses on that side of the lake are ours, and the fire department, the police department, the water works, the power company..." He paused and thought for a moment. "We built the marina and the yacht club, too." He saw how I was looking at him. "My father enjoys sailing. It's a matter of convenience."

I shook my head, laughing helplessly.

My favorite nights were when we let Prince and Sali race each other down a long, wide clearing behind the old manor house. Prince almost always won, which annoyed me and Sali, but occasionally I rode close enough to bump shoulders or legs with his rider. That always seemed to divert Jesse's attention long enough for Sali and me to sprint ahead.

"You're distracting me," he accused after we beat him to the finish line. "On purpose."

"I have to. Your horse is bigger and faster than mine." I dismounted and took an apple cookie out of my jacket pocket as a reward for Sali. "We girls have to use whatever tactics we can."

He gave Prince a consolatory rub on his strong neck. "You mean, you have to cheat."

"There are no rules against accidental bumping," I informed him.

"There should be," he muttered.

While we were together Jesse and I talked about everything: his family, mine, life at home, things that had happened in the past and what we looked forward to in the future. I learned that when Jesse was younger he had traveled with his parents all over the world, and spent months exploring countries like Spain and France and Germany. He'd even gone to Egypt and seen the great pyramids.

I started to feel a little jealous until I told him about all the places where we had lived. Despite trekking all over Europe, the only part of the U.S. he'd seen was Central Florida.

"You have to go to California someday," I told him after describing the place we'd rented outside Napa Valley. "It's like the best of the whole country packed into one state. There are mountains, beaches, deserts, valleys…" I sighed. "One time my brother took us all the way down the Pacific highway, from Eureka to Baja. The sea is on one side, the mountains on the other, and every now and then you see a house up on a cliff or a sailboat gliding across the waves." I sighed. "I think I miss California the most. I loved so many places out there."

He watched my face. "Maybe someday we could travel there together."

I couldn't imagine the logistics involved with making travel safe for someone like Jesse, who could never be exposed to sunlight. "You'd take a vacation with me?"

"I would go anywhere with you," he assured me.

Fourteen

The only time I couldn't get away to see Jesse was on Friday night, when I went with Trick to Gray's weekly football game, either at Tanglewood or at another area high school.

I knew Trick didn't approve of Gray playing football, although when we went to the first official game of the season he outwardly behaved as if nothing were wrong. When we arrived at the field, he told me to go and find us some seats while he went to the concession stand to buy us some hot dogs and sodas.

I didn't know whether to sit as close or as far away as we could, so I picked a spot in the middle of the center section of the bleachers. While I waited for my brother, I saw the seats to the right and left filling up with students wearing Tanglewood jerseys, T-shirts and ball caps.

A couple of the rowdier guys had painted their faces with brown and white stripes, and one blonde girl sported spray-on brown streaks in her hair.

"Looks like the kids are infused with school spirit," Trick said as he sat down next to me and handed me a hot dog. "Why didn't you paint your face?"

"After you're six it stops being cute." I scanned the field looking for Gray, who trotted out to the sidelines a few minutes later with the other players. "There he is." I pointed toward him. "See? Number three."

"He looks like a professional in that uniform." Trick didn't sound very enthusiastic.

"I had no idea the pants high school players wear would be so tight. They look like they're painted on." I leaned forward. "Did you know his butt was that shape? I didn't." I tilted my head. "Kind of looks like an upside-down heart, doesn't it?"

My brother didn't say anything, but I felt him relax a little.

After playing the national anthem, the announcer introduced the teams as they took the field. As the visiting team kicked off I got to my feet and started cheering for our players along with everyone else. By the time Gray made his first successful pass, Trick was on his feet and yelling, too. We got the first touchdown two plays later.

The visiting team wasn't a pushover, however, and Gray and the Tigers had to fight for every yard. I saw my brother get tackled repeatedly, and a couple of times he went down hard. But he always threw the ball before anyone touched him, and the Tigers started racking up points.

When he was on the sidelines, Gray would take off his helmet and go down on one knee. Once he turned around and spotted me waving at him, and grinned.

The only time I got worried was when one of the opposing team threw a punch at my brother after the play had ended. Gray added insult to injury by ducking and avoiding the blow, but the officials saw it and penalized the visiting team. As Gray was walking back to take his position, the penalized player shoved my brother from behind, knocking him flat on his face.

I grabbed Trick's hand as he started to stand up. "Wait."

Gray pulled a piece of turf from the faceguard on his helmet before he stood and turned around. Instead of hitting back, Gray said something and held out his hand. The other boy rudely turned his back on him, but everyone had seen it, and began clapping for Gray. A minute later the penalized player was ejected from the game.

"Way to go, Grim," I said, loud enough for Trick to hear.

When the whistle blew on the final play, the score was 42–17 Tanglewood. The screaming, jumping and hugging in the stands didn't stop for a full ten minutes.

Trick kept an arm around me and looked down at the Tigers, who were trotting across the fifty yard line moving opposite the visiting team. As each player passed another, they slapped hands.

"That was a good game." My brother sounded relieved, and then he caught my expression. "It was a great game." When I punched his shoulder, he chuckled. "Fine. You were right."

We walked down to join the crowd of parents waiting outside the exit door of the locker room, and several of the dads there spoke to Trick and praised Gray's performance. I watched all the shoulder-slapping and loud guffawing my oldest brother had to endure while I tried to keep a straight face.

Gray got pummeled quite a bit himself as he emerged from the locker room. He sported a band-aid over his right cheekbone and a fresh graze on his chin, but he nodded and smiled as he worked his way through the crowd to us.

"Hey." He was trying not to beam and failing miserably. "You waited for me. So, what did you think of the game?"

"You were terrible," I told him after I gave him a hug. "Really. Only six touchdowns, Grim? Beyond pathetic. We were so embarrassed that we're thinking about moving to Tibet. Without you."

"Brat." He messed up my hair, but his expression became more uncertain as he turned to Trick. "Thanks for coming, bro." He moved his shoulders. "I know football isn't your thing."

"Yeah, well." The stern set of Trick's mouth slowly stretched into a wide smile. "It is now."

The final surprise of the night was waiting for me when we got home. I knew Trick and Gray would probably want to talk about the game—guys loved to analyze sports to death—so I said good night and went upstairs to shower. When I went into my bedroom, however, I smelled something sweet and followed my nose to my bed.

I drew back the covers and found on my pillow a long-stemmed white rose. Then I looked over at the window and saw it had been left open a few inches.

"Jesse." I lifted the delicate bloom to my face to breathe in the fragrance, which was subtle and slightly sharp, the way the air smelled after it snowed. I knew there wouldn't be a note; the rose said it all. "I miss you, too."

———

As Jesse and I continued to meet in secret every night, school gradually stopped being an ordeal for me. Whenever I saw other kids looking at me or heard them whispering—which happened in every class—I just thought of Jesse and smiled at them.

Grayson's stellar performances at the weekly football games also helped. By the time September turned into October, my brother was being called the best quarterback Tanglewood had ever had, and being his sister didn't hurt. On the contrary. I never sat at an empty table during lunch again, and kids in all my classes started being more friendly to me. Most of the girls who talked to me mainly wanted to know if my brother had a girlfriend, but I didn't mind. Gray was finally fitting in, and I was happy for him.

Tiffany was still there, and three days after spraining his ankle during tryouts Boone came back on crutches, but I hardly noticed them anymore. Their popularity had ebbed to the point of where most of the kids ignored them. Sometimes I caught Boone watching me, but he never again tried to corner me the way he had in the cafeteria.

Barb also finally reappeared after being absent for a week, but she seemed as miserable as I was happy.

"Why were you out for so long?" I asked her at lunch on the day she came back. "Ego said you were sick, but did you have the flu or something?"

"No, it was my teeth. One of my molars cracked, and it got infected." She took out a little pill bottle and opened it. "My whole face swelled up. I looked awful." She nodded toward the pink pills she shook out into her palm. "Now I have to take these every day until I'm like thirty."

"Antibiotics?" I asked.

"I guess." She put them back into the bottle. "I can't stand it anymore. I'm going to flush them. I hate pills. I really hate doctors." She looked down at her tray before she got up, threw away her food and left the cafeteria, as if she'd completely forgotten about me and Ego.

I frowned. "Is she going to be all right?"

"I don't know," Ego said, sounding just as mystified. "But I can tell you, those aren't antibiotics she's taking." When I glanced at him he added, "They're only effective for seven to ten days."

"Well, maybe they're painkillers." Barb had seemed a little sluggish. "Are you going on that zoo field trip at the end of the month?"

"For that night-with-the-animals thing?" He shook his head. "My foster parents work at night, so I have to stay home and make sure the dogs don't eat the furniture." He yawned. "Why are you going? You don't seem like the zoo type."

I smiled. "I like the night life."

The real reason I'd signed up for the trip was the unique timing, which I explained to Jesse that night at the manor.

"In biology class we've been studying the habits of nocturnal animals," I said as he finished building a fire for us in the old hearth. "This is also the month that the zoo has a 'Night with the Animals' week and stays open until dawn. Our teacher decided to take the class there. We're supposed to go on a guided tour and write a lot of notes on what we see."

He sat back on his heels as flames enveloped the old dry branches he'd stacked over a mound of browned pine needles. "Creatures who hunt at night are interesting. You should enjoy it."

"I want you to go, too." I crouched down beside him. "It's perfect for us. The tour doesn't start until after sunset, so there's no danger of you getting burned." He wasn't saying anything, and it was beginning to make me nervous. "You could meet me there and we could check out all the critters together. I'll introduce you to my friends. It'll be fun." I watched him stand up and frowned. "Jesse?"

"I'm flattered that you would want me to escort you on this trip." He sounded upset now. "I would also very much like to meet your friends. But I can't go with you, Catlyn."

"Why not?" I got up. "My brothers aren't going to be there. It'll be a bunch of kids from school, our biology teacher and a couple of parent chaperons. They probably won't even notice you."

"What if they do?" He tossed another log onto the fire. "Have you thought about how you're going to explain who I am? Why I'm there?"

"I was just going to say that you're one of the kids who takes classes by computer from home, and that I'm your tutor." I didn't understand why he behaving as if he were upset. "If you're worried about your parents finding out, we can come up with a fake name. How about George?"

He smiled sadly. "I can't ride Prince to the zoo."

"So meet me at the high school, and I'll sneak you on the bus," I told him. "You can walk to the school from the docks, right?"

"I can't do that."

"Why not? You ride across town to meet me every night." A thought occurred to me, and I stepped back. "Jesse, are you ashamed of being seen with me? Is that why you don't want to go?"

He didn't answer me.

"I see." I turned away. "I'm sorry, I didn't realize *why* you wanted to keep our friendship secret."

"Catlyn, you're not..." He made a frustrated sound.

"Every time I come here to see you, I break a promise I made to my parents. I do that because I can't stay away, but also because I know now that nothing bad will happen. When you're with me, you're safe. Away from here…"

He wasn't making any sense. "What could happen at a zoo, Jesse? We walk around. We get some popcorn. We look at animals with insomnia. How is any of that going to hurt me or you?"

"There are reasons my family lives on an island," he said. "Every time I leave it, I'm vulnerable. Every night I come here, I put myself and my parents in danger."

"I don't understand why you're afraid. Jesse, whatever your parents want, you can't live on that island forever." He gave me such a bleak look that I caught my breath. "Is that what they made you promise? That you would never leave? How could they ask you to do that?"

"I'm not like you, Catlyn. I'm sick, and I'm not going to get better." He looked up at a dusty medallion carved into the plaster ceiling. "Being around all those people is dangerous. I can't risk it."

I felt a sharp pain in my chest, as if my heart had just broken in two. "Why didn't you tell me it was this bad?"

"Don't you see? When I'm with you, I can be just like anyone else. You've never treated me as if I were different. Do you know how wonderful that feels? To ride and talk and laugh. To be normal." His head sagged. "But I've been fooling us both. I can't have this life. We live in two different worlds, and I can't walk out of my shadows into your sunlight."

I felt tears sliding down my cheeks. "You don't have to be alone, Jesse. No one does."

He cradled my face between his hands. "Do you mean that?" He sounded desperate.

"Of course I do." I closed my eyes and hugged him. "I've never felt like this with anyone but you."

He put me at arm's length. "I have to show you something. Will you come with me?"

I nodded, and he seized me hand and almost dragged me out of the house. After he tossed me up on Prince, he jumped onto the saddle in front of me and we took off.

We rode down the trail that led to an enormous old barn about a mile from the manor, where Jesse brought Prince to a halt and helped me down.

"Open the doors," he said, pointing to them.

When I pulled the old sliders aside, he walked Prince into the barn, and I followed them.

Once inside he dismounted and handed me the reins. "This is where I used to practice before we moved to the island. I used to live in this barn." He went around and began lighting oil lamps, setting them into high shelves on the walls until a golden glow filled the air.

I saw a center ring, just like the kind they had in the circus, surrounded by little colorfully-painted wagons and racks of some sort of equipment. Sawdust had been scattered all over the ground, which felt as hard as cement under my feet. I turned to Jesse, who was removing Prince's saddle and blanket.

I felt completely bewildered now. "You wanted to show me that you used to practice for the circus?"

"I want you to know who I am," he said, and removed Prince's bridle before he slapped the big black on the haunches. Prince leapt neatly over the rim of the foot-high, red and white painted wooden ring and began galloping in a circle.

I drew back. "Jesse, this isn't a good idea. You could get hurt."

He smiled at me. "I was practically born on horseback, Catlyn." He walked backward toward the ring, and then sprang into a high, long backwards somersault. When he landed, he was standing on Prince's back.

I would have shrieked if I hadn't clapped my hand over my mouth. He'd just jumped onto a galloping horse without looking back. I'd never seen anyone perform such a stunt, not even in the movies.

Prince kept galloping in circles while Jesse turned around and flipped head over heels, landing on his hands this time and lifting his legs straight up in the air. He turned his head to look at me, and his hair fell back from his face.

All the strength went out of my legs, and I sat down hard on the sawdust-covered floor. I'd seen this before. The horse was black instead of white, and the ring was in a barn instead of under the big top. They were different, but the trick rider performing the handstand wasn't. He'd done this before, and it had been captured on black-and-white film.

Geza Ravenov in performance, 1873.

Fifteen

Jesse reversed his handstand before rolling to one side of Prince and then the other, lowering his legs as he held onto the stallion's neck. He used the ground like a springboard and the horse like a piece of gymnastic equipment. I watched him do things I'd never thought were possible on the ground, much less a galloping horse.

And all the while I kept seeing the image of Geza Ravenov, frozen forever in a handstand he performed over a hundred years ago.

Prince slowed to a trot as Jesse straddled him and used his hands on his neck to guide him to the center of the ring. The big black turned in a tight circle, faced me, and went down on his forelegs, dipping his head. Jesse vaulted up and over Prince's head and landed on his feet, lifting his face and spreading his arms as if expecting applause.

That was my cue. I got to my feet and clapped a few times, but my heart wasn't in it. "Bravo."

He bowed low and then came up with a grin. "What did you think?"

I thought that he and Geza Ravenov were twins, or doppelgangers, or clones of each other. A thousand things ran through my mind as I walked over to the ring. "Riding like that, you should be in a full-body cast."

He seemed to see my face for the first time. "You didn't enjoy it."

"I don't know. I was too busy prying my heart out of my tonsils." I looked around the barn. "Jesse, why are you doing this? Do you how dangerous it is to perform acrobatics on the ground, much less on the back of a galloping horse? If you'd fallen off—"

He looked annoyed. "I never fall." He put Prince's bridle on and led him past me out of the barn.

I turned around and called after him. "I know better, remember?"

I could hear the sounds of pumping and water gushing into a trough, and the horse drinking, but I stayed inside. My thoughts were as jumbled as puzzle pieces rattling around in a box with a picture of Geza Ravenov on the outside. I couldn't make anything fit. Jesse lived on an island; he had a house in the woods. He was dependent on his parents; he owned half the state. He came to see me every night; he couldn't go to the zoo.

Nothing connected. Nothing belonged in the same box.

A hand touched the back of my neck. "Catlyn?"

I didn't know why I blurted it out, I just did. "Are you Geza Ravenov?"

He flinched. "How do you know that name?"

"I found a picture of him on the internet. Geza Ravenov, making a handstand on the back of a white horse in the eighteen hundreds." I glanced down at his right hand. "He had your ring. And your body. And your face."

"Geza Ravenov died in eighteen seventy-four."

I felt impatient. "Jesse, just tell me the truth."

"I am not lying to you, Catlyn. He is dead. The Ravenov performers were attacked in the mountains. Most of them were murdered." He recited the facts as if they meant nothing. "That was the reason my family came to America. The show could not go on."

I tried to regroup. "Do you think you're him? That you've been reincarnated or something?"

He smiled a little. "No. I may look like Geza, but I can never be him." He looked over at the ring. "No matter how hard I try."

"Then explain this to me," I demanded. "Why are we here? Why did I need to see you do this?"

Before Jesse could answer me, Prince let out a loud screech and slammed into the side of the barn. We hurried outside, only to see the big black galloping off into the woods.

"Something must have spooked him." I caught Jesse's

arm as he started to go after him. "It's only a mile. We can walk back."

"We can't walk." His eyes shifted to the trees behind the barn. "The sun will rise in less than an hour."

I checked my watch, and saw it was close to five a.m. "All right, then you'll have to stay here."

"I can't," he insisted. "The barn has too many gaps; it won't protect me."

We'd ridden Prince together from my house; Sali was still in our barn at the farm. I thought hard. "Will Prince go to the manor?"

"I don't know. He might follow the trail." He took my hand. "Can you run?"

I nodded, and took off with him. He had a longer stride so I had to run a little faster to keep up. Halfway down the trail Jesse picked me up off my feet.

"Put me down," I said as soon as I'd grabbed his neck. "You can't carry me and run."

He didn't listen. "Hold onto me."

I laced my fingers together as he picked up his pace, and a moment later he was running so fast the trees started blurring around us. I didn't know how he could move faster while holding me than he had when I'd been running beside him, but I wasn't afraid. Jesse was different, I understood that, and he'd taken me to the barn to try to explain how.

Now he might die because of it.

The closer it came to sunrise, the slower Jesse moved. We arrived at the manor just as the sky began to turn a dark blue, and his arms trembled as he put me down on my feet. Prince wasn't there waiting for us, and didn't answer Jesse's whistle.

"I'll look for him," I said. "Go inside the house."

"There are too many windows, and nothing to cover them." He sat down on the steps and braced his arms against his knees, leaning against them as if he were tired.

I saw red dots speckling his brow. "You're bleeding."

He wiped his forehead with his sleeve, leaving a red streak across it. "Is there a vault in your house?"

"A vault?"

"It would be under the house," he said, panting the words. "Like a cellar, but no windows."

I tried to remember what Trick had told me about the house. "There used to be an old root cellar, but it wasn't safe so they filled it in." I looked at the manor. "Is there one here?"

He shook his head. "It flooded after a storm, and the walls collapsed."

I thought of the surrounding farms. "Maybe one of my neighbors has one."

"It's too late now." He sounded dull.

"No, it's not. I don't know any of the neighbors, and asking will waste time, so I'm taking you home." I went over and pulled him up. "Come on." I put his arm around my shoulder and led him down the path to the road between our properties and up the drive to my house.

"I'll be right back out," I told him, propped him against Gray's truck. "Don't run off anywhere."

He gave me a wan smile. "No, I won't."

I ran to the front door and jerked it open, hurrying through the house to the kitchen and the rack where Gray kept his spare keys. I changed direction to grab a quilt I'd washed and left folded in the laundry room, but the sound of Trick's bedroom door opening made me race back into the kitchen to grab the spare keys before I flew back outside.

"I can get you as far as the docks," I told him as I unlocked Gray's truck and threw the quilt in on the seat before I helped him inside. "How do you get to the island from there?"

"I have a boat." He looked through the windshield at the sky. "There are only a few minutes left. We're not going to make it in time."

"Yes, we are." I got in behind the wheel and started the engine. "Fasten your seat belt."

I put the truck in reverse and hit the accelerator, looking through the back window as I sped down the drive. I ran off onto the grass before I could maneuver the truck onto the road, and muttered as I shifted into drive.

Jesse glanced back at the house. "Your brothers are going to be very angry with you."

"They'll live." I should have felt horribly guilty for stealing Gray's truck, but I was too worried about Jesse.

"If Trick had let me get my learner's permit, I wouldn't have to be a carjacker now."

"You'll be punished for this." He closed his eyes and sank back against the seat. "For me."

"You're worth it." I glanced sideways, and nearly ran off the road when I saw how ashen he was. "Cover yourself up with that quilt."

I ran stop signs and red lights all the way from the farm into town, but it was still early and there were hardly any cars on the road. I pulled into the lot by the docks just as the sky lightened to a soft pale blue.

Jesse stumbled out of the truck as I raced around it to help him. "Where is the boat?" I asked after I draped the quilt over his head and shoulders.

"Over here." He pointed and then staggered, almost falling before I caught him. "Do you know how to drive one?"

"Trick taught me last summer when we went on a fishing trip." He sounded so weak I felt my heart constrict. "You've never shown me all the good fishing spots around here, you know."

"Next time," he promised.

I hauled him toward the small black-hulled boat at one end of the pier, and once he had climbed down into it I uncoiled the two rope lines securing it to the dock.

After I stepped off the pier onto the boat I went to the console and turned a key that was sticking out. The boat vibrated as the outboard engines started, but when I turned around I saw Jesse collapse, the quilt falling away as wisps of smoke rose from his body.

"No." I dragged him under the canopy over the console and covered him up. "Hang on. We'll be there in a few minutes."

The engines roared softly as I drove the boat away from the pier. Once we were in deeper water I throttled up, increasing the boat's speed until we were jetting across the surface of the lake.

The wind blowing in my face made me squint, and lake water sprayed over the bow to pelt me like needling rain. I felt Jesse's hand on mine and looked down at his eyes, which were weeping tears of blood. "We're almost home. Don't you die on me now. You have to introduce me to your parents."

"I'll try." His voice was barely a whisper. "Catlyn, whatever happens … I'll always be with you."

"I know." I held onto his hand. "Stop talking now, or you'll make me crash into the island."

As we crossed the last quarter mile, I saw a small pier where I could dock the boat. I also felt the first rays of the sun on my neck and smelled smoke. Once I'd pulled up alongside the concrete posts of the dock I didn't bother with the ropes, but hauled Jesse up and helped him onto the weathered, silvery wooden planks. I put my arm around his waist and supported him as we stumbled toward the tree-lined embankment on the other end.

A man hurried to meet us, and got on Jesse's other

side to help support his sagging body. To me he said, "This way. Please, hurry."

Between us we got Jesse from the pier and through the trees to a small cinderblock structure where two more men were waiting. They took Jesse from us to help him inside, where they went down a flight of stairs into the dark. I picked up the quilt from where it had fallen on the ground, but when I tried to follow them the man who'd met us at the dock stopped me.

"You can't go with him, miss."

I gave the man an impatient look. "I just want to know if he's okay." I tried to yank my arm from his tight grip. "I have to explain what happened to his parents—"

"You can't be here," was all he said as he turned me around and marched me back to the pier.

Despite my protests the man forced me back into the boat and made me sit down. "I'll take you back to town now."

"What if I wait here while you go check on him? I won't move a muscle, I swear." The man ignored me as he started up the boat. "Will they take him to a hospital? Is he going to be okay?"

The man spared me a glance. "You saved his life by bringing him home, miss. For that, I know his family is grateful."

Grateful, but not enough to let me stay on the island.

All the frantic energy drained out of me, and I sat down on the bench seat behind the console. I had to go home and face the music now, something I didn't look forward to. Trick had been awake; he would have heard the truck when I'd pulled out of the drive. He'd be waiting for me at the front door.

At least things can't get any worse.

I looked across the water at the dock where I'd left Gray's truck. I hadn't remembered to take the keys out of the ignition, but it was still where I'd parked it. Then I saw someone walking out on the pier to meet the boat and frowned. Trick wouldn't have known where I was going. Something flashed from his face, and it took me a moment to realize that it was the sunlight reflecting off the silver lenses of his sunglasses.

Things just got a lot worse.

————

Sheriff Yamah watched me climb out of the boat, but he didn't acknowledge my existence. To the man who'd driven me back, he said, "Morning, Larry."

"Jim." Larry inclined his head toward me. "This young lady needs to get on home. Would you make sure she does?" When the sheriff nodded, he started up the engines and drove off back toward the island.

I felt my stomach clench as I watched him go. "I can explain, Sheriff."

"No doubt you can, Ms. Youngblood." He didn't look at me. "Right now I'd like to see your license, and the registration for this vehicle."

I thought about lying and saying I'd left them at home,

but if he checked—and he probably would—it would only make the situation worse. "I think the registration is in the glove box." I looked at the ground. "I don't have a license yet."

He took the radio clipped into his belt and spoke into it. "Bob, I've got a blue pickup truck parked down here by the dock. Seems it was stolen. I need you to come on down here and drive it back to the Youngblood place. Yeah, I'll meet you there." He waited for an acknowledgment before he shut off the radio.

"I didn't steal my brother's truck," I said as soon as he turned to me. "I borrowed it. I can take it back home right now."

"You're an unlicensed driver, young lady," he reminded me. "You're not taking it anywhere." He pointed toward his cruiser, which was parked next to the truck. "Let's go."

He didn't handcuff me or read me my rights, but he did make me sit in the back like any other criminal. I thought about trying to talk to him about Jesse and what had happened, but I suspected the sheriff would only use that information against me.

"I found a girl your age last week down in the park," the sheriff said, glancing at me in the rearview mirror. "She'd violated curfew to go out joyriding with some friends. Only they didn't turn out to be such good friends, and now she's in the hospital."

I met his gaze in the mirror. "I'm sorry to hear that."

"Not the first time something like that has happened,"

he continued. "Last month we had two girls attacked outside the movies after the midnight show. They were robbed and beaten. Then there was this little girl from the middle school who disappeared after sneaking out one night to meet some boy. We found her three days later, wandering in the woods, covered with cuts and bug bites and ticks. Another night and she likely would have died out there."

Bile rose in my throat. "That's terrible."

"That's what happens to kids who don't consider the consequences of their actions." He shook his head. "Maybe you should think real hard about that, Ms. Youngblood. Because the next time you decide that the law doesn't apply to you, you might not be so lucky."

I knew he was trying to scare me, and it was working, but I felt a little indignant, too. "I took my brother's truck so I could help Jesse Raven get home. He told me that you're a friend of his parents, so you have to know about his condition."

His voice turned cold. "I know all about Jesse."

"What I did," I continued, "I did it for him. He's my friend."

Yamah didn't say anything for a while, and then he glanced back at me. "I don't know how you got mixed up with Jesse, but it ends now. After this, his folk won't let him see you again."

Anger made me tremble. "They can't stop us from being friends."

"You don't know what the Ravens can do to you,

young lady." He sounded bored. "But just in case you're thinking of trying to see him again, don't. If you're caught trespassing on Raven Island, the Ravens will press charges. You'll spend a minimum of six months in juvenile detention."

Trick was standing in the drive when the sheriff pulled up, and came over to open the back door as soon as the cruiser stopped. "Are you all right?"

I nodded.

"Mr. Youngblood," Yamah said as he climbed out. "I apprehended your sister in town. I have enough evidence to bring her in on suspicion of car theft, boat theft, and trespassing on private property. Certainly you can appreciate how serious these charges are."

Trick put his arm around me. "I'm sure my sister has a good explanation for what happened."

"There is no excuse for breaking the law, but I'm willing to let her off with a warning this time," Yamah said. "I won't do that again, Mr. Youngblood. Unless you want to see how your sister looks in an orange jumpsuit, you'd better do whatever it takes from here on out to keep her in line." He glanced back as his deputy drove Gray's truck up the drive before he spoke to me. "I'll be keeping an eye on you, too, Ms. Youngblood."

I worked up a tepid smile. "Thank you for the ride home, Sheriff."

Trick waited until the officers left in Yamah's cruiser before he took me inside. He marched me back to the kitchen and sat me at the table while he stood looking down at me.

For once I couldn't joke my way out of the situation. "I'm so sorry about this, Patrick."

"You're something," he agreed. "You stole your brother's truck. You were driving without a license. But that wasn't enough? You had to steal a boat? You had to be caught trespassing? Have you lost your mind?"

Gray came to stand in the doorway. "Is she all right?" I heard him say.

Trick spared him a glance. "Yeah. You'd better get to school." When I tried to stand up, he gripped my shoulder and pushed me back down. "*You* aren't going anywhere. Not until I get to the bottom of this."

Sixteen

I did want to tell Trick everything that morning, but I knew when he found out about me and Jesse he'd go ballistic. There was no way he'd understand why I'd been sneaking out for weeks to meet a boy at night, or believe that it had been completely innocent. He really would ground me for life, or see to it that I'd never step foot outside the house again without him or Gray hovering over me.

If I told him the truth, I'd never see Jesse again.

For that reason I gave him a severely edited version of the facts. I told him that I'd found Jesse after he'd been thrown from his horse, saw how hurt he was, and thought only of getting him home. There hadn't been time to ask permission, so I'd taken Gray's keys and the truck. The only way to get to Jesse's home was by taking his boat. Everything I'd done, I insisted, had been to help an injured, helpless boy.

Trick paced around the kitchen. "Why didn't you come and get me when you found him? I could have driven him to the emergency room."

"There wasn't time, and he didn't want to go to the hospital," I said. "I guess I just reacted."

He stopped and studied my face. "You're lying."

"I didn't think." I resisted the urge to hunch my shoulders as I stared at the cracks in the table. "I only wanted to help him. That's all."

"So you drove him to town, stole a boat, and took him out to this island. Because you didn't think." He dropped down in the chair beside mine. "Who is he?"

"His name is Jesse—"

He slammed his fist on the table. "Who is he to *you*?"

I looked into his furious eyes. "He's just a boy. That's all."

He sat back. "And you expect me to believe this story." He got to his feet and started pacing again. "Go get cleaned up. I'm taking you to school." When I stood he glared at me. "You're grounded until you tell me the truth. Then I'll decide what to do with you."

Arguing was pointless; he was too angry to listen to me. I nodded and went upstairs.

Trick didn't simply take me to school; he parked and escorted me to the admissions office, where he signed me in. "I'm picking you up today. You wait for me out front."

"But Gray doesn't have practice until …" I trailed off when I saw his expression. "All right."

After Trick left, I had to wait for a pass, but the secretary was busy with another kid who had to call home. She let him use a phone sitting on small table beside her desk, and when he couldn't reach his mother she gave him a telephone directory to look up the number for her office.

After the student left the secretary made out my pass and handed it to me. "Here you are, Katie. Thank you for waiting."

"No problem." I didn't bother to correct her on my name. "Ma'am, I forgot some homework, and I have to turn it in today. Could I call my brother real quick?"

She nodded and turned back to her computer, and I went over to the table and opened the telephone directory, flipping through the white pages to the letter *R*. I didn't know Jesse's parents' first names, but there couldn't be that many Ravens in Lost Lake.

As it happened I found no listing for anyone named Raven, but there was a number for Raven Island Property Management. Quickly I dialed it and waited for someone to pick up.

"Property management," a woman answered.

"Hi," I said in a low voice. "Is … is Jesse Raven there?"

Her voice sharpened at once. "Who is this, please?"

"My name is Catlyn. I'm the one, I mean, I brought Jesse home this morning." I glanced over my shoulder and saw that the secretary was frowning at me. "Please, can I speak to him?"

"I'm sorry, miss," she said, her tone a little softer now, "but the family doesn't accept outside calls."

I bit my lower lip. "Can you at least tell me if he's all right?"

"Don't call this number again, or I'll have to report you to the police." She hung up on me.

I put down the receiver, grabbed my backpack and left the admissions office. Jesse's family probably had a private number; like most rich people they'd only give it out to people they trusted. I couldn't even call back to try to persuade the lady in property management to give Jesse a message from me; she'd call Sheriff Yamah. Who would be delighted to arrest me for making crank phone calls.

I trudged through my classes, and since I'd forgotten to make my lunch I almost didn't go to the cafeteria. Then I remembered that Ego's foster parents worked for the Ravens, and went to find him.

"You can't call them," he told me after I asked if he knew the family's private number. "The only telephone on the island is in my dad's office."

"Is his office Raven Island Property Management?" I asked, and he nodded. "Does your mom or dad take messages for the family?"

He thought for a minute. "I don't think so. My parents usually just talk to vendors to place orders and schedule drop-offs." He eyed the soda I'd bought for myself. "What are you, dieting?"

"I forgot to pack something this morning. No, that's okay," I said when he offered me the bag with his free lunch. "I'm not hungry."

His expression turned shrewd. "Tell you what. You explain why you're so interested in the Ravens, and I'll give you half my PB&J."

I saw Barb standing in the lunch line. If she heard me talking about this morning, she'd gossip to everyone. "I need to find out how Jesse Raven is. He was hurt this morning."

"You *heard* about that?" Ego looked impressed. "My foster mother got a call about it right before I left for school. So who told you?"

"It doesn't matter," I said quickly. "Did she tell you what happened to Jesse? Is he all right?"

"Are you kidding? Marcia lectured me about it," Ego said drily, and then raised his voice to imitate a nagging woman's tone. "'Diego, I hope you're never as inconsiderate or ungrateful as the Ravens' boy. After sneaking off and staying out all night, he comes home in such bad shape they had to medicate him. This is what happens when you give kids too much. They get spoiled.'" Ego grinned and shifted back into a normal tone. "Anyway, Marcia said Jesse's going to be fine, although he's not going anywhere for a while."

"What do you mean, he's not going anywhere?"

"His parents didn't know he'd left the island or was out after curfew, so now he's in hot water with them. You know what that means among the obscenely wealthy?"

He handed me half his sandwich. "No yachting privileges, no caviar snacks before bed, no private screenings of unreleased blockbusters in the family's private theater."

"Who has a private theater?" Barb asked as she sat down beside Ego.

"I do." He bumped her shoulder with his. "Come over sometime and I'll show you my extensive collection of Three Stooges movies."

I bit into the half-sandwich Ego had given me, but it tasted like PB&J-flavored cardboard. As I chewed and listened to Barb detailing the latest brouhaha, which had gotten Tiffany Beck and two other cheerleaders lunchtime detentions, I felt someone run a finger along the back collar of my T-shirt, and turned around.

Boone, no longer on crutches, smirked at me as he walked on by.

———

That afternoon I went out after the dismissal bell to find Trick waiting on his Harley just outside the exit doors. After that, he showed up there every day I got out of school to pick me up.

From that day my big brother kept his word and held me under house arrest, forbidding me from leaving my room except for meals and chores. Indoor chores, of course; I wasn't allowed to ride Sali, feed or brush her, or even go to the barn. Trick refused to speak to me except once every night after dinner, when he'd ask if I was ready to talk to him.

I knew what I'd done was wrong. I knew my brother was punishing me not because he wanted to see me suffer but because he loved me and he was worried about me. I also knew that telling him what he wanted to know would not make things better.

The first couple of nights when he spoke to me I simply didn't answer. Trick would try to stare me down for a few minutes (I quickly learned to focus on his earring instead of his eyes so it ended in a draw) and then he would tell me to go back up to my room.

Gray didn't talk to me or look at me. He did, however, take his spare set of keys off the rack in the kitchen and hid them somewhere else.

I used my domestic imprisonment to study, read, rearrange my closet and write some poetry. I soon got bored of that, especially when all the poems I wrote started sounding the same and only described how sorry my brothers were going to be when I died of loneliness.

After school on Friday Trick (who had been doing all of the cooking since I'd gotten grounded, much to everyone's despair) set only two places at the table. When Gray didn't show up I felt like saying something; if I had to eat Trick's singed sausage and peppers, so did he. Then I remembered he wasn't coming home because it was game night. Tanglewood would be playing a team everyone had said was their bitterest rival, the Silver Lake Sentinels.

I'd gotten used to going to the games, and I liked

them, and the thought of missing this one really bugged me. Trick seemed to pick up on that because he made a point to rub salt in my wounds.

"Kickoff is in an hour," he said as he carried his plate over to the sink. "Are you ready to talk to me? If you tell me the truth, I'll let you go to the game tonight."

I inspected my fingernails. They'd grown a bit because I wasn't allowed to touch Sali or work in the barn; I'd already filed them into perfect ovals. Maybe I'd borrow some nail polish from Barb and paint them.

"If you can't go, I can't go," my brother continued. "Gray won't have anyone there to watch him."

I gave him an ironic look. At the last game dozens of girls had shown up wearing number three jerseys over gray jeans. They all sat together, and when they weren't shrieking "Go, Gray, Go!" at the top of their lungs they made up their own cheers that rhymed with my brother's name, even when he wasn't on the field.

"The paper says the Sentinels are favored to beat the Tigers by three touchdowns," Trick added. "Be a shame to miss your brother showing them how wrong they are."

I began softly whistling the POW's tune from the movie *The Bridge Over the River Kwai.*

"I know how stubborn you can be, little sister," my brother told me. "But you're not only one in this family who inherited that mule-headed gene. And I'm not the one sitting and staring at the same four walls every day."

True, but I had a lot more to lose than he did, so I was clinging to my silence.

"Have it your way," he said. "Go back to your room, and I'll see you in the morning."

I went upstairs, and flopped on my bed, and wondered if it were possible to die of loneliness. Aside from the general misery of being grounded, I'd been feeling unsettled and depressed, just as I had after finding Jesse's ring. I'd gotten so used to seeing him every night that even when I fell asleep early, I always woke up just after midnight, my heart racing and my fingers itching for the reins. A few times I opened my window and stared at the pine tree as I imagine climbing down it and sneaking over to the barn. But as much as I loved my midnight rides with Sali, without Jesse it wouldn't be the same.

The worst part was not knowing what was happening to Jesse. Ego didn't know anything more than what he'd told me, and I stopped asking him about the Ravens when he started to become suspicious.

"What is it with you and the rich and famous?" he teased. "Are you angling for an invite to the island?"

I knew I wasn't welcome, but it would be a consolation to know that Jesse was having some visitors. "Do they invite people there?"

He coughed a chuckle into his fist. "No, but they do have anyone who comes within ten feet of the shore arrested."

"Why?"

"Because they're rich and they can."

"What if a friend of Jesse Raven's came out to the

island?" I asked. "What would happen? Hypothetically speaking, I mean."

Ego considered that for a moment. "Jesse Raven doesn't have any friends. Not in this town, anyway."

"Say he makes a new friend in town, and the friend wants to go out to the island to check on him." I knew I was pushing too much, but I had to know. "How can they make that happen? Without getting arrested."

"I guess this friend"—he glanced up at the light fixture—"would have to find a way to get to the island first. That means buying a boat, because none of the charter operators will go out there. Yamah would yank their licenses."

The only way I'd get a boat was to actually steal one. "What about your foster parents? Would they be willing to take a friend of Jesse's with them when they go to work?"

He pursed his lips. "Larry, he actually likes kids, so he'd just say no. Marcia is more preemptive. She'd say no, smack the kid with her purse, and call the cops."

I touched my arm where the man on the island had gripped it while marching me down the pier. "Your foster father's name is Larry."

He nodded. "My social worker said I didn't have to call them Mom and Dad because they're not my birth parents. I do it because it annoys Marcia. But I digress." He itched his chin. "This *friend* of Jesse Raven's can't get out to the island unless she swims there, so I think you should tell her to forget about the whole idea."

I saw how he was looking at me. "It's not me. It's a hypothetical friend."

"I know. I have plenty of those." He looked at his milk carton and my unopened soda can. "Want to trade?"

Barb, who was back to her normal self, tried her best to cheer me up. "I know why you've been so blue lately. You've been hitting the books too hard."

I hadn't told her or Ego that I'd been permanently grounded. "Yeah, that must be it. Educational depression."

"Tonight will be a lot more fun." She giggled. "I wonder if any of them, you know, get busy right there with everyone watching." At my blank look she grinned. "You forgot, didn't you? Tonight's the field trip. You know, we're spending the night with the animals."

I hadn't remembered the field trip, and being reminded made me think of the argument I'd had with Jesse. "I don't think I'm going."

She frowned. "But you already signed up and paid for your ticket. You've got a spot on the bus. You have to go."

"My brother isn't too thrilled about me going out at night." Or anywhere, for that matter. "I'll ask him, but he'll probably say no."

"If you need a ride to the school, call me and I'll ask my mom if we can pick you up," Barb said. "And if your brother fusses, remind him: it's educational."

Because the bus was leaving at sunset, I had to ask

Trick about going on the field trip as soon as we got home from school.

"You signed the permission slip a month ago. Weeks before I committed the crime of the century," I added. I wanted to go on the trip just so I could get out of the house for a little while, but I wouldn't admit that to him. "So it's no big deal. I won't hold you to it."

"I think it would do you some good to get out," he said, astonishing me. "We'll have an early dinner, and then I'll take you over to the school."

"You're letting me out of solitary?" I didn't like the smug tone in his voice. "Why? What's the catch?"

"No catch." He lifted his brows. "Would you rather I say 'no' and 'go to your room'?"

"That's okay." I wasn't a gift-horse mouth checker.

After dinner I showered and changed before I met my brother downstairs. Instead of taking me to the school on his Harley, he drove me over in Gray's pickup truck. I found out why as soon as he pulled out of the drive.

Trick wanted to talk.

"I've heard this zoo has some nice exhibits," he said.

I leaned back. "They generally do."

"You and your friends should have fun."

I doubted he even knew where the zoo was. "I'll be sure to report your kindness and generosity to Amnesty International the next time they visit."

"What if I ask you one question, and you answer it without deliberately trying to tick me off?" he countered. "Do you think you could do that?"

"Depends on the question." I folded my arms. "Go ahead, give it a shot."

He kept his eyes on the road. "Did you steal Gray's truck because you got yourself involved with this boy?"

I frowned. "I don't understand the question."

"Allow me to clarify." His hands tightened on the steering wheel until his knuckles bulged. "That morning, were you two trying to run away together?"

I turned toward him, completely dumbfounded. "You thought I was *running away* with him?"

"That's not an answer."

"Of all the—" I stopped myself and covered my eyes with one hand while I took a steadying breath. "No, Patrick. I did *not* steal Gray's truck so I could run away from home with a boy. Among the many excellent reasons I would never do that, the boy in question desperately needed medical attention."

"I want to believe you, little sister," he said slowly.

I dropped my hand. "So I'll take a polygraph. And I'll pass it. Will that satisfy you, or should we discuss more reliable interrogative methods, like injections of sodium pentothal? Or beating the soles of my feet with a cane?"

"Stop being sarcastic," he snapped.

"Then stop being ridiculous." I was so angry I could have hit him. "I took Gray's truck without permission, which was wrong. I drove without a license; also highly illegal. But I did it to help someone who was in trouble, and that, big brother, is the truth. If you want to turn that into a soap opera, be my guest. I don't have to convince you of anything. I don't care. I *know* what I did."

He didn't say anything more until he pulled into the school parking lot behind the field trip bus. When I reached for the door handle, he said, "Catlyn."

"The bus is going to leave," I said flatly. "Am I going on this field trip or not?"

"You're fifteen years old," he said, ignoring my question. "The same age Mom was when she met Dad."

"Check the dates on the letters," I advised him. "She was seventeen."

"Close enough. Have you read all of them yet?"

Thanks to all the turmoil in my life, I realized I hadn't even thought about them. "I have a couple more to finish."

"I'm the reason Mom's family disowned her," Trick said. "She ran away with Dad because she was pregnant with me."

I hadn't known that, and it shocked me until I realized why he was telling me. He thought Jesse and I were…

Through my teeth I said, "I'm not pregnant."

"Right before all this happened, you were happier than I've ever seen you. I may seem ancient to you, but I'm not blind. You were acting like a girl who had fallen in love." He sighed. "I just don't want to see you end up like Mom."

Unbelievable. "I'm not in love."

"Then why are you shouting at me?" he countered.

I covered my face with my hand and then dropped

it. "Because we're talking about me. Me, Patrick. The girl who has never had a boyfriend or gone on a date."

His mouth flattened. "That doesn't mean anything."

"Where and when do you think I'd have a chance to conceive this imaginary baby? In the girls' restroom, in between classes? Under a cafeteria table during lunch period?" He didn't answer me. "Okay. I really don't think it's any of your business, but just to ease your mind, I haven't even had my first kiss yet. So I think it'll be a while before I work up to premarital sex. Can I go now?"

He sighed. "Go."

I didn't slam the truck door after I'd climbed out, and I made a point to plaster a smile on my face as I walked toward the other kids gathering by the bus.

"Hey, Cat." On the other side of the crowd, Barb waved. "Over here."

I glanced back at my brother, who was still parked and watching me. He'd made such a drama out of the whole thing that I wanted to laugh. Stealing a truck to run away with a boy. Getting pregnant. No wonder he'd kept me locked up in the house all this time. He probably thought Jesse and I had been doing it in the woods.

You were acting like a girl who had fallen in love.

I stopped walking, and in that moment, I knew. While I'd been seeing Jesse, I had felt happier and more alive than I'd ever been in my life. Now, without him, I drifted through every day, miserable and hopeless. Trick was right.

I was in love with Jesse.

Seventeen

Barb sat next to me on the bus and talked nonstop for the entire trip. "My cousin Ronnie works part-time at the zoo taking care of the cages and habitats and feeding the animals. I told him our class was coming tonight and asked him if he could get us into some of the places in the park only the employees can go, like the nursery. You can't believe how cute the baby animals are."

I usually felt a little jealous of my friend's perpetual energy and enthusiasm, but the shrill jabber of her voice grated on my ears. I didn't want to go to the zoo anymore; I should have stayed in the car and told Trick to take me home. Caught between Barb and my depression, I knew it was going to be a long night.

Once we arrived and were led through the front entrance by our Biology teacher, Mrs. Richards, who was already lecturing, I felt a little better. The night air washed over my face, cool and crisp, and walking through the shadows toward the exhibits made me imagine I was in the jungle. The zookeepers had switched off most of the electric fixtures in the park, so the only light we had came from flaming party torches they had staked here and there along the walkways.

The first habitat we stopped at was in the reptile exhibit, where one of the herpetologists who worked at the park explained the nocturnal habits of alligators, frogs, snakes and other scaly critters.

"Florida's reptile population has always had a bad reputation, especially in the lakes region where gators have been known to attack and kill humans," the scientist explained. "But the swamp is the kingdom of the reptile, and they all serve as an important part of the food chain. Frogs, for example, are extremely helpful in curtailing the insect population, and serve as nourishment for many of our aquatic birds."

"Okay, I get how frogs are important," one of the students said, "but what good are snakes?"

"Snakes may seem repulsive and frightening, but without them the rodent population would quickly multiply out of control," the herpetologist said. "In areas where land development and pesticides have wiped out the local snake population, we've even seen mini-plagues of mice and rats."

"Hard to tell which is worse," a girl's voice sneered behind me.

Beside me Barb shrank down, as if she wished she could disappear, which surprised me as I glanced back at Tiffany and her posse. I wondered why they'd bothered to wear their uniforms and jackets on a field trip, but at least it made them easy to spot.

"What do you think is more disgusting, girls?" Tiffany smirked before she glared at Barb. "The squealing little rats"—she shifted her gaze to me—"or the slithering slimy snakes?"

"I wouldn't know," I answered before anyone could shake a pom-pom. "But I'm sure you and your friends have some redeeming qualities."

A few kids around us hooted their admiration for my comeback, but Tiffany wasn't amused, and took a step toward me. "Yeah, we do. Like not stealing someone else's boyfriend."

I scanned the group until I spotted Boone, and then I looked back at her. "But why steal a guy who you don't even want, and who you can have for free?"

As everyone around us laughed, Tiffany's face twisted. "You're going to regret this," she promised in a low voice.

The hatred in her eyes chilled me, but I was tired of being blamed for her breakup. "You're going to need therapy."

The teacher called out for us to move on, so I turned my back on her and followed the rest of the class to the next exhibit. Barb clutched my arm and pulled me away, putting some distance between us and the cheerleaders.

"Geez. For a minute I thought she was going to jump

you." She blew out a breath. "Maybe we should walk with the teacher. You know, before we end up getting pushed into a pit of poisonous snakes."

I faked a yawn. "They keep a pit filled with cheerleaders?"

"Good one." Barb looked over at a group of park employees standing a few yards back. "Maybe one of them knows where my cousin is working. You go ahead and I'll catch up with you."

We had to wait behind another school group at the next exhibit, mainly because some of the students couldn't be coaxed away from the glass panels that provided an underwater view of the alligator pond. It was understandable; the other group was made up of elementary school-age kids, who obviously thought seeing the underside of a gator swimming was the best thing since recess had been invented.

"It will just be another moment," our teacher said when some of our group began grumbling. "The students ahead of us are from Sunshine School."

I didn't recognize the name, but heard a boy near me mutter, "Great, we have to wait on the retards."

"Hey." The girl standing next to him pushed him. "They're called special needs kids, moron."

"Whatever." He sounded bored.

After the short delay the tour guide rerouted the children from Sunshine School, and we worked our way through two more exhibits. Because Barb hadn't returned from talking to her cousin I began jotting down notes to give to her.

After the second presentation Tiffany rudely pushed past me and walked up to speak to the teacher. Although I couldn't hear what they discussed, the cheerleader pointed back at us and made several big gestures with her hands. When the teacher shook her head, Tiffany actually stamped her foot before she stalked off in the direction of the last exhibit we'd toured.

"We'll take a break here," our teacher said after we finished the tour of the insect exhibits. "Does anyone have to use the facilities?"

I went to sit down and wait on one of the benches by the restrooms, but some of Tiffany's friends beat me to the only empty one left. I changed direction and wandered over to the gift shop, which was closed, and examined the souvenirs in the display window.

"Pretty boring, isn't it?"

Of course it was Boone, standing directly behind me, looking over my shoulder at the stuffed elephants. Whenever Tiffany messed with me, Boone was sure to follow up with his own brand of harassment. I felt like banging my forehead into the window until either the glass or my skull smashed. "Go away."

"That's what I'm doing." He looked over his shoulder before he asked, "Want to get out of here? We can take a drive over by the lake, maybe sit and talk. I could use some advice."

I turned around which I immediately realized was a

mistake, because he was so close he was practically on top of me. Sure, he wanted to talk. "You're planning to steal the school bus?"

"I missed the bus, so I drove over in my car." His eyelids drooped as he braced an arm against the window. "Come on. No one will miss you."

I smiled at him as I imagined driving my foot into his newly-healed ankle and listening to it snap. "Okay, let's go."

He lifted his head, his expression bewildered. "Really?"

"I'm bored, too." I just needed a little more space to make my escape. "So, where's your car parked?"

He took a step back and turned, lifting his hand to point toward something. That gave me enough room to duck under his arm and take off.

I ran around the short alley between the gift shop and the park's ice cream parlor, and as soon as I was out of sight I backtracked to the restrooms. I noticed another building behind the public facilities with lights on, and went in that direction. It turned out to be a visitor's center, which due to the all-night event was still open.

A receptionist looked up as I walked inside. "May I help you?"

I thought of Barb. "One of my friends left our group to see her cousin who works here, and our teacher wants her to come back before we get too far ahead on our notes," I said. "Her cousin's name is Ron Riley. Do you know him?"

"Sure, Ron is assigned to the big cats habitat, which

is right behind the elephant and giraffe enclosures," the receptionist said. "He might have taken your friend to the nursery in building seven over there. One of our cheetahs had a litter in June, and everyone loves to see the little ones."

I thanked her, slipped back out and checked on my class. Since there were long lines of kids still waiting to use the restroom, and Boone might have a bright moment and realize what I'd done, I decided to go and find Barb.

I couldn't help stopping at the giraffe pen for a few moments to admire the towering, awkwardly elegant creatures. My presence drew the attention of one seven-foot-tall youngster, who lumbered over to the fence to have a look at me with his big, soft dark eyes.

"Don't tell anyone I'm AWOL," I said in a loud whisper, and chuckled as he dipped his head as if inviting me to tell him another secret.

I followed the walkway from there to the beginning of the big cats exhibit, where I looked down the small side paths for the caretaker building where Ron Riley had his office. Although the other kids had complained about how dark it was even with the scattered torches, I had no problem reading the small signs posted outside the employee areas. I didn't find the building, so I stopped at the directory map across from the lions' habitat to check my location.

A deep, hunking sound made me turn around, and at first glance I thought I saw a series of small light-colored boulders lining the inside of the high chain link fence surrounding the enclosure. Then I caught the backshine of feline eyes and realized I was being watched by some of the lions. I looked past them at the concrete shelves of the mock cliff that comprised their living area, but they were empty, and what I had thought were boulders were blinking and breathing.

I was being watched by *all* of the lions.

Lions had been mentioned several times in the section of our class textbook that covered nocturnal predators. Although they were excellent night hunters, they were also short-sighted so they preferred to sneak up on potential prey.

"Nice kitties," I murmured, taking a step back. I wasn't a coward, but I wasn't used to being stared at like a limping gazelle. At the sound of my voice some of the females began stirring around the big male, who shook out his enormous mane and then seemed to grin at me. "I think I'll move along to the next exhibit."

My footsteps echoed as I walked down past the lions' habitat and into a darker section of the exhibit. I thought I might be walking a little too fast, and then I heard the echo split into two sounds: my walking and someone else running. I peered ahead and saw the back of a cheerleader's jacket in the distance. It disappeared a moment later, but not before I read the name BECK above the tiger decal.

What was Tiffany doing over here? Had she followed Barb in order to harass her?

The sound of her running steps had disappeared by the time I reached the next habitat, and I couldn't tell which direction she had gone. I turned to go back the way I came when I noticed that there was a piece of the fence around the cheetah compound missing. On closer inspection the gap in the fence turned out to be a gate that had been left open.

That wasn't what made me go still. The cheetah standing directly on the other side of the gap did that.

The long, lanky feline stretched out its head, sniffing the sides of the fence and the ground. Silently I prayed it would lose interest, turn around and walk off so I could grab the gate and close it, but the sound of laughter drew its attention, and it sauntered through the gap and onto the walkway.

I turned my head toward the sound and saw that the students from the special needs elementary school were gathering at another enclosure fence only a few yards away. The big cat saw them, too, and her ears flicked as her orange eyes tracked over them, not curious but assessing.

I thought frantically. I knew from my studies that cheetahs were diurnal predators who hunted early in the morning and late in the afternoon. Because they depended on their sight instead of smell to identify prey, they liked to climb up into trees and up cliffs so they could survey a wide swath of the surrounding area, too. Which they could cover very quickly, as they were the fastest animal on land in the world.

My textbooks had said nothing about how to make a cheetah go back into its habitat, or stop it from attacking grade-schoolers.

"Hey, pretty thing," I said, keeping my voice low and even. "Over here." The cheetah swung her head around toward me, and uttered a sound like a bird chirping. "That's right. Look at me."

I couldn't shout out a warning without startling her, but I could put myself between the cheetah and the children. I moved slowly, taking care not to make any sudden movements, and tried to think of what I could do to keep her attention focused on me. On some level I knew what I was doing was insane, that I should run for safety. I also knew that if I did she might see that as prey behavior and chase me down. In a race against the fastest feline on the planet, I would definitely lose.

"You have gorgeous eyes," I told the cheetah as I took a step forward and closed the gap between us. "I've never seen any kind of cat with orange eyes. But what do you wear to bring out the color? Other than your furs, I mean."

The cheetah's tail twitched, and she chirped again.

"Of course it would be more fun to chase down those little kids instead of listening to me. Kind of like getting take-out at one a.m., right?" I stopped two feet in front of her, and saw the regal power coiled in her bunched muscles. "But you know it's not good for you to eat before you go to bed."

This close I could count the uneven spots on her pelt;

they looked like smudged fingerprints on her sides and then began blending together into uneven stripes along her spine. Her lower jaw dropped, flashing the daggerlike tips of her teeth as she started to pant and pace back and forth in a small circle.

I could almost sense her conflicted instincts. She was built for speed, not compassion or mercy. In her world it was eat or be eaten; hunt to live or starve to death. But maybe she also understood that young had to be protected, even in this artificial world built by humans who came here to gawk at her.

"They're only little ones," I assured her. "Let them go, okay?"

She swung her head back to give the grade-schoolers one final look, and then sat down on her haunches.

"Thank you." Somehow I'd gotten close enough to touch her, and held out my hand, turning the palm up and spreading my fingers. Her whiskers prickled my skin as she rubbed her head against it, and she made a rough sound like a purr, as if she were nothing more than an oversize house cat. "Now, how can I convince you to walk back through that gate and let me close it?"

The chaperons escorting the Sunshine School kids must have finally noticed me and the big cat, because a woman let out a terrified scream while someone else shouted for the kids to run. The noise broke the spell between me and the cheetah, and her ears flattened as she rose on all fours.

When I saw her muscles bunching I knew I had to

give her a different target, something she couldn't resist. I dug my fingernails into my palms as hard as I could and then spread my hands as I felt blood pool in the crescent-shaped wounds. I was afraid, and I really didn't want to die, but if someone had to it was going to be me.

The cheetah's nostrils flared as she picked up the scent of my blood, and she crouched down, ready to spring.

Out of the corner of my eye I saw a man with a rifle pointed at me. An instant later a shadowy streak shot through the air, and something slammed into me, but it wasn't the big cat. It was big and powerful, and hit me so hard it knocked me across the walkway. Then I was on the ground and rolling into a wide swath of bushes until we stopped. I threw up my arms to cover my face, and kept my eyes tightly closed as I waited to feel fangs sinking into my flesh.

"Catlyn."

I opened one eye and peeked through the gap between my arms. Predatory eyes stared down at me, but they weren't orange or feline. These were solid black, with a strange opalescent sheen that moved over them in a hypnotic swirl. That those eyes glittered down at me framed by the beautiful face of my dark boy confused me.

"Jesse?" I was probably hallucinating. Or I'd already died and gone to heaven. I lowered my arms anyway. "You can't be here. You said you couldn't... be here." Why was it so difficult to speak?

Jesse's hair fell against my cheek, blocking out the

light, and then he cupped my cheek with his hand. "Close your eyes," he whispered.

My eyes closed on their own. Then I felt a whisper of breath against my neck, cooling my heated skin. It felt wonderful. Everything was wonderful now that he was here.

His cheek brushed mine, and then I felt the touch of his mouth against mine, another whisper, this one soft and gentle. I felt my name as he breathed it there before he kissed me again.

My whole body became one huge flush, but I didn't care. Nothing existed except that kiss, my first kiss. *Now I can die*, I thought as I fell into him, drifting away into some silent place, some nowhere only the two of us shared.

I thought I'd be awkward, and not know what to do, but I kissed him back as if I'd done a thousand times. Everything inside me untangled, stretching out through my veins, rushing over my heart like a wave of warm water.

I would have lay there and kissed him forever, until the stars winked out and time ended, and all that had been faded away. I didn't mind. Jesse and I were the only universe I needed.

A heartbeat later he lifted his mouth from mine, and when I opened my eyes, the dark silver of his smiled down at me.

"Hi." I didn't know what else to say.

Jesse drew back and lifted me up in his arms as he

pushed through the back of the bushes to another walk-way behind them. He set me on my feet but kept his hands on my arms. "Where are you hurt?"

"I don't know." And I didn't care. "What are you doing here?"

"I felt...I thought you might need me." He glanced over the bushes at the zookeepers, who were gathering around the cheetah where it lay on the ground. "How did that animal escape?"

"Someone left a gate open." My dreamy euphoria ebbed away as I realized Jesse was really here, at the zoo, where there were hundreds of kids. "You can't stay here. There are too many people."

"It doesn't matter." He hesitated, and then said, "I'm not as sick as I thought I was."

I smiled. "You're better? Really? I've been so worried about you."

His mouth hitched. "I know."

"I tried to call. I would have come back to see you if there had been any way, but your island is like Fort Knox." I winced as he took my hand in his, and made a face as he examined the small wounds on my palm. "I had to distract the cheetah from some little kids." I looked over the bushes at the big cat, who was sprawled on the walkway, a red-fletched cartridge dart sticking out of her neck. "I thought the smell of my blood might do it."

"It is very distracting," he agreed, and lowered my hand while he studied my face. "You are thinner. There are shadows under your eyes. Have you been sick?"

"My brother has been keeping me on the bread and water diet." I explained what happened after Ego's father had brought me back to the docks, and Trick's reaction. "This is the first time since that day that I've been allowed to do anything but sit in my room and go to school. Did your parents punish you?"

"They forbade me to leave the island." He brushed my hair back from my forehead. "I thought it would be best if I stayed away, but I was wrong. Without you, I was lonely and miserable and empty. Every night I could think of nothing but you."

"I know exactly what you mean." I saw one of the zookeepers peering into the bushes. "They're coming. You should go."

"No." He put his arms around my waist. "I'm not going to leave you again."

Eighteen

I told the zookeepers that I wasn't hurt, but they took me to the park infirmary anyway to be checked out. The doctor who cleaned the scratches on my palms praised me for not trying to run from the cheetah, which he said saved my life. I knew better but I didn't contradict him him.

Jesse never left my side. Not for a second.

The man who had tranquilized the cheetah also came in, and asked me to tell him what had happened. I described everything from the time I passed the lions' habitat to the moment when I knew the cheetah was going to spring. Then I glanced at Jesse, and left it at that.

"You have a very cool head, young lady," the zookeeper said at last. "It's probably what saved your life tonight. Did you see anyone else around the exhibit?"

Another reason not to mention Jesse's presence; he might get blamed for messing with the gate. "Just one of the kids in my class. She left, though, just as I got there." I heard the door to the infirmary open and saw Sheriff Yamah and one of his deputies walk in. "Am I in trouble?"

"For keeping a cheetah from running loose in the park?" The man laughed. "Ah, no."

The sheriff wasn't wearing his creepy sunglasses, and I was a little startled to see that he had rather nice, pale blue eyes. He kept them on me as he crossed the room, and then he stopped in his tracks as he noticed Jesse on the other side of the exam table. His eyes went to our linked hands and then to Jesse's face.

I saw Jesse shake his head a little, as if to warn Yamah.

"Doctor," the sheriff said, his voice tight, "can I have a word with Ms. Youngblood?"

"Sure. She's going to be fine." The doctor patted my shoulder. "Soap and water for the cuts on your hands, young lady. Leave them open at night, and other than that, get some rest."

"Thank you." I watched Yamah take out a notepad and wondered how he was going to use this against me. He'd probably tell Trick the whole thing was my fault.

To my surprise the sheriff was polite, and only asked me what had happened. I repeated everything I had told the zookeeper, and while I spoke he made some notes.

"So the gate was already open when you arrived," Yamah said when I'd finished. "Did you see anyone inside the fence or around the exhibit?"

"Other than the cheetah? Just one of the cheerleaders from our class," I told him. "She was walking ahead of me."

He asked for her name, and then said something to his deputy, who left the room. To me, Yamah said, "Would you like me to call your brother, Ms. Youngblood?"

I tried to keep a straight face. "No."

"The cat handlers told me what you did kept that cheetah from attacking the kids from Sunshine," he said, sounding a little sheepish. "It was a very courageous, unselfish thing to do."

The deputy returned with Tiffany Beck in tow, who scowled as soon as she saw me.

"Is this the student you saw outside the exhibit before the cheetah got loose?" Yamah asked.

I nodded.

"What are you talking about?" Tiffany wrenched her arm out of the deputy's grip. "I didn't go anywhere near her or that cat exhibit."

"I saw the back of your jacket when you ran away," I said.

"Really." Tiffany spread out her bare arms. "What jacket?"

"You were wearing it when we got here." If we'd been in school and this had been another prank, I might have let it go. But if Tiffany had opened that gate, she had deliberately endangered everyone in the park. "I know what I saw."

"Where is your jacket, Ms. Beck?" the sheriff asked.

"I don't know." She dropped her arms. "I took it off and put it down for a second, and someone stole it. And I don't care what she says; I didn't open that stupid gate."

"How do you know a gate was opened?" the sheriff asked.

"I heard what happened from my friends." Tiffany wrapped her arms around herself. "Someone must have told them."

"So someone stole your jacket, and someone told your friends about the gate." Yamah sounded skeptical. "But you don't know who it was. That sounds a little too convenient, young lady."

A sullen look came over Tiffany's face. "It was probably *her*. It's not the first time she's lied to get me in trouble. I bet she's the one who opened that gate, just so she could blame it on me."

"If Ms. Youngblood was the one to open the gate," the sheriff said, "then why would she stay there after the cheetah got out?"

"So you'd believe her," Tiffany shouted.

"Yes, that's it. I wanted you to get a detention so badly that I was willing to die for it." I climbed off the exam table. "Can I go now, Sheriff?"

He never got a chance to answer because the cheerleader shrieked and rushed toward me. Jesse pushed me behind him while the sheriff grabbed Tiffany and pulled her back.

"Yes, Ms. Youngblood, I think we're finished here," Yamah said. "Jesse?"

"I'll take her home." He put his arm around my waist, guiding me around Tiffany.

"Does your boyfriend know that you're cheating on him?" Tiffany sneered as she fought the sheriff's grip. When Jesse looked down at her, she smirked. "That's right. She's been sneaking around with Aaron Boone, my ex-boyfriend, since the beginning of school."

"You're mistaken," Jesse told her. "Catlyn is not seeing anyone else."

"How do you know? She lies about everything."

He gave her a pitying look. "I know because she's been too busy sneaking around with me."

I managed not to make a sound until after we walked out of the infirmary. Then a giggle escaped me.

"I think," Jesse said in a grave voice, "that girl does not like you very much."

"You noticed." I was not going to give into the laughter bubbling up inside me, because I suspected it was mostly hysterical. "Thank you for setting her straight."

His arm tightened around my waist. "You're welcome."

My thoughts were still in a muddle, so much so that I didn't notice where we were headed until we reached the turnstiles. "This is the exit for the park."

"It is." He stood aside so I could go through first.

"I should go back with my class." I made a face. "We took a bus here."

He gave me a gentle push through the turnstile and

followed after me. "I told James that I would take you home."

"I appreciate the offer," I said, "but it's kind of a long walk from here."

"We're not walking." He took my arm and steered me toward a shiny dark green convertible. "I am driving you home."

"*You're* driving."

He opened the passenger door. "I was not exactly honest. I did not spend all my time thinking about you. While we've been apart, James taught me how to drive, and obtained a license for me."

I got in and sank back against the leather seat. "So I got grounded, and you got a gorgeous, brand-new convertible."

He went around the car and got in behind the wheel. "I think my parents purchased it as an incentive." He glanced at me. "Don't worry. James says I am a good driver."

"That's terrific." I fastened my seat belt. "Do you think your parents would adopt me?"

Jesse proved to be a very good driver, but when we reached Lost Lake I remembered my brother and touched his arm.

"Trick was coming to the school after the field trip to pick me up," I told him. "Can you drop me off there?" At his frown I added, "It's okay. He won't be there for at least a half an hour."

"I'm not worried about meeting your brother." He

slowed down and turned down the road that went past the school. "I was hoping that we would have a little more time to be together. To talk."

That reminded me that I was still grounded. "Don't you have a phone on the island? I mean, besides the one in the property management office?" I could probably sneak down to the kitchen and call him after my brothers went to sleep.

"There is one in the main house, but my parents never use it." His expression turned rueful. "They don't care for the new technology."

"Jesse, the phone has been around for like a hundred years. It's not exactly what you'd call new. It doesn't matter; Trick probably won't let me get near the phone." I thought of my mother's letters. "What if we write to each other? Will your parents let you receive letters?"

"They don't accept postal deliveries." He slowed to make the turn into the pickup area at the school. "You could leave letters for me in your hayloft. Hide them under the blanket over the old trunk."

"There's no…" I paused to swallow hard. Jesse's joke made me feel so nauseated I thought for a moment I might throw up.

The hayloft. The old trunk. The hayloft. The old trunk.

At first the words hammered inside my head like two sledges, and then I remembered all the conversations I'd had about the hayloft and the old trunk. Jesse kept telling me that the old trunk was in the back the hayloft, and then when I asked my brother about it… I'd forgotten it again. Why was I having the same lapse in memory over and over?

By that time Jesse had parked, and I looked out at the cars of parents who were already there and waiting for the bus. Trick hadn't arrived yet, which was probably a good thing. I decided to keep my recurring amnesia to myself, at least until I went up into the hayloft and saw for myself whether or not the old trunk was there.

"Assuming my brother ever lets me out of the house again," I said, "would your parents be okay with us seeing each other?"

"I don't know." He shut off the engine. "I haven't spoken to them about you, but I don't need their consent."

"Jesse, you're their kid," I reminded him. "Whether you like it or not, they love you. And until you're eighteen, they own you."

He started to say something, and then a passing car grabbed his attention. "Perhaps it's time that I introduced you to them."

"You don't have to. I mean, if you don't think it's the right time." I glanced at the car he was watching, which was a beautiful old-fashioned Rolls Royce. "Wow, great car. Like something out of an old movie, isn't it? Do you know those people?"

He nodded.

The Rolls pulled into the lot next to Jesse's convertible, and a driver wearing a formal chauffeur's uniform got out to open the rear door. I tried not to stare, but as soon as the young couple sitting in the back emerged it was hard not to.

The girl, a petite brunette with a lovely face and large, cornflower blue eyes, looked like a perfect little porcelain doll. The handsome guy with her was big and dark and exotic-looking, with narrow brown eyes and a thick mustache that framed the corners of his mouth. Both wore formal evening clothes that were suitable for a much older couple, which seemed odd.

Maybe they're college students who had to dress that way for a costume party, or prom. Except it wasn't Halloween, and it would be another eight months before proms started.

Jesse got out of the car and came around to open my door, and then took my hand and walked with me over to the young couple, who were watching us.

"Jesse." The woman smiled. "James told us you might be here."

He nodded. "Catlyn, this is Sarah and Paul Raven."

"It's nice to meet you." I shook hands with both of them before I glanced at Jesse. "Are these your cousins?"

"No." His mouth tightened. "They're my parents."

"Sure they are." I waited for him to say he was joking, but no one but me was smiling. "They are?" I turned to stare at them. "But you—you're both—"

"So young-looking?" Sarah suggested. When I ducked my head, she chuckled. "My husband and I have always appeared much younger than we are. The illusion is something of a family curse."

"Mother." Jesse didn't say anything else, but I could feel how tense he was.

"I am very happy to meet you, my dear," Sarah continued. She had a pretty voice and a faint accent I couldn't quite place. "I've wanted to personally thank you for saving our son's life."

"Indeed." Jesse's father regarded me with a far more reserved expression in his slanted eyes. "I have been curious about you as well." He spoke English with a stronger version of Sarah's accent. "How did you meet our son and become such a good friend to him?"

"Well, we sort of bumped into each other one night." Jesse hadn't told his parents anything about me, but they could clearly see he was holding my hand, so I felt a little embarrassed. "We started talking and found out we have a lot in common."

"Such as?"

"We both love traveling, and old houses, and horseback riding." I smiled at Jesse. "I'm not quite the accomplished rider he is, but I can usually keep up."

"So you have gone riding together." Paul Raven didn't sound as if he approved. "What more have you done?"

"Paul, really." Sarah gave me apologetic look. "Excuse my husband, he likes to interrogate more than converse."

"I have a brother who's exactly the same way," I assured her. "Our parents died when I was young, so he's my guardian."

"This brother, he allows you to go out alone at night?" Paul frowned. "A proper guardian would not, I think."

Jesse saved me from having to answer him. "Father, Catlyn's family is not your concern. Neither is our friendship."

"Have you made yourself known to this brother?" His father glared at him. "I thought not."

I saw Gray's truck pulling into the parking lot. "I don't think that's going to be a problem any longer, Mr. Raven."

Trick parked on the other side of the Rolls and came toward us, only to stop short and stare at the Ravens. He seemed to recover a moment later and came straight to me.

"The sheriff called me from the zoo and told me what happened," he said, and took my hands in his to look at the fingernail marks. "You're all right?"

"I'm good. Trick, this is my friend, Jesse, and his parents, Sarah and Paul." I turned to them. "This is my oldest brother, Patrick Youngblood."

I saw Mr. Raven's lips move as he silently repeated our name. Sarah also went still.

Trick didn't offer his hand to anyone, and the measuring look he gave Jesse stopped just short of insulting. "I appreciate you bringing Catlyn back to the school." To me he said, "It's late. We'd better go."

"It was very nice meeting you," I said to the Ravens before I turned to Jesse. "Be careful with that new car."

"Catlyn." He almost took a step toward me, but his mother put her hand on his arm, and he subsided. "Good night."

———

Trick didn't talk to me on the way home, and I guessed he was angry over finding me with Jesse. I considered trying to explain things, but his silence felt like a warning sign in a library: *No talking*.

With every mile that passed, I missed Jesse a little bit more. I'd thought being grounded and not knowing how he was had been bad, but this was worse. I'd had a night filled with terror and wonder; Jesse had saved my life and given me the most amazing first kiss of all time. After tonight, how was I going to bear being locked in my room forever?

When we arrived at the farm I went into the house and started for the stairs, but Trick asked me to wait for a minute.

"Tomorrow morning I want you to start packing up your room," he said, stunning me. "Use the suitcases in your closet for your clothes, and the plastic bins in the laundry room for your books and things. I'll go into town early and pick up some empty boxes."

I thought of how I'd joked about military school, but surely he wouldn't... "Where am I going?"

"We're all going," Trick said. "You liked California best, didn't you?"

"We're moving again?" I couldn't believe it. "Why?"

"It's not safe for us to stay here any longer." He looked over as Gray came out of the hall. "Grayson, we're going to pack up and head out to California. Would you mind..."

He stopped and watched my brother stomp off into the kitchen.

We both heard the kitchen door slam.

"You could tell him that he can play football at our next school," I suggested. "Maybe then he won't hate you so much."

Trick rubbed a hand over his scalp. "I have to protect you and your brother, Catlyn."

"From what? Did Grandma and Grandpa drop in while I was at the zoo? No?" I put my hands on my hips. "You can't do this to us. You told us that we were staying, that we were settling down. Now that we have, suddenly it's not safe. Are we in imminent danger of becoming happy, normal kids for the first time in our lives?"

Trick's jaw clenched. "Go to your room and get some sleep. We have a lot to do to get ready for the move."

"What if I don't pack?" I snapped. "What if I refuse to go?"

"Then I'll leave your things here and take you to California with the clothes you're wearing. This is not your decision, and the discussion is over," he added when I started to protest. "Go to bed, Catlyn."

He waited to watch me go upstairs, but once I slammed my bedroom door shut I heard him walk through the kitchen and go out the back door. I went to my window to see him heading out to the barn after Gray.

The hayloft. The old trunk.

As soon as he was out of sight I ran downstairs to

grab his key ring from the rack in the kitchen. I removed the key to his desk and hurried back to his room.

All I took from Trick's desk was the old key from the box that had held my mother's letters. I locked the desk, left his room, replaced the key on his ring, and was back upstairs before my brothers returned to the house. I hid the key under my pillow and switched off my lamp.

As I suspected he would, Trick came upstairs to check on me. He didn't bother to knock this time, but opened the door and looked in on me.

I rolled over in bed, turning my back on him.

"I'm sorry about this, Cat," he said, and the regret in his voice sounded genuine. "But someday when you're a parent, you'll understand."

When my brother closed the door, I slipped the key out from under my pillow and held it in my hand as I listened to the sounds downstairs. As usual Gray locked himself in his bedroom, but I heard him slam something into one of his walls, so hard it made the house shake a little. Trick walked down the hall, said something to my brother, and then went around the house switching off lights and checking the locks. The last sound he made was opening and shutting his bedroom door, and then the house fell silent.

I didn't make the mistake of leaving just then; I waited for another hour until I felt sure my brothers were asleep. Then I opened my window, climbed over the sill and jumped to the pine tree.

I hadn't been in the barn for so long that all of the

horses put their heads over their stall doors to whinny at me. Even the surly Flash nuzzled my hand when I stopped to give him a pat.

I lingered with the horses until they all got bored of me. Although I'd come here on a mission, I didn't want to go up in the hayloft. The thought of it made me feel frightened and sick, as if it were the worst thing I could do. It made my skin crawl, as if I were covered in bugs. I could even picture it, armies of them swarming out from under the old horse blanket.

Strong as they were, I knew the feelings and sensations and mental images were completely wrong, especially when I remembered Jesse's voice telling me about the old trunk that Trick said was there. And wasn't there. And was there. And wasn't there.

If I kept thinking about it I was going to be sick, so I forced myself to walk over to the ladder and start climbing up the rungs. The feelings of dread only got stronger from there, and by the time I reached the top sweat drenched my clothes and I was shaking all over.

I knew I wouldn't see the trunk because it wasn't there.

But I could see that something was under the old horse blanket. Something big and rectangular and waiting for me.

I couldn't seem to lift my feet anymore, so I shuffled through the loose hay toward it. I reached down and with both trembling hands I tugged the horse blanket away.

The old trunk sat there, its black-painted wood scarred with scratches and gouges and stains; its gray metal fittings pitted and dull. I took the key from my pocket and crouched down to slip it into the lock stamped with the letters *AVH*.

From the squeal of the hinges I guessed it hadn't been opened regularly in a long time, maybe years. Someone had packed it full of papers and books and newspapers, and I took one heavy volume out and trained my flashlight on the cracked spine. The embossed title was still readable, but the words were in Greek.

I opened the book, which had pages as thin as tissue paper, and saw they were also printed in Greek. The first illustration showed a man half-buried in a grave, and a group of other men surrounding him, their arms holding pointed sticks as if they meant to stab him.

I put the book aside and sifted through the other papers. Nothing was written in English but I recognized some of the languages as French, Spanish and German. Under a bundle of brittle, yellowed newspapers I found an old knife in a cracked leather sheath. I removed the blade, which had been engraved with dozens of tiny crosses. It was made of the same pewter metal as the trunk fittings.

Not pewter, I thought as I turned it over and saw *AVH* stamped at the base. *Iron.*

I set the knife and sheath aside and began unloading the trunk, separating everything I found into four piles: papers, books, sketches and weapons. There were seven knives, a short sword, a hammer with a spiked ball on the end, and what looked like an antique version of brass knuckles. All of the weapons I removed were made of iron and engraved with crosses or words in what I thought was Latin.

The only knives we owned were the ones we kept in the block holder in the kitchen, so the collection confused me. Why would Trick, who didn't even own a penknife, be saving these antiques?

The books and sketches were even creepier than the weapons. I couldn't read the books, but most of them were illustrated so I looked at the pictures. They all seemed to date back to medieval times, and showed horrible things: people being attacked by demonic-looking creatures; beautiful women being burned at the stake; the fallen bodies of men who had been beheaded by soldiers. The sketches were cruder version of the same type of nightmarish scenes.

Finally I found one slightly newer book written in what I thought might be Dutch that contained portraits of evil-looking men and women with pointed teeth and gouged-out eyes. On closer inspection I saw that the eyes in the portraits weren't missing, but had been filled in with solid black ink. I didn't understand what they were until I came to one man's portrait, which showed some dark fluid stained his sharp teeth and streaming from the corners of his mouth.

They weren't people. They were vampires.

Nineteen

I felt him slip into the barn before I heard him call my name. "Catlyn."

I closed the vampire book and discovered the paralyzing dread that had made me so dizzy and sick had gone. Or maybe it was knowing that he was there, and why.

I went over to the side of the hayloft to look down at Jesse. "You shouldn't have come."

"You said no more spying." He went over to the ladder, but instead of climbing it he jumped up and over it, landing on his feet in the hayloft. As soon as he looked at my face his smile faded. "What is it?"

I knew what he did was impossible, that things like this only happened in dreams. I also knew I was wide awake. "I found the trunk. I opened it." I held out my hand. "Come and see."

We went to the back of the hayloft, and he knelt down to look at the things I'd taken out and piled on the floor.

"These books are very old." He picked up one I'd left open to an illustration of a vampire dropping down to attack a man on horseback. He looked around at the others and then reached down to close each one. When he picked up the book of portraits, he looked at the man with the bloody mouth for a long time before he closed that one, too.

"Jesse." I sat down beside him as he put the book down. "Look at me. Please."

He turned his head, and his eyes had turned an opal-sheened black, just as they had at the zoo. He closed them, and when his eyelids lifted they had shifted back to dark, glittering gray.

Only then did he take my hands in his. "Don't be afraid."

"I'm not." This was Jesse, my friend, my dark boy, and I knew he would never hurt me. "But I do need to understand."

"I don't have a disease," he admitted in a low voice. "I can't eat food or go out in the sunlight because of what I am."

"And you don't live on island because your parents are snobs," I guessed. He shook his head. "How long have you been like this, Jesse?"

"One hundred and thirty-six years." He looked down

at our hands. "I lied to you about the photograph you found. Someone took it of me when I was still human."

I laced my fingers through his. "How did this happen to you?"

The story Jesse told me put together all the things that hadn't made sense to me. He and his family were the last generation of the Ravenovs, whose circus had traveled through Europe during the end of the nineteenth century. They had performed for peasants and kings, in hamlets and at court, always riding their famous white horses.

At the end of each season they returned to their homeland in Romania, where they bred their horses, practiced their acts and rested up over the winter. It was on the final leg of one journey that their encampment was attacked in the middle of the night.

"The horses tried to warn us," he said slowly. "They sensed the brigands approaching, but my uncle said they were only being fractious because of the long journey. The first vampire I saw ran into the camp and seized my youngest cousin, Marta. He plucked her right out of her mother's arms. He moved so fast. When I blinked they were gone, and my aunt was screaming."

He described how the Ravenov men, who were accustomed to the dangers of traveling, had fought back against the vampires. They quickly realized how unnaturally strong the monsters were, and that only by piercing their hearts or beheading them could they kill them, but by that time nearly all of the men in camp were mortally wounded or dead. His mother herded the women into the wagons and then came to fight alongside her husband and son.

"My parents and I fought hard, but there were too many of them," he said. "The vampires surrounded us, and disarmed us, but they did not kill us. They admired us, their leader said, because we were fierce fighters. They wanted my parents and I to join them."

"You refused, I hope," I said.

He nodded. "The vampires dragged us out of the camp and took us to the caves where they lived. Their leader had his men hold us down while he took our blood, and made us take his."

Hearing that made my stomach roll, but it wasn't his fault. "Is that when you and your parents were changed?"

"Yes. When we woke, most of the vampires lay around us, sleeping. Everywhere we saw gold and jewels and other treasures that the vampires had stolen from their victims. Our movements roused their leader, but he only spoke to us as if we were his servants. He told us that to finish the change we would have to attack a mortal and drain their body of blood. He ordered us to return to the camp and kill all of the surviving women and children. He was so sure that we would obey him that he turned his back on us. That was when my father picked up a sword and beheaded him. Then my parents and I killed the rest of them where they lay."

Jesse's voice became strained as he described how it was for him and his parents when they returned to the camp to help the survivors. "They saw the paleness of our skin and the blackness of our eyes, and they were afraid. For us, the sight of their wounds and the scent of their blood were a torment, but my father said we could resist it. He was determined that we would not become like the monsters who had killed so many of our kin."

I let out a breath. "So what did you do?"

"We bandaged the wounded and buried our dead, and then completed the journey to our horse farms in the mountains. We used some of the vampires' treasures to help the members of our family who had survived." He sighed. "By that time we knew we could live on the blood of animals, but we also knew our human lives were over. We left Romania and came to America."

Some of the circus performers came with them, Jesse told me, to help protect him and his parents during the daylight hours of their journey, when they had to take refuge in sealed stone coffins carried by covered wagons. After Jesse's parents had bought what in that time had been remote, uninhabited swamp land in Florida, their human friends stayed to help them establish the first of many cattle ranches, and then built the town of Lost Lake for themselves and their families.

"We offered them enough gold to pay for their passage back to Romania, and assure that they would never want for anything, but our friends were very loyal and refused to abandon us," Jesse admitted. "Some of their descendents still watch over us."

"Like Sheriff Yamah?" I guessed, and he smiled. "Now I understand why he lets you come in his house and rummage through his fridge." A thought occurred to me. "If you and your parents never completely changed, then you're not really vampires."

"We have not escaped the curse entirely," he warned me. "We're very strong and fast, and we don't become sick or age. When we're hurt, our injuries heal in a matter of hours instead of days or weeks. We share some of their vulnerabilities as well. Sunlight burns us, and garlic and iron are poisonous to us. We have never tried to end our lives, but beheading, piercing our hearts, or exposing our bodies to sunlight would probably kill us."

I picked up one of the iron daggers. "These weapons were used to do that. To kill vampires."

"I think they were."

I didn't want to think about why they were hidden in my barn, so I put the blade back in the trunk and focused on him. "This is why you don't live in town, or go to school."

"Being near human beings is dangerous for us and them," he admitted. "After so many years people begin to see that we don't age. We have never wanted to hurt anyone, but our instincts are very powerful. We can see in the dark, and hear the sound of a heartbeat from across a room. Our sense of smell is particularly keen. We can track the scent of blood for miles. Even a single drop can cause us to shift into our predatory state." He gestured toward his face. "Our eyes turn black, and our fangs descend."

I didn't remember seeing fangs when he had tackled me at the zoo, but the solid-black eyes were burned indelibly in my memory. "You smelled my blood tonight, didn't you?"

"The urge to attack is strongest when we are wounded, but fierce emotions can also trigger a shift. I saw you and the cheetah before I smelled the blood on your palms. I thought that she would spring before I could get to you." He turned my hand and gazed down at the crescent marks.

"I'm not complaining," I assured him. "You saved my life, Jesse. I can deal with the scary eyes."

"It's not that. It's … " He paused as if to find the right words. "My parents have always loved each other, Catlyn, but since we were changed they have shared a deeper bond. Wherever they are, they are always aware of each other, and happy only when they are together. They share their thoughts and feelings without speaking. The old stories say that vampires can forge such bonds, but only with others of their kind. Perhaps they were wrong."

What he was saying finally registered, and I felt a little flustered. "Makes a girl almost wish she wasn't human." I began putting things back into the trunk.

"If your brother Patrick has been keeping these"—he gestured to the weapons—"then he knows vampires exist. Every book here was written about how to identify them, how to hunt them, and how to kill them."

"This is just some old stuff Trick inherited from our parents," I insisted. "It doesn't belong to him. I doubt he could read any of these books."

"Then why does he keep the trunk hidden?" He caught my wrist. "Catlyn, your brother used iron barbed wire for the fences, and hung clusters of garlic on the posts. He must know."

"It could be a family superstition," I said quickly. "My grandparents were Dutch; maybe it was something they did in the old country and Trick is just carrying on the tradition."

"The traditional defense against vampires is to keep horses," Jesse said. "They react violently whenever a vampire is near. If they can get loose, they will try to trample him."

I frowned. "That can't be right. You ride Prince all the time. And Sali likes you."

"That is one part of the curse we have escaped," he said. "Father believes that because we don't feed on humans, we have a different scent; one that doesn't aggravate the horses."

"Wherever we've lived, we've always had them." I picked up a book and held it between my hands. "I can't believe it was only because my brother wanted a vampire alarm system."

"What about your parents?" he asked. "You said this trunk might have belonged to them."

"Now that I've seen what's in it, I don't think so," I said. "My father was a horse trainer, and my mother was just a girl who ran away from home to be with him. After they married they lived here for a little while, and then they moved up to Wyoming."

He touched the letters stamped into the trunk's lock. "Whose initials are these? Your mother's?"

"No. Her name was Rose Fanelsen." I saw the way he stiffened. "What is it?"

"I know that name, Fanelsen. I heard my father and James mention it once when they were talking." He gave me a worried look. "It was soon after you came here. The sheriff paid a visit to the island, and told my father about you and your brothers. He insisted that you were a threat. My father insisted we were safe on the island, and that you couldn't do anything to hurt us."

"Your father never saw the stuff in this trunk." I felt him take his hands from mine. "Jesse, I didn't mean that. We would never try to hurt you or your parents. We're just normal people with one trunk of weird things in our barn."

"If anyone is a threat, it's me." He stood up. "My parents told me tonight that they don't want me to see you again. They were quite insistent."

"As soon as we got home tonight, my brother told me that he's selling the farm," I said. "He plans to take us to California."

He looked down at the open trunk. "Perhaps that would be best."

"No. You would never hurt me, and I am not a threat to you. Jesse." I scrambled up after him. "Please, listen to me."

He jumped down to the barn floor, and without

thinking I followed. My landing wasn't as graceful as his, but I stayed on my feet and I didn't break anything.

"Catlyn, what are you doing?" he demanded. "You could have broken your neck."

"I don't care." I strode over to him and took him by the arms. "I'm not moving to California. You're not going to spend the rest of your life alone on that island."

"It's for your sake, not mine." He tried to set me aside, but I held on. "My parents know how dangerous I am to you. Catlyn, think. What if I'd lost control tonight? What if instead of kissing you, I tried to kill you?"

"Your eyes are black now, Jesse." I touched his cheek. "I'm not bleeding. Do you want to hurt me?"

He closed his eyes.

"I am *not* afraid of you." I knew I had to prove that, so I stood on my tiptoes, curled my arms around his neck, and pressed my lips against his.

This time I felt the sharp ends of his fangs against my lower lip as we kissed, but he didn't bite me or even scratch me. I sank against him as his arms came up around me, and I felt tiny explosions under my skin, as if my body were erupting in hidden fireworks.

I never understood what glorious was, until that moment.

The feeling didn't end when our lips parted. Jesse kissed the corners of my mouth, and the curve of my cheek, and one single tear that hadn't yet fallen from my eyelashes.

"Catlyn." He folded me against him so that my hot

face pressed into his cool throat. "Are you sure about this?"

I drew back so I could look in his eyes. They were still black, and swirled with that dark rainbow sheen, but I saw nothing in them that frightened me.

"You're the only thing in this world that I am sure of." I drew my hands down from his shoulders. "There is more to this than what our families are telling us. We have to know *why* my brother has been hiding these things, and how the sheriff and your father knew my mother's maiden name." At his frown, I added, "Even if our parents met when mine lived here, my parents were married by the time they moved to the farm. My mother didn't want my grandparents to find them, so she never used her maiden name."

"I will see what I can find out," Jesse promised.

———

I waited every night for Jesse to come back to the farm, but after a week had passed with no sign of him and no notes left for me in the barn I suspected his parents were keeping him on the island. That left it up to me to find out what connection there was between our parents.

Trick insisted we continue to prepare to move, and checked daily on our progress, but neither Gray nor I made any particular effort to hurry. Grayson said nothing, but I knew why he wanted to stay in Lost Lake. He was the school's hero now, and the football team's perfect record had made him all the friends he would ever need.

Although news of what had happened at the zoo as well as Tiffany Beck's suspension was all around the school, from that day on I was treated as if I'd turned the cheetah loose. None of the kids looked at me or spoke to me; as far as they were concerned I was the invisible classmate. My teachers stopped calling on me during class, and only spoke to me when they absolutely had to. Even Barb avoided me and started sitting with other girls at lunch.

I had no proof, but I suspected Jesse's parents had something to do with my outcast status. Nearly everyone in Lost Lake either worked for them, rented property from them or financially depended on them. Anyone the Ravens disliked had to be considered a threat to the entire community.

The only person in school who didn't treat me like a leper was Ego. He sat with me every day at lunch and when he saw me in the halls would come over and walk with me.

"You don't have to do this," I told him one day at lunch when I noticed some of the nasty looks the kids at other tables were giving him. "I'm moving away soon."

"I wonder why." He made a hideous face at a cluster of scowling girls passing by us. "I heard your golden-armed brother is none too happy about it."

"Gray is never happy, period." He still hadn't talked to me at home, and the few times I'd tried to speak with him he'd simply turned and walked away. "My point is, you're going to have to live here after I'm gone. You shouldn't make yourself a bunch of enemies just so I don't have to sit by myself."

"I know Barb told you that I was dumped here like garbage when I was a baby," Ego said. "It's okay; she tells everybody. The people here have taken care of me, but they've never cared about me or how I feel. No one has ever tried to find my birth parents and ask them why they left me behind. I'm just a stray they're going to feed until I'm old enough to hit the road."

I'd never heard him talk this way. "But your foster parents care about you."

"Larry's not a bad guy. Marcia hates me. She's already told me, the day I turn eighteen, and they can't collect anymore checks for me?" He kicked the table. "Out I go."

"I'm sorry."

"Don't be. I've been saving every paycheck I've made for the last three years. I've got ten thousand dollars in the bank, and I'll have fifteen thousand more by the time I graduate." He seemed pleased by my shocked expression. "I'm going to move to Texas, get my own place, and open a landscaping business. I'll cut lawns during the day, go to school at night, and on weekends I'm going down to Mexico and see if I can find my mom and dad."

"You are the smartest kid in this school." My sympathy became a mixture of admiration and envy. "But how are you going to find your birth parents?"

"Internet records," he told me. "My parents' first names aren't all that common, so that gives me an edge. Right now

I'm searching through all the migrant worker sites to see if they've registered and are still working in the U.S. Haven't found anything yet, but I'm going to keep trying."

I hadn't thought of using a computer to learn more about my mother's family. "Can you run a search for information on a couple who lived in Virginia back in the eighties? They're my grandparents, and I don't know anything about them."

"Sure. What's the name?"

I wrote it down for him. "I know they're both Dutch, and they had a horse farm. That's about it."

"Fanelsen is definitely an uncommon name, so that helps." He folded up the note and stuck it in his pocket. "I'll run a search tonight and print out whatever I can find. Don't thank me yet," he said when I started to do just that. "Grandparents are usually old people. They might have sold their farm and retired, or went back overseas, or even passed away."

"I won't get my hopes up," I promised.

Ego looked past me. "Uh-oh. We've got paparazzi at two o'clock."

I followed his gaze and saw the Goth girl I'd talked to at Gray's tryouts; she had a camera aimed at us. "Does she like you?"

Ego gave me an ironic look. "Cat, she's wearing death camouflage and a guy haircut. She probably likes *you*."

Kari put her camera away and then strolled over to our table. "Since you caught me, I thought I'd ward off a summons to the dean's office and explain. I think you two make such a cute couple that I was overwhelmed by warm fuzzies and had to capture the moment for posterity."

"Try again," I told her drily.

"I'm a hired gun," she said bluntly. "I'm getting paid a pittance to take pics of you for the Lost Ledger."

Ego laughed, but I was still mystified. "I beg your pardon?"

"The Ledger's kind of an underground subversive newswire thing," Kari said. "It's passed around school in unmarked notebooks every week. Whoever gets one of the notebooks reads the stories in it, adds their own, and then drops it in someone else's locker or backpack when they're not looking."

"You know who writes the Ledger?" Ego asked.

"Wish I did," Kari said. "I love the guy. I'd have his babies. But no, I just get an envelope in my locker with the pittance and instructions. I leave the photos I take in a certain book at the media center. It's all very anonymous."

"But why have an underground notebook newswire or whatever it is?" I asked. "And why does it have to be anonymous?"

She grinned. "First, because a lot of creepy things happen in this town that don't make it into the official media sources."

I wondered what Kari would think if I told her that the wealthiest, most important family in town were not human. She'd probably agree.

"Second," she continued, "our benevolent dictator, I mean, the school principal, has sworn that when he finds out who started the Ledger, they're going to be expelled. Thanks for the warm fuzzies and all." She sauntered off.

"Ego," I said, watching her leave, "why does the Ledger need pictures of us?"

He buried his face in his arms. "You really want me to tell you."

"I really do."

"It's not me, it's you," he said. "You're the cover story this week."

"What's this story about?" When he didn't answer, I glared at him. "Ego. Tell me."

"The story's about the incident you had at the zoo," he admitted. "The headline is, *Who Wants to Kill Cat Youngblood?*"

———

I saw Ego in the halls the next day a few times, but he would only produce a painful smile and abruptly change direction. He also didn't show up at lunch. Since he was the last friend I had left, I wasn't going to let him dodge me without an explanation.

I knew his schedule, and asked my last period teacher if I could leave a few minutes early to go and make an appointment in Guidance. She couldn't write the pass fast enough. I then went and waited outside Ego's classroom until the bell rang, and he filed out with the other kids.

"Oh, no you don't," I said, grabbing his arm when he tried to dart off. "We need to talk." I hauled him over to a quiet corner behind the stairwell. "Who told you to stay away from me? Was it your foster parents, or the Ravens?"

"No one told me to do anything." He dug some folded papers out of his pocket and shoved them at me. "Here's the stuff I found out about your grandparents. I gotta go."

I yanked him back by his collar. "Is it Jesse? Have you heard something?"

"Cat, you don't want … ah, here." He took the papers back from me and unfolded them. "Your grandparents aren't Dutch, they're Americans. Your grandfather's ancestors came here from Amsterdam in the nineteenth century. And it turns out that they're a big deal. Millionaires. The family made their fortune breeding hunting horses, and now they breed race horses. You're an heiress. Congratulations."

"This is why you've been ducking me all day?" I didn't believe him.

He gave me a resentful glare. "Fine. When the first Fanelsens came over here, they changed their name. The government probably made them do it, considering. It's kind of the same, but it's … ah, come on, Cat. You don't want to hear this."

I rolled my hand.

"It's all in here." He took out another bunch of papers but these he didn't give to me. "Your grandfather's name was originally Van Helsing."

"Van Helsing." I blinked. "As in—"

"Professor Van Helsing, the vampire hunter. The guy

who tried to kill Dracula." He flinched as I ripped the papers from his hand. "I swear to God, I'm not making it up."

"I didn't say you were." I shuffled through the papers, skimming through them rapidly. "This is wrong. *Dracula* was a work of fiction. The author invented the characters. They weren't real."

"Actually they were based on real people. Dracula was modeled after Vlad the Impaler." He tried to smile. "Stoker just never bothered to change the name of the guy he used for the vampire hunter."

"It has to be a coincidence." I found the printout with the ship's manifest. In 1875, Mr. and Mrs. Abraham Van Helsing had traveled to America. Another page was a copy of a newspaper article written about my grandparents and how they had been breeding horses since my grandfather's ancestors, the Van Helsings, had immigrated to the states. "This doesn't prove anything."

He took the papers from me and sorted through them until he found one and handed it back. "This does. It's a research paper written by a literary professor who spent thirty years researching Bram Stoker's inspirations for the novel. He discovered that Stoker and the real Van Helsing met a few times in England. In an interview one of Stoker's friends claimed Van Helsing gave the author details about vampires and how they could be killed. It's all there."

I read everything twice while Ego waited. The connections were tenuous, but he was right, they were there.

My mother's family had been vampire hunters, and guessing from what she'd written in her letters to my father, were still hunting them. I was Abraham Van Helsing's direct descendent.

Abraham Van Helsing. *AVH*. The same initials stamped on the trunk filled with vampire books and vampire sketches and vampire-killing weapons.

"I appreciate this, Ego." I folded the papers and put them in my backpack. "Are you going to tell anyone about this?"

"Who would believe me, besides that weird chick Kari?" He ducked his head. "I wasn't going to tell you. I was going to lie and say I didn't find anything. But I know what it's like to have family you've never met." He gave me a hopeful look. "You're not mad at me, are you?"

"No." I reached over and kissed his forehead. "But I need one more favor."

His shoulders drooped. "Please, don't ask me to look up your dad's family. They'll turn out to be werewolf slayers or zombie sharpshooters."

"I need the number to the phone in the main house on Raven Island," I said. "Jesse told me about it."

"Yeah, but why? My mother is the only one who will answer it, and she'll just hang up on you."

I thought of Jesse's parents and my brother, and how much all of them had been keeping from us. That was going to stop, tonight. "Not this time."

Twenty

Trick was letting Grayson bring me home from school again, and when I went out to the student parking lot my brother was waiting in his truck. He didn't look at me when I climbed in but started the engine and took off.

"Sorry I was late," I said. "I like to wait until the halls are empty before I leave school. It's safer for me now that I've turned invisible and inaudible. What if I fell down and got trampled in the rush? No one would ever find me."

He muttered something under his breath.

"What's that?" I cocked my head. "Trick hates me, everyone at school hates me, and I've utterly destroyed the beginning of your brilliant athletic career? I know. Lately I do nothing but marvel at my own capacity for destruction. You're driving too fast again. That also my fault?"

He slowed down. "You're my sister."

"Tragic, isn't it." I released a heavy sigh. "Can you disown a sister? We should check into that when we get to California."

He shook his head. "I don't hate you."

"This is the first time you've spoken to me in a week," I pointed out. "Your idea of sibling affection needs some fine-tuning."

He fell silent for so long I thought conversation time was over. Then he asked, "Why is Trick doing this?"

"Didn't he tell you?" I beamed at him. "It's a great reason. We're moving because we're not safe here anymore."

The steering wheel creaked under his hands. "What did you do, Cat?"

I glared at him. "See? We're back to *it's my fault*. Does it matter? We're packing. We're leaving. In ten days we'll be unloading the horses, unpacking the boxes, and registering at a new school. Then in six months we'll do it again, and again next summer, and again next winter, and—"

Gray hit the brakes, so hard only my seat belt kept me from going face first into the dash. He pulled off onto the side of the road and shut off the engine.

"What is the matter with you?" I demanded.

He turned toward me. "He hasn't been the same since

the night you went on that field trip. He won't talk to me and I have to know. *What did you do?*"

Gray never yelled at me, so I just sat there for a minute with my jaw in my lap. "I committed the unspeakable crime of introducing him to my friend Jesse and his parents. He was rude to them and when we got home, he said we were moving. That's it." I saw his hands were shaking and all my own anger evaporated. "Grayson? What is it?"

"It wasn't you. It was me."

I folded my arms. "Okay, then what did *you* do?"

Gray turned away, closing his eyes as he put his head back. "I told him about a nightmare I had. In it I saw you standing by silver water, and then something pulled you in. I tried to get to you, Cat, but I was too far away. By the time I reached you, you were gone."

"Gray, I don't mean to be insensitive here," I said gently, "but no one moves out of town because their brother had a bad dream." He mumbled something, and I leaned closer. "Sorry, what?"

"I said, my dreams come true." He gave me a defensive look. "They do. I'm not joking."

I thought of the dream I'd had of Jesse jumping up into my bedroom. "I'm not laughing. When did you have this dream?"

"The same night you were at the zoo. I was reading and I fell asleep. It was so real that when I woke up I was yelling, and he was there shaking me, and ... " He bent over and rested his forehead against the wheel. "I shouldn't have told him."

"You'd rather let me drown than move to California?" As soon as he turned his head, I said, "I'm kidding."

He straightened. "We have to talk to him. We can't live like this anymore. It's not just about football. I'm tired of being afraid."

When we got home we found a note instead of Trick.

"He's gone into town," I told my brother as I read the note, "and he won't be back for a couple hours. We're supposed to finish our rooms and start packing up the stuff we don't need out in the barn."

"I'm taking Flash for a ride." He stopped by the kitchen door and looked back at me. "We will talk to him tonight, together. We'll make him listen this time."

I doubted we could make our older brother bat an eyelash if he didn't want to, but I wasn't going to discourage Gray. For once he was on my side. "Sounds good."

I waited until sunset before I picked up the phone in the kitchen and dialed the number Ego had given me. As I listened to the rings I rehearsed what I was going to say in my head. I'd be polite. I'd be honest. And I *would* talk to Jesse before I hung up the phone.

His foster mother Marcia answered with "What is it now, Diego?"

"Hello," I said. "I'd like to speak to Paul Raven."

"Who is this?" Marcia demanded. "How did you get this number from my son?"

"I beat it out of him," I said, keeping my tone pleasant. "Now would you please go and tell Mr. Raven that Rose Fanelsen's daughter wants to speak to him."

For a moment I thought she was going to slam down the phone, but then she said, "Please hold."

I stayed on hold for a couple of minutes, and then heard the line engage and Paul Raven's deep voice. "Why are you calling, Miss Youngblood?"

"To talk to you, sir." He didn't respond to that. "Obviously you know about my mother's family, and I'm sure they're the reason you don't want me to see your son. But I've never ever seen my grandparents. My brothers and I have had no contact with them at all. We would never do anything to Jesse or your family."

"You cannot help what you are, Miss Youngblood, any more than we can." His voice softened. "You do not understand the nature of the abilities you've inherited. Perhaps you are not yet aware of them."

"I don't have the ability to do anything, sir," I assured him. "Except maybe get into trouble."

"You and your brothers were bred to do this work, as all of the Van Helsings have been," he said flatly. "From what Jesse has told us, you and your younger brother are coming into your abilities now. Soon you will understand."

"We've never met the Van Helsings," I repeated. Was this what Trick was so afraid of? That Gray and I would find out from our grandparents that vampires existed, and our mother's family hunted them? "They haven't taught us what they do."

"These abilities are not taught. Van Helsing children are born with them." His voice became sympathetic. "Have you never wondered why cats follow you everywhere? Why your brother does so well at a sport that he has never before tried to play?"

The man had been living on an island too long. "Mr. Raven, those aren't special abilities. Lots of kids like animals and play football."

"Do those children win every game they play," he asked, "or stop wild beasts in their tracks?"

I didn't know what to say.

"No one knows how the Van Helsings acquired their abilities, but they have been hunting and killing vampires for centuries," he continued. "In every generation there are two who are born to hunt the vampire. A brother and a sister."

"I have two brothers," I felt I had to point out.

He ignored that. "When your mother came here with your father, we were still living in the manor house. Rose knew what we were from the moment we met, but like you, she was not afraid. She told us of her family, and how she had left them, and that she would never hurt us. She believed that humans and vampires could live together in peace." He hesitated. "One night my wife found your brother in the woods. He was drawn to us, as all Van Helsings are. Sarah brought him back to the farm, but when Rose saw her with your brother in her arms, she attacked my wife. If not for your father, she would have killed Sarah. Your parents left Lost Lake the next day."

I closed my eyes.

"Miss Youngblood, I have seen how you are with my son. I believe you are genuine in your regard for him. But my wife and I know what you are, and that is something that can never be changed. That is why you and your brothers must leave Lost Lake. If you stay, Miss Youngblood, Jesse will die. You will kill him."

———

The truth was supposed to set you free, but all it did was turn me into a robot. After I spoke to Jesse's father, I hung up the phone and went to my room, where I sat by the window and watched the moon rise. At some point Trick came in and spoke to me, but I didn't hear what he said.

I didn't care anymore.

I went to bed, got up when the alarm went off, and went to school. I did everything I was supposed to, but my brain remained disconnected. Vaguely I wondered if I'd be this way for the rest of my life, and even that didn't bother me. Maybe it would be better this way, not feeling, not caring. Maybe in a few years I'd forget what Paul Raven had told me.

Jesse will die. You will kill him.

"You look like you just lost your best friend."

I frowned. I was standing in front of my locker with my Calculus book in my hands. Generally my books didn't talk to me, so I turned around.

Boone stood there, not smirking or crowding me, but just waiting.

"I don't have any friends." I turned back to my locker. "Leave me alone."

"The Halloween dance is tomorrow night," he said. "Are you going with anyone?"

Why was he still talking to me? "No."

"So go with me."

"No." I slammed my locker shut, locked it and went around him.

Boone caught up with me. "Is it because your brother's going with Tiff? They don't care about us."

"There is no 'us.'" What he said finally penetrated my fog. "My brother isn't going to the dance. He's not interested in your ex-girlfriend."

"You really are out of it." He took my arm. "Come with me."

I don't know why I went with him to the student parking lot. Idle curiosity. Complete apathy. Who knew? But when we arrived Boone stopped and pointed at my brother's truck. Gray was standing next to his truck. So was Tiffany Beck. She was talking to him. Gray smiled at something she said, bent down and kissed her.

Tiffany wrapped her arms around his neck and kissed him back.

"I heard they've been leaving campus together every day," Boone said. He looked like someone had just punched him in the stomach, which was exactly how I felt. "Doesn't look like they've been going out for lunch."

Grayson and Tiffany. Tiffany and Grayson. No matter how I arranged their names in my head, it didn't work. Gray was my brother, and I loved him. Tiffany Beck had tried to kill me, and I hated her. They didn't belong together. They couldn't be together.

But there they were, kissing. Holding hands. Walking off to class.

"How long has this been going on?" I asked Boone.

"A while now" he said. "One of my friends said your brother started dating her a couple of weeks ago."

Seeing it all with such crystal clarity felt almost painful, but I welcomed it. My brother watching the cheerleaders at lunch. My brother talking to Tiffany, and defending her after the stunt she pulled in the media center. My brother trying out for Boone's position on the football team. My brother, who hated everything, being happy with the world. My brother becoming so furious about moving away.

"Cat?" Boone peered down at me. "You okay?"

Gray didn't care about making friends or being popular. He'd done everything for her. He'd wanted Tiffany, and now he had her. She loved him. Everyone loved him. He was our hero.

I took a moment to let the fury settle inside me, and then I gave Boone an empty smile. "Thank you."

"Yeah, sure." He looked uncertain. "Talk to you later?"

I nodded and headed back to the cafeteria.

Ego was happy to accept the lunch I no longer felt

like eating, and observant enough to know I didn't want to talk to him. As I sat there and stared at the top of the table, Barb came over and sat beside me.

"Hey." She sounded tentative, as if she expected me to explode any second. "I haven't seen you guys in a while. How's it going?"

"Fine. I'm Diego, and this is Catlyn." Ego sat back. "And you are...?"

She made a face at him before she glanced at me. "I asked Boone if he would tell you about your brother and Tiffany. I thought you should know."

I stared at her.

"Why didn't you tell her?" Ego demanded. "Oh, right, you've been too busy not being seen with us." He waved his hand. "You can run away and sit somewhere else now."

"Look, I wish it could be different." Barb sounded miserable. "I'm not like you, Cat. I want to have friends. I want people to like me."

"Why don't you just shut up and go?" Ego snapped.

Barb ignored him. "I came to talk to you because I know what Tiffany's doing. She's only been dating Gray to get back at Boone for breaking up with her. She knows you and your brother are close. I heard that she's planning to embarrass him at the dance. She's going to make a big scene and blame him for doing something really awful. You should warn him." She saw some kids watching us and got to her feet. "My friends are waiting for me. See you later."

"Her friends are waiting for her." Ego threw down the remains of his sandwich. "I can't believe she's turned into such a snot."

"She was trying to be nice. Let it go." Already I could imagine Tiffany making a scene at the dance, and humiliating Gray in front of the whole school. "I've got to talk to my brother."

"You believe her?" He sounded incredulous. "Cat, she's just trying to start trouble between you and Tiffany again. It's like the girl's only hobby."

Doubt started to set in as I tried to think of what to say to my brother, but not because I thought Barb was lying. From what Boone had told me and what I'd seen with my own eyes, Grayson was obviously crazy about Tiffany Beck. Gray also knew how much I disliked her, which was probably why he'd been keeping the relationship a secret.

My brother would listen to me, I knew, but he wouldn't believe a word I said about his girlfriend. His heart wouldn't let him.

I thought it over until the dismissal bell rang. I had to try to warn my brother, but I also needed a back-up plan.

I intercepted Boone on the way out of class. "Do you still want to take me to the Halloween dance?"

He grinned and pulled two tickets out of his pocket. "When can I pick you up?"

I was about to tell him that I'd meet him at the dance, but there was no way I was riding in Gray's truck with him and Tiffany. "I'll be ready at seven."

Confronting my brother about his relationship with

Tiffany Beck was my next unpleasant task. But when I met him at his truck, he tossed me a small drawstring black bag.

I caught it reflexively. "What's this?"

"Candy gram. The players have been selling them to kids to send to their friends tomorrow." He looked sheepish. "I know you're not into candy, but … it supports the team."

What he meant was he knew that no one else would send one to me. "That's nice. Thanks."

On the way home Gray brought up cornering Trick about the move. "I tried to wait up for him last night, but he didn't get home until real late. We should talk to him after dinner."

Jesse will die. You will kill him.

"Cat?"

"Yeah, okay." This was the perfect chance for me to tell him that I knew he was dating Tiffany on the sly, but my heart wasn't in it. I'd had all my dreams crushed, why ruin his? Why did I have to be the bad guy? Tiffany would do that at the dance, and then Gray would be happy to leave Lost Lake, and everything would be fine.

I just wished I believed that.

Trick left another note at home saying he was out repairing some fencing at the back of the property. Gray went to his room, but once I was alone I couldn't stand staying in the house another minute. I dropped my backpack on the kitchen table and headed out to the barn.

Sali, who I'd been neglecting too much over the last

weeks, was happy to see me, and I spent a little time pampering her with a thorough brushing. My bottle of mane-and-tail detangler was almost empty, though, so I went out to the cabinet where Trick stored our grooming supplies. On the way I noticed some trailing marks on the floor that ran from the barn door to the hayloft ladder, as if someone had dragged something heavy into the barn.

I glanced up at the hayloft. *Or out of it.*

I climbed up the ladder and went over to the old horse blanket, which lay in a crumpled pile. When I lifted it, I found nothing but some loose straw and a wolf spider, which scuttled off under the edge of a bale.

The trunk had vanished.

"Cat? Where are you?"

I dropped the horse blanket, went over to the edge, and looked down at Gray. "What do you want?"

He frowned. "You shouldn't be up there. Trick told you to stay out of the hayloft."

Grayson appeared uncomfortable, and sounded worried, and he wouldn't look me in the eye. That gave me my second moment of painful clarity.

Gray knew about the trunk. He knew about the Van Helsings. Trick hadn't been hiding it from both of us; he and Gray had been working together to keep it from me.

I jumped over the railing and landed on the barn floor in front of him, as agile as if I'd never needed a ladder.

Gray's face whitened. "Are you nuts?"

"No, I'm a Van Helsing." I paused to appreciate the moment; he looked ready to keel over. "Getting rid of the trunk was a waste of time. I already opened it and saw all the goodies inside."

My brother finally recovered, shoved his hands in his pockets and kicked at some straw on the floor. "Don't be such a drama queen. It's not ours. Trick picked up that trunk at an auction. He didn't want to move it again."

"Liar." I walked over to Sali, who was getting nervous, and stroked her neck. "Our mother was a Van Helsing. They were teaching her the family business when she ran away with Dad. Now it's on you and me. How do you feel about a career in hunting down and killing vampires? Do you think they have any job pamphlets in Guidance about who's hiring?"

He still wouldn't look at me. "I don't know what that guy Jesse told you—"

"He doesn't know anything." Or perhaps he did, and that was why he'd stayed on the island. "His father told me. The Ravens knew our parents, Grim. They were neighbors. At least, they were until Mom tried to kill Jesse's mother."

"Then he lied to you," Gray said. "There are no Van Helsings. Mom's name was Fanelsen, and she would never hurt anyone. She was a sweet, gentle person—"

"—who had been trained by her parents to hunt down and kill blood-sucking monsters," I finished for him. "Give it up, Gray. I know everything."

His expression turned stubborn. "Vampires aren't real, so whatever that man told was just bull. Stop deluding yourself."

"Speak for yourself." I turned to him. "You've been dating Tiffany Beck since you got on the team. You think she's your girlfriend, but she doesn't care about you. She's never cared about you."

He stiffened. "Tiffany loves me."

I hooted a laugh. "Yeah, right. Do you know what she's planning to do tomorrow night? While you're at the dance, she's going to make a scene. A nice, big, nasty scene that will make you look like a total idiot. Her relationship with you was only to use you to get back at Boone, and me."

He dragged his hands through his hair and tried to say something, and then shook his head.

"I know you don't believe me," I continued. "Which is fine. Just remember when this blows up in your face that I told you the truth. The real, ugly, painful truth. Which is a lot more than you and Trick have ever done for me."

"It doesn't matter," he said slowly. "By tomorrow you'll forget all about this." He stalked out of the barn.

If Gray wouldn't talk to me about the Van Helsings, it was because he'd promised our brother that he wouldn't. If I was going to get any answers, I had to face Trick.

Sali was delighted when I went into her stall to saddle her, and nuzzled my neck as I tossed the blanket over her back.

"Don't act so happy," I warned her. "You're probably going to have to listen to a lot more yelling."

"No one has to yell." Trick opened the stall door. "Come out here, Catlyn."

Twenty-One

On the way back to the house from the barn I asked Trick if I was going to be grounded forever.

"That would make it pretty hard to move next week," he said. He inspected my face. "I think you can be paroled for good behavior."

"Does my parole include going to the Halloween school dance tomorrow night?" I batted my eyelashes at him. "I've already got a date."

He stopped me. "With who?"

"Aaron Boone." The way he was scowling made me chuckle. "Come on, Trick. I'm fifteen, and it's just a school dance. Gray's going, and we'll be chaperoned to death. Please?"

"I suppose so."

"Great. Ouch." I winced and rubbed my throbbing temple. "I can't seem to get rid of this headache."

"You're overheated." He rubbed my back. "Go upstairs, take a couple of aspirin and get some rest. I'll wake you for dinner."

I leaned my head against his shoulder. "Have I ever told you that you're a prince?"

I went into the bathroom upstairs to get my bottle of aspirin, but found it empty. "Who's been stealing my drugs?" I grumbled as I tossed it into the trash can.

I trudged back downstairs to get some from the bottle in the kitchen, but stopped just outside as I heard Trick's angry voice.

"We can't keep doing this," he was saying. "I said it had to stop when we moved here. Those headaches she had in Chicago were too severe. We could be causing permanent damage."

"I told you what she said." Gray sounded sulky. "You'd rather have her know?"

"You're the finder. Why aren't you watching her?"

"I told you to change our schedules, but you said nothing would happen," Gray snapped. "That guy's father talked to her. He told her about them."

"When?" Trick asked. "You were here last night. Did Raven come to the house? Did he call?"

As Gray answered no, I remembered that I'd made a call last night. I'd called someone from the phone in the kitchen, but why would I talk to a bird?

"Trick, we can't just take away a couple of things. We

have to make her forget it all this time," Gray said. "Moving here, school, that boy, everything. It's the only way it'll work."

I almost laughed out loud. Make me forget my life? Was he kidding?

"It's not just the trunk or the letters," Gray said. "She thinks she's in love with this guy. The Ravens know who we are. How long do you think those monsters will wait before they come after her?"

I took a step back. In love? I wasn't in love. I'd never been in love. And why was he talking about birds knowing me and being monsters?

"So far they've done nothing," Trick said. "They're not like the others. They seem to be able to control themselves. If we stay here, that will change."

"Is that right? Then why did Tiffany say Jesse was all over her at the zoo?" Gray demanded.

From the moment my brother said the name 'Jesse' my heart began to pound faster. I moved away from the kitchen door, groping my way along the furniture as I dragged myself to the stairs. I couldn't let them see me like this. I couldn't let them know I'd been listening.

I don't know any Jesse. There is no Jesse.

I crawled up the stairs, panting as tears of pain streamed down my face. The headache swelled until it pressed against the inside of my skull, so hard I expected to hear it crack. At the top of the stairs I nearly fell as the hammering agony became the world, and one low, beautiful voice began whispering in my mind.

Go back where you came from, girl.
It's dangerous to ride in the dark.
I won't let you fall.
When I'm with you, I can be just like anyone else.

"Jesse." I staggered inside my room and fell on my bed, holding my pounding head between my hands. "Help me remember. Help me."

His voice became my guide: Every hello and good-bye, every complaint, every compliment, every single word he'd ever said to me. They brought with them images: Jesse riding Prince, the moonlight gilding them silvery white; Jesse holding my hand and walking with me through the cool silence of the woods; Jesse standing with me next to the tiny jewel of a lake we'd found hidden on his land. Jesse frowning and smiling and laughing. With each memory I dragged from the dull gray void in my head the pain began to fade, until my headache itself was only a memory.

Catlyn, whatever happens… I'll always be with you.

Once I remembered Jesse, the rest of what I'd forgotten unfolded around his memory like a moonflower blooming in the night. I had found out about the Van Helsings from Ego and from Paul Raven. I'd confronted Gray in the barn, and had been saddling Sali when Trick came into the stall. Then there was another void, a space of time I couldn't recall. After that, Trick and I were walking back to the house.

Something had happened to me in the barn. Something

that had made me forget the most important person in my life: Jesse, the boy I loved.

I sat up slowly, holding my head in anticipation of more pain. Nothing hurt, but I felt sluggish and a little disoriented, as if I'd woken up after sleeping too long.

A knock sounded on the door, and Trick looked inside. "How are you feeling?"

"Better. I think the aspirin is starting to work." I wanted to throw my lamp at his head, but I managed to keep my cool. "I'm not really hungry. Would it be okay if I skip dinner tonight?"

"I could make you some soup," he offered, as if he really cared.

"That's okay." I made a show of stretching. "I think I'll just take a shower and sleep off the rest of this."

He nodded. "See you in the morning."

I kept my smile pinned in place until the door closed, and then I got up. Trick knew what had happened to me in the barn, and he was hiding it from me. Had I fallen and hit my head? That would explain the headache and the gap in my memory. Or had Trick given me a drug? How much of my life had been stolen from me to protect our family's secrets?

Worse, how much more would I lose?

I couldn't live like this, but I had nowhere else to go. I could run away, but I didn't have any money or transportation, so I wouldn't get far. I could call the sheriff, but he wanted us to leave town, so he wouldn't help. Neither would Jesse's parents. I was so desperate I even thought of contacting my grandparents, but they were Van Helsings. If they helped me get away from my brothers, it would only be so they could use me for their own purposes. They wouldn't feel an ounce of sympathy for a granddaughter who had fallen in love with a vampire.

Jesse was my only hope.

Several hours later, when the house was quiet, I climbed out of my window and dropped to the ground. I still had no idea how I would get to Jesse, or if he even wanted to be with me anymore. I was sure his father had told him about the Van Helsings, and my mother attacking Sarah. Maybe he hated me now.

If he hated me, I had nothing left.

I was tempted to take Sali for one last midnight ride, but instead I walked over to the Ravens' land, and followed the trail to the manor. Along the way Soul Patch, Princess, Terrible and a couple other strays joined me. They followed me up to the steps, and when I sat down they piled around me, purring and rubbing their heads against my jeans.

More cats crept out of the woods and padded over to us, joining the pile-up. I was so preoccupied that I didn't notice the newcomers getting bigger and wilder until a brown spotted bobcat trying to nestle at my feet swatted at a lynx cuddling in the same spot.

That shook me out of my thoughts. So did seeing a large, cream-colored panther approaching the steps, trailed by her two energetic, fluffy cubs.

I held my breath as the other cats began to slink away

on either side of me, making way for the panther as she climbed the steps and sat down beside me. She nudged me under my chin with her blunt head, baring her sharp teeth as I carefully scratched around her ears. The cubs tumbled onto my lap and curled up together.

"She's beautiful."

I looked up to see my dark boy walk out of the woods, and when the panther reared her head I stroked her back until she calmed. "I didn't think I'd ever see you again."

He smiled. "I am happy to disappoint you."

Maybe Paul hadn't said anything to him yet. "Did your father tell you that I'm a Van Helsing, and I was born to hunt vampires?"

"He did, in great detail." He picked up Soul Patch and sat down with him on the bottom step. Some of the other strays began swarming around him. "My father sees everything in black and white. He doesn't know you."

"Something happened to me today that made me forget you." I ran my fingers through the cub's soft, downy fur. "It didn't stick, though."

Jesse let Princess climb up on his shoulders and drape herself around his neck. "We are both stubborn."

"But we're not enemies." Gently I lifted the cubs from my lap to set them by their mother before I stood. "Why don't they understand that?"

"They're afraid because they love us," he said softly.

"Some love." I walked down and took Princess from his shoulders, setting her on the ground as he stood up and took my hand. "I'm going to the Halloween dance tomorrow night with a boy I don't like just so I can protect my brother from his evil fake girlfriend. Now *that's* love."

He frowned. "Why didn't you ask me to be your date?"

"Hmmmm." I pretended to think. "It might have something to do with the fact that your parents hate me and won't let me talk to you and have armed men guarding the island where you live. Also, girls never ask boys to go out with them. It's the law."

"I'll have to remember that." He kissed my forehead before his expression turned serious. "We can be together, Catlyn. I have my own money, and friends who will help us. We can go away together and make a life somewhere else. Somewhere they can't find us. We can go tonight."

For a moment I was tempted. My mother had run away with her love, and they had been happy. But she had never escaped her past, or what she was, and she had left behind that burden on me and my brothers.

Jesse and I might escape our families, but we would live the rest of our lives looking over our shoulders, expecting my brothers or his parents to appear and try to tear us apart again. I was human; I would age and someday die. Jesse would always be eighteen, and after I was gone, alone forever.

He deserved better than that. So did I.

"We're not running away," I told him. "We're going

to face this, and our families, and make them under-stand."

He cradled my cheek with his hand. "How can we do that?"

"I don't know," I admitted. "Maybe the first step is to show them that we're not afraid."

He pulled me close. "I think I know how to do that."

———

Jesse promised we'd see each other again soon, and after making sure I got back in my room safely vanished into the shadows. I went to bed, tired but happy. When I was with him no problem seemed impossible, even one as complicated as ours.

The next day I had to keep up the smiling oblivi-ous Catlyn act in order to fool my brothers into believ-ing I had forgotten all about Jesse. All I wanted to do was knock their heads together, so it was a strain to smile and chat and laugh with them as if nothing were wrong. But I was discovering that I was a pretty good actress when I needed to be, and managed to keep up the pretense with-out a hitch.

After dinner I went up to change into the one Hallow-een costume I owned, a garnet-red velvet gown trimmed in black lace and golden braid that I wore every year. I had bought a matching red velvet hat with a golden veil from a RenFaire we'd gone to in Chicago, and once I shook out the hoop skirt and adjusted the angled sleeves I made a passable medieval princess.

I came downstairs a minute before seven o'clock, just in time to meet Boone at the door. I tried not to wince as I surveyed his classic vampire costume, and wondered if I should call the whole thing off. Then Trick came out, and I made myself introduce them.

"Nice to meet you." My brother shook his hand. "Be careful driving, have a good time, and remember the curfew."

"I will, sir." Boone looked over as Gray walked out of the hall.

My brother wore his only Halloween costume, a blue velvet version of a doublet and hose with a broad-brimmed feathered hat. He'd left his hair loose and looked exactly like a prince from a fairytale.

For a minute Boone stared at him with visible dislike before he offered me his arm. "Let's go, Princess."

The narrow seats in Boone's sports car didn't like my hoop skirt, and I spent most of the drive over to school trying to keep it from getting hooked on his gear shift.

"You look really nice, Cat," Boone said, glancing at me. "You should wear red often."

"Thanks." I'd been prepared for him to behave like the jerk he usually was, so I didn't quite know how to handle this new, polite Boone. "Why did you decide to dress up as a vampire?"

"They didn't have a decent werewolf outfit at the costume shop." He grinned at me. "Besides, girls love vampires."

I hid my own smile. "Do they."

The Halloween dance was being held in the gymnasium, which was already overcrowded by the time we arrived. I saw a lot of homemade costumes, and a couple of boys dressed in flannel shirts and jeans who were probably telling everyone they were lumberjacks. Most of the girls had dressed to look more beautiful than scary, and there were so many princesses that I didn't feel out of place. A few brave souls were dancing between the basketball hoops to the music blaring out of the loudspeakers, but most of the kids were either milling around the room or sitting on the bleachers with their friends. At one end of the gym the chaperons had set up long tables with bowls of punch, platters of doughnuts, fruit and cookies, and several decorated sheet cakes.

"Would you like some punch?" Boone almost had to shout for me to hear him over the music.

I nodded and followed him over to the refreshment tables, where he handed me a cup of black cherry soda with a chunk of frozen pineapple floating in it. I took a sip and discovered it tasted much better than it looked, but shook my head when Boone pointed to the snacks.

No one came up to talk to Boone, and everyone was still avoiding me, so we ended up sitting one of the bleachers and watching the other kids dance. Boone seemed to forget about me as he watched the doors, which was why I knew the moment my brother arrived with Tiffany Beck, who was dressed as Sleeping Beauty.

Boone never took his eyes off her, I noticed.

The music dropped a few thousand decibels as someone put on a slow ballad, and I saw Gray lead Tiffany out onto the dance floor.

"Want to dance?" I asked Boone.

He gave me a startled look, as if he'd forgotten I was sitting next to him. "Yeah, sure. Come on."

We walked to the edge of the court, and then Boone took my hand and put his arm around my waist. With several respectable inches between us, he maneuvered me toward the center of the dancing couples. He looked past me and over my head and to one side and the other, but I might as well have been a teacher for all the notice he gave me.

"If you really want to make her jealous," I said, "you should pay attention to me, not her and Gray."

Boone looked down at me. "I don't want to make anyone jealous."

I smiled. "And you're doing an excellent job of that."

He ducked his head, clearly embarrassed. "If you want to go home, we can leave."

"It's okay. I have my reasons for being here, too." I glanced over at my brother, who had Tiffany in a virtual bear hug. "If you still have feelings for her, why did you break up?"

"She was acting weird. Always talking about you and

how she was going to get even." He sounded uncomfortable. "I know how girls are when you fight, but she started blaming you for stuff I know you didn't do, like trashing her locker and putting roaches in her desk. She got totally obsessed."

I thought of my own trashed locker. "That day in the media center, did you really see her spill that soda?"

"Cat, that's why she had me buy it." He sighed. "No, I didn't actually see her spill it, but another girl did, and she told me while the teacher was yelling at you."

"What other girl?"

He thought for a moment. "I can't remember her name, but her mom works for my dad. She's that chubby girl with the braces. You know her; you used to hang out with her."

"You mean Barbara Riley?"

His expression cleared. "Yeah, that's her."

"Excuse me," a familiar voice said. "Would you mind if I cut in?"

Boone gave the boy dressed as a highway robber a startled look. "Who are you?"

"I'm Jesse Raven," my dark boy said, "and you're dancing with my lady."

Twenty-Two

Boone reluctantly turned me over to Jesse, and as soon as I was in his arms he whirled me away.

I saw my brother frowning at us, and wondered if Gray would try to start something. "Jesse, what are you doing?"

"I think it's a waltz," he teased. "Would you rather try a tango? I used to be quite good at that, too."

"Well, I'm not, thanks." I laughed as he twirled me down the length of his arm and then tugged me back to him. "I meant, why did you come to the dance?"

"You said we can't run away or hide," he reminded me. "That means being together where everyone can see us. Out in the open. Unafraid."

"Unafraid." I closed my eyes and rested my cheek against his chest. "Okay."

We danced through that song and the next, and I stopped caring who was staring at us or what my brother would do. Being in Jesse's arms was heaven; he was so handsome, and he made me feel beautiful. When the second song ended, and someone put on a fast, heavy rock song, he took me by the hand and led me out of the gym.

"No one can see us out here," I said as he guided me to the sidewalk that led down to the lake.

"I want you to myself for a few minutes." His arm came around my waist. "I also want to persuade you to wear more gowns. You look like a grand duchess."

I smiled up at him. "Tonight, I feel like one."

When we reached the dock, Jesse steered me to an old oak tree, where the wide trunk hid us from view. "I also brought you out here so I can ask you something."

"I don't think I can move to the island," I warned. "But maybe, if we talk to your parents, I might visit."

"That would be wonderful." He took the ring from his finger and slid it onto mine. "Catlyn, will you wear this for me?"

"After all the trouble I had getting it back to you?" I smiled as I traced the outline of the raven, and then I glanced up. "Why?"

"I can't be with you all the time," he admitted. "When you look at it, I hope you'll think of me."

"I don't need a ring. You're always with me." I touched my heart. "Right in here."

He lifted my chin with his hand, and bent down to brush his mouth over mine.

"What do you think you're doing?" Boone's angry voice demanded. "Let her go."

Jesse and I were wrenched apart as Boone dragged me away.

Jesse's eyes darkened. "Take your hands off her."

"Go back to the gym, Cat," Boone said, giving me a push in that direction as he tore off his cape and rolled up his sleeves. "I'll deal with this clown."

"Aaron, stop it." I stepped between them. "Jesse is my boyfriend. He didn't doing anything wrong. I wanted him to kiss me."

"You don't know what he is. No one does." Boone shoved me aside as he rushed at Jesse, and I fell, hitting my head against something hard.

I propped myself up, holding my aching head as I heard water splash. Boone had pushed Jesse in the lake and was wading in after him.

"Why are you just sitting there?" a girl screamed.

I looked up at Barb, who was dressed like a vampire. I almost didn't recognize her, her face was so red and contorted.

"Get up," she shrieked, dragging at my sleeve and ripping one seam as she pointed toward the lake. "Go down there and tell him to leave Boone alone."

I staggered to my feet when suddenly Boone came flying back out of the lake, landing on the ground in front of us. I heard bones crunch and he howled as he rolled over and grabbed his arm.

"Oh God, oh God." Barb dropped on her knees

beside him and clutched at him frantically. "Aaron, are you all right? How could she do this to you? No, don't try to move. I'm here now, you'll be okay, you'll be fine—"

"Get off me." Pale and shaking, Boone tried to get to his feet.

I saw Jesse wading out of the lake and started toward him to help, when someone grabbed me from behind and threw me to the ground.

"No, you don't." Barb stood over me, and she had an oar in her hands. "You're not going to ever put your dirty hands on him again. Aaron doesn't love you. He loves me."

"Barb, what are you talking about?" I saw the wide, crazy way she was staring down at me and wondered if she even recognized me. "Barb, it's me. Cat, your friend."

As she brought the oar down, I threw up my arm to protect my head. Then I saw a dark blur knock into Barb, and the oar flipped through the air, smashing into the trunk of the oak and landing in pieces all over the ground.

Barb cringed and sobbed as she crawled on her hands and knees away from me. "Boone? Boone, he hurt me. Make him leave me alone."

Jesse helped me sit up, and held me in the circle of his arm as he looked over at Barb. "Who is that girl?"

"I thought she was my friend." The sound of running footsteps made me turn my head, and I saw Tiffany, Grayson and some other kids running down from the sidewalk toward us. "We need to get some help for Boone," I called out to my brother. "He's been hurt."

"The sheriff is just down the street," one of the boys said. "I'll get him." He turned around to take off in that direction.

Jesse made sure I was all right before he went over to check Barb, who sat with her arms wrapped around her knees. As soon as he tried to help her up, she made a shrill sound and cowered away.

I got up and went to her, kneeling down beside her. "Barb? Are you hurt?"

"It wasn't supposed to be this way," she said, moaning the words as she rubbed her forehead from side to side against her knees. "He was going to ask me to the dance. I got my costume so we would match. We're in love. He doesn't want anyone else."

"Barb?" When she didn't answer me, I met Jesse's gaze. "She's not like this. She's never like this."

"Let me try something." Jesse touched Barb's shoulder, which seemed to immediately calm her down. "Why did you attack Catlyn tonight?"

"Catlyn?" She lifted her face, and the blankness of her expression gradually turned into a mask of hatred. "She wants to take Aaron away from me. She's been flirting with him since the first day at school. I saw her by the bathrooms. I saw how she looked at him. I can't have that. He's mine."

"None of that is true, and Boone isn't dating her," I murmured to Jesse. "He doesn't even know her name."

Tiffany came to stand beside me, and for once she didn't look angry. "Barb told me that day that you were after Aaron. She said that's why you deliberately ruined my uniform."

"I didn't." Something Barb had said once came back to me. *I know plenty of ways to get to Tiffany.* "I tripped, that's all. It was an accident."

"Yeah," Tiffany said, looking down at Barb. "I think I know who tripped you."

Things began to make sense now. Barb, who had been my friend since the beginning of school. Who had been at my side every time Tiffany and I had clashed. Who had been at the library, using the same terminal. Who was taking art, and knew exactly where my locker was. Barb, who had such a crush on Boone that she covered the insides of her notebooks with his name.

"It was her," I said slowly. "All this time, it's been her."

"But you never knew." Barb struggled to her feet, her lips peeling back from her braces in a wide smirk. "I made sure of it. You were so perfectly clueless."

"You knew we were sitting at the cheerleaders' table, that first day," I said, remembering. "You picked out the table, hoping to start trouble."

"She called me that night," Tiffany said. "She said you and Boone had a good laugh over me. She called me practically every day after that, always about you and the lies you were spreading about me, and how much you wanted to break up me and Boone."

"At lunch she'd tell me the same things about you. How you hated me and wanted revenge. She said you were dating my brother and planning to hurt him to get back at me." I sighed and shook my head. "And I believed her."

"Aaron never wanted you," Barb told Tiffany. "You're nothing but a cheap slut." She jutted her chin at me. "Just like her."

Jesse came to stand beside me. "Her mind is not right," he murmured. He breathed in and touched the shoulder of my gown. "You're hurt."

For the first time I felt the blood trickling down my skin from the gash on my shoulder. "It's not bad," I told him.

Tiffany bent down to look into Barb's eyes. "Did you steal my jacket at the zoo, Barbara? Did you put it on before you opened that gate to the cheetah enclosure?"

"I had to." Barb gave me a sullen look. "But that stupid cheetah didn't do anything to her, and you hardly got into any trouble."

"I owe you a huge apology," I said to Tiffany.

She nodded. "Same here. Barbara told me one time that her mom was making her go to see a therapist. I think she was on medication, too."

I shook my head. "She told me she hated pills. She threatened to flush the last prescription she had."

Sheriff Yamah arrived a few minutes later, and after checking Boone he spoke with Jesse about what had happened.

"An ambulance is on the way for Aaron. I'll deal with Ms. Riley." He bent over to help her up. "Barbara, I'm going to take you home now. Your mother is very worried about you."

"She said I couldn't go to the dance, but I had to." She gave Yamah a blank look. "I had to stop Aaron. He doesn't love her. Look at what she did to him. You have to arrest her, Sheriff. She tried to kill him. She has to pay for this."

"This is just a misunderstanding," Yamah told her. "You can talk it over with your mom." By then half the kids from the dance had gathered on the walk above the lake, and he turned and called out to them, "We're all done here. You youngsters go on back to—"

Barb wrenched free of his hands and darted around him. I saw the sheriff's gun in her trembling hands first because she was pointing it at me.

"You hurt my Aaron," Barb whispered, and pulled the trigger.

Three things happened at once. Boone lunged between us, Tiffany screamed and Jesse snatched the gun from Barb.

Boone staggered backward, and I caught him as he sagged. His dazed eyes met mine. "A guy should always pay on the first date."

I saw a black hole and the blood seeping down the front of his shirt in disbelief. "Aaron, no."

Jesse helped me lower him to the ground and then handed the gun back to the sheriff. His eyes had turned solid black, and his voice shook when he spoke. "James, where is that ambulance?"

"*You killed my Aaron.*"

Barb grabbed a piece of the broken oar from the ground and hurled herself at me, but Jesse caught her and spun her away. When the sheriff dragged her off him, Jesse looked down at the jagged wood embedded in his chest, and then at me, before he stumbled away toward the boat house.

I knew why he was going there. His eyes had turned black, he'd been shaking, and now he was hurt. *The urge to attack is strongest when we are wounded.*

"Grayson, Tiffany, come here." When they knelt down beside Boone, I tore the veil from my hat and folded it into a layered square, which I put over Boone's gunshot wound. "Can you keep pressure on this?"

"I've got it." Gray clamped his hand over the make-shift bandage. "Go."

I glanced over at the sheriff, who had handcuffed Barb, and then took off after Jesse. The door to the boat-house stood open, and when I hurried inside I found him sitting by one of the roof posts, his arm curled around it.

"Don't come any closer," he whispered. "Please, Cat-lyn. Go back with the others."

"We're being unafraid, remember?" My voice trembled as I sat down on the deck beside him, and saw that the broken oar shaft penetrated his chest between his ribs. "Tell me what to do."

He closed his eyes. "Push the wood in so that it pierces my heart."

Jesse will die. You will kill him.

"I can't," I whispered.

"I need blood, Catlyn, and there is too much in the air." His voice shook as his fingers curled into my torn sleeve. "I can't hold myself back much longer. You have to stop me now, before I become a monster. You're the only one who can."

I knew why he was telling me this. I was a Van Helsing; killing vampires was my family's legacy. If anyone could keep Jesse from attacking Boone and Tiffany and the others, it was me. I had a duty, not to my family, but to the innocent people outside. I had to protect them from what Jesse would become.

But Jesse wasn't a monster, not yet.

"I won't let you die." I wrapped my hand around the wood and jerked it out of his chest. "You're going to live."

I pulled aside the shoulder of my gown, exposing the bleeding gash beneath it, and cradled the back of his head. I brought his mouth to my flesh, and felt his lips against the wound, but still he kept his mouth shut.

He was afraid, but I wasn't. "Take my blood, Jesse."

He closed his eyes, wrapping his arms around me as he drank from my wound.

His scent filled my head, and the tug of his mouth made stars explode behind my eyes. I didn't go limp or become paralyzed; I held onto him, soothing him with my hands and my voice.

When he lifted his head, his eyes were no longer black. "Catlyn," he whispered. "What have I done?"

"You didn't take too much. You didn't hurt me. You are not a monster." I touched his cheek. "Neither am I."

His eyes shifted past me. "Your brother."

I turned my head to tell Gray that Jesse was all right, and then fell silent as I saw it was Trick. I held onto Jesse's hand as we both stood up, and then I stepped in front of him.

"I'm not going to hurt him," Trick said.

"I know you're not, Patrick, because you'll have to go through me first." I felt Jesse's hand tighten over mine as little shadows began slipping in through the door and padding over to me and Jesse, gathering around us like a small, silent army.

When Trick took a step toward us, the cats crouched down, ready to spring.

"I wouldn't do that," I advised him. "I don't know how much control I have over them yet. This ability of mine is apparently still in development."

"They respond to your thoughts," Trick told me. "All cats do."

"Then let's all think happy thoughts." I didn't want to hurt my brother, but I wasn't going to let him do anything to my dark boy.

He looked at Jesse for a long moment before he said to me, "Your friend's parents are here. I'll wait for you outside."

When Trick left, the cats settled down and I turned

to Jesse. "I think this unafraid idea of yours might actually work."

He smiled. "So do I." He touched his ribs. "I am not completely healed, so I must return to the island with my parents. Will you come with us?"

I wanted to. I never wanted to be apart from him again, not for a single moment. But Aaron had been shot, and my brothers were waiting for me, and I couldn't turn my back on the rest of the world to be with my dark boy.

Not just yet, anyway.

"Another time." I reached up to kiss him. "Go home. Tell them everything. Oh, and warn your Dad, I'm going to call you tomorrow night."

He glanced at the boathouse door. "Will your brother allow that?"

My smile slipped. "They can't keep us apart now, not after this. We've proven to them we can be together, that we can love each other." I rested my cheek against his shoulder. "I did mention that I'm in love with you, right?"

"Boone interrupted us before you could." He smiled down at me. "But I thought you might be."

Outside the boathouse Jesse gave me one final kiss before releasing my hand and walking up to where the big Rolls was parked by the curb. I went over to where my brothers were standing and watching Aaron being lifted onto a gurney by two paramedics.

"Is he going to be all right?" I asked Gray as I joined them.

He nodded. He was watching Tiffany, who was standing by the gurney and holding Boone's hand. She didn't look back as she walked with the gurney and the paramedics up to the waiting ambulance.

I felt sorry for my brother, but I wasn't surprised. On some level I'd always known that Tiffany and Boone belonged together. It was just a shame that Gray hadn't.

The sheriff had already left with Barb, and once the ambulance and the Rolls drove off the kids began walking back to the gym. I followed my brothers up to the street, and waited with Trick by his Harley while Gray went to get his truck.

"That thing could have killed you tonight," my brother said.

"*That thing* is a boy. His name is Jesse, and I love him." I turned to him. "He asked me to run away with him, but I said no. I'm not Mom. I'm not afraid of you or Gray, and I'm not ashamed of how I feel about Jesse. I have the right to a normal life."

"Yes," he said, sounding regretful. "You do."

I looked down as he wrapped his hand around mine. The same way he had taken my hand in the barn while I was saddling Sali. The same way he had when he'd found me looking through the old trunk in Chicago.

We all had abilities, I remembered Paul Raven telling me. Gray and I were the vampire hunters, but he had never explained what Patrick was, or what ability he had.

"I'm sorry, Catlyn."

Twenty-Three

"at."

I opened one eye and saw Trick standing over me, a folded newspaper under one arm and a mug of something hot in his left hand. The scent of hot chocolate warmed my cold nose. The rest of me felt heavy and sluggish, as if I'd slept too hard. "Hmmm?"

"Time to get up." He put the mug on my nightstand. "First day of school."

"Sorry. Must have hit the snooze button." I rubbed my eyes and sat up to look out the window. "Why is it so light outside?"

"You keep forgetting that I set all the clocks back last weekend for daylight saving time." He ruffled my hair. "Look at it this way: you'll get an extra hour of sleep every morning until spring. Or you could get up early and catch up on school work."

Naturally; thanks to the rotten timing of our move from Chicago and Gray's truck breaking down in Georgia I was starting school two months late. "Excuse me for not cheering." I got up and reached for my robe. That's when I felt the bandage under the shoulder of my T-shirt, and turned my head, trying to see it.

For an instant I didn't remember how I'd hurt it until an image of Trick picking me up from the ground flashed through my mind. He'd explained how I'd been thrown from Sali after a snake spooked her, and landed wrong.

"My shoulder doesn't hurt anymore," I told him, hoping I wouldn't get another lecture about being careful when I rode. "Can I take this off?"

He nodded. "How's your head?"

"Fine." I rubbed the back of it. "No lumps or bumps." I yawned. "You know, if you homeschooled me, among other things we could both sleep in."

"Among other things." His smile didn't quite reach his eyes. "Even though you're starting a little late, you'll like this school. I promise."

"You always say that," I called after him.

I felt too tired to work up a new argument against going to school, and went to the bathroom to splash my face with cold water. When I straightened and looked in the mirror, my eyes looked darker than usual. I'd also bitten my lip in my sleep, and winced as I touched the raw spot. I also felt a little sore all over; I must have landed really hard when Sali bucked me off.

Did she buck me off, or did I slip? Weird that I couldn't remember.

I tugged aside the collar of my T-shirt to pull off the bandage and inspect my shoulder. A big scab covered the gash I'd gotten when I'd fallen, and the oval bruise around it had faded to a light yellow-brown, but the wound still looked awful against my pale skin.

I wrinkled my nose at my dark-eyed reflection. "No wearing tank tops for a while."

Gray followed me into the kitchen, where Trick had plates of scrambled eggs, bacon and toast waiting for us.

I studied mine closely. "Who made this?"

Trick looked up from his paper. "Why?"

"The eggs aren't brown, the bacon isn't half-raw and the toast isn't black." I grew suspicious. "Did you sneak out to a restaurant and get take-out breakfast for us?"

He gave me a disgruntled look. "Shut up and eat."

I didn't know what girls at this new school were wearing, so I dressed in faded jeans, a white T-shirt and a red plaid flannel shirt. Normally I would wear all blue on my first day—blue being my lucky color—but this morning I liked the look of the red shirt better. I didn't fuss with my hair, which was too long for any sort of style, but pulled it back in a ponytail.

Gray looked in the bathroom. "Are you ready yet?"

"Quit asking me that." A sense of déjà vu came over me as I realized it was the first time he'd asked me. Or maybe it wasn't. I couldn't remember. "I'll be down in a minute."

We always lived in small country towns, and on the way to school I saw this one was just as tiny and boring as all the others. This one seemed to be all antique shops, gift shops, and sandwich and coffee shops. At school I knew there would only be a couple hundred kids, and dinky classrooms, and nothing to do. Life in a small town offered about as much excitement as movie night at a nursing home.

"Do you like it here?" I asked my brother.

He glanced at me. "It's okay. Probably."

Gray hated everything, so that was kind of a shock. "You think so? Why?"

"I just do." He made a turn and pulled into the student parking lot. "Give it a chance, Cat. I have a feeling it's going to be a good place for us."

"If you say so." I felt mildly astonished that my brother would be such a fan of a place stuck in the middle of the swamps. Even the town's name, Lost Lake, sounded dismal.

Some of the kids in the parking lot stared at us, or more precisely, at Grim, but my brother's size always drew a lot of attention. I ignored the kids and went with him to the front office, where we picked up our schedules from the secretary. As usual all of our classes were in the same buildings, and we even had the same lunch period.

Before we left, the secretary smiled at me. "Nice to see you back."

"Thanks." I'd never been here, but maybe she'd mistaken me for another kid.

Gray walked me to my first class, and promised to meet me at lunch.

"You can go and sit with the other juniors, you know," I told him. "I'll be fine."

"I know. See you." He trudged off.

My first class was Calculus, and after giving my transfer slip to the teacher I sat down in the empty desk behind a pretty redheaded cheerleader. She turned around at once.

"You're Catlyn Youngblood, right?" When I nodded, she smiled. "I'm Tiffany Beck. I've been assigned to be your student mentor."

"Sorry you got stuck with that job." I hated being the new kid. "I'll try not to be a big pain."

"Not a problem," she assured me. "I know you're a couple months behind on school work, but I can come in early and help you catch up. Just let me know what mornings are good for you, and we'll meet in the media center."

"That would be fantastic." I didn't know why she was being so nice to me, but I wasn't a gift horse mouth-checker. "Thanks a lot."

Between classes Tiffany walked with me and introduced me to some of her friends and her boyfriend, a tall, handsome boy named Aaron who had his arm in a sling.

"I took a bad fall during practice," he explained, lifting his arm. "Broke two bones and got spiked in the shoulder, so I'm benched for the season."

"But you're okay, right?" Seeing his arm like that made me feel particularly anxious.

"Don't encourage him," Tiffany said. "He thinks having a broken arm means everyone should wait on him hand and foot."

"Not everyone." He put his good arm around her and stole a kiss. "Just you, sweetie."

They were such a cute couple, and so obviously crazy about each other that I felt a pang of jealousy. *Someday I'm going to someone who makes me feel that way.*

The rest of the day went amazingly well. Tiffany and Aaron sat with me and Gray at lunch, and while my brother was his usually grumpy, silent self, I chatted with them and heard about the search for a new quarterback to replace Aaron. A Hispanic boy in a work uniform stopped by our table and frowned at me before he went to sit with some other kids.

"Do you know him?" Tiffany asked. When I shook my head she said, "That's Diego. He's one of the smartest kids in school, but he's been out with the flu since Halloween."

"A lot of kids have been," Aaron said. "They even had to shut down the school for a couple days to keep it from spreading around. Hey, maybe we'll get lucky and there'll be another outbreak."

Tiffany prodded him. "You just want to lay around all day and watch TV."

"That's not what we did the last time," he teased.

As Tiffany protested I leaned over to Gray, who hadn't said a word. "What's wrong with you?"

"Nothing." He abruptly stood up. "I've gotta go."

After my brother left I gave my new friends a wry look. "Sorry. He's shy."

"Most big guys are," Tiffany said. "Present company accepted, of course."

"Your brother ever think about playing football?" Aaron asked me. "He'd make a great front lineman."

"Gray's really not into sports." I felt a little dizzy. "Both of us love to ride, though. Do you guys have horses?"

As we talked the dizziness faded, and didn't come back for the rest of the school day. I met Gray out by his truck in the student parking lot feeling pretty good about our new school. Maybe this time we'd be able to make some real friends and be more like other teenagers.

My brother didn't say anything on the way home, but once we were home he offered to help me make dinner.

"Are you running a fever?" I demanded.

Gray shrugged. "Trick said you shouldn't have to do all the cooking."

"I like doing the cooking," I reminded him. "It gets me out of clearing the table and washing the dishes. Don't ruin things for me."

I decided to make spaghetti for dinner, and I was browning the ground beef and onions when Trick came in from the barn.

He went to the sink to wash his hands. "How was your first day?"

"Unusually terrific," I told him as I added some diced garlic to the skillet. "My student mentor is the school's head cheerleader, and she's great. So is her boyfriend. I like all my classes and my teachers. I just wish Grim weren't so … grim."

"A new school is always an adjustment. Give him some space," my brother advised. "Any problem today with your head or your shoulder?"

"I felt a little dizzy at lunch, but it went away. It was probably because I was hungry." I glanced at him. "I know you're worried about me, but you need to lighten up, too. I'm good."

Trick sat with me and talked about his plans for the farm as I made the salad and garlic bread. While he was setting the table I took my backpack upstairs and unloaded it so I could do my homework after dinner. I dropped one book, and as I bent down to pick it up I noticed something sticking out from under the edge of my mattress. It was a note written in block letters on thin, stiff paper.

Meet me tonight by the moonflowers.

I stared at the note as I slowly straightened. My head pounded as I kept reading the words over and over. Meet who? What moonflowers?

A moment later the sensation passed, and I calmed down. Gray must have stuck it there as some sort of weird practical joke. I'd have to pay him back by leaving a note in his underwear drawer: *Stay out of my bedroom, you sneak.*

My spaghetti turned out as it always did: tasty but nothing special. For once my brothers didn't seem to have much appetite, and I remembered what Boone had said about the flu.

"We should get flu shots this year," I said. When they both stared at me, I laughed. "Someone told me today that it's been going around the school. What, do you *want* the flu?"

"I've got to check on Flash." Gray got up, took his dishes to the sink and then stalked out.

"What is with him?" I asked Trick.

"He's a teenager," my brother said, as if that explained it all.

I thought about mentioning the note Gray had stuck under my mattress, but something stopped me. I couldn't tell Trick about the note because...I didn't know why, but I couldn't.

Gray never came back to the house, so I helped my brother clear the table and wash the dishes. Then I went upstairs to do the rest of my homework, but I kept looking at my bed. Finally I got up and went to the side, lifting the mattress to see if the big grump had hidden anything else under there.

The bundle of letters I found was very old, and the envelopes each had my father's name written on them in beautiful script.

I sat down on the bed, holding them as if they might crumble into dust. I'd never seen them before, but they looked so familiar. My fingers slipped the last envelope out of the bundle, and I opened the flap and took out the folded sheet inside.

Thomas,

I heard my parents talking in the library. Someone saw us together, and now my father knows about us. He knows what you are. He's going to gather the family and hunt you down. Thomas, he intends to kill you.

I can't stay here or let them hurt you. I know you said we can't be together because of what we are, but I know you love me. You're the only one who can protect me and the baby now.

I'll be at the mill after midnight. We have to go tonight. Please, be there.

Your Rose

The letter floated from my fingers to the floor beside my feet as I heard someone calling me. I got up and turned around, but no one was there.

I picked up the letter, put it back in the envelope, and hid the letters in my sock drawer. I couldn't read them anymore. I couldn't know what my mother wrote to my father. The compulsion was so strong I almost took them out of the drawer to tear them into pieces.

But a part of me knew I had already read the letters. I knew. I knew.

I didn't look at the drawer again. Instead, I made myself finish my homework, and take a shower, and get ready for bed. When Trick came up to say good night, he found me reading the book for my English class.

"*Moby Dick* again." He sounded amused. "What is this, the sixth or seventh time you've read it?"

"Eighth," I told him, closing the book and setting it on my nightstand. "At this point? I'm cheering for the whale."

He chuckled and bent over to kiss the top of my head. "Get some sleep."

I didn't sleep. I waited. I listened to the sounds downstairs, and when they quieted and I knew my brothers were asleep, I got up and changed into my riding clothes. I wasn't supposed to go riding at night, but I needed to get out of the house. I needed to find the moonflowers, and see who was waiting for me there.

Sali whickered to me as I went to her stall, and once I saddled her she trotted out eagerly. I didn't try to guide her but let her have her head, and she loped across the pastures, taking me to the very back of our property where it bordered a dense, thick woods.

I reined her in as we reached an old black oak with low-hanging branches, and after I dismounted I tied her up there. Then I walked toward the fence, and the brush hanging over it, and the dark boy standing next to a cluster of white flowers that were just now blooming.

"You shouldn't ride alone at night," the boy said. "It's dangerous."

I glanced at the big black tied up on the other side of the fence. His name was Prince, and he was very strong, and very fast. Sali liked to race him.

"Do you know who I am?" the boy asked.

I reached out to touch one of the moonflowers. I looked up into his beautiful gray eyes, like dark, glittering marcasite. Then I held up my bare fingers, but the ring I expected to see wasn't there.

"He took it away from you and gave it back to me." The boy took my hand in his and slid a heavy, old-fashioned ring on my finger. "It was part of the bargain he made with my parents. They made me swear I would not try to see you again."

"But you're here."

"I've come every night since the dance." His mouth hitched. "I even thought about having Prince throw me into the fence again, if I saw you out riding Sali."

I closed my eyes and crumpled, but the dark boy caught me in his arms. He held me as my mind filled with voices and images rushing into my mind, and my body shook, and I cried out as the pain grew and built and then shattered.

When I opened my eyes, he was still holding me in his arms. My dark boy. My love. "Jesse. Oh, God."

"I'm here." He held me close, rocking me as I wept, stroking my hair and murmuring to me.

I felt empty by the time my tears ebbed, and tired, and filled with despair. "It was Patrick. He took away all my memories of moving here, meeting you, everything that's happened. I thought today was my first day of school." I remembered how friendly Tiffany had been. Tiffany, who had first despised me, and then had helped me during Barb's attack. "They didn't shut down the school because of the flu."

He shook his head. "Your brother's ability is very powerful, but he needed time to erase you from the memories of the people who live here. The sheriff helped him by conducting interviews about the incident during the dance. They were very efficient."

"So everyone's forgotten me. Diego. Boone." I closed my eyes briefly. "What about Barbara?"

"She had a complete breakdown that night." He brushed some hair back from my cheek. "Her parents have taken her for treatment at a mental health hospital in another state. They will not be returning to Lost Lake."

Trick couldn't have done this all on his own. "Your parents helped my brother do this." He nodded. "Why?"

"He promised that he would keep their secret, and help protect them, if they would do the same for him." He used his thumb to wipe the last tears from my face. "He loves you very much." Then he looked away from me.

"There's something else." When he didn't reply, I drew back. "Jesse, tell me."

"You remember that you gave me your blood?" When I nodded, his expression grew tentative. "It should have finished the change, but it didn't. It only strengthened the bond we have. I can hear your thoughts now, as plainly as if you were speaking to me." He stopped talking and looked into my eyes. Inside my head, I heard his voice. *And now that you are listening, you can hear mine.*

"Yes. I can." As stunned as I was, I still didn't understand. "You said that vampires can only bond with other vampires."

"That is true." He looked as if he were groping for words. "Catlyn, I didn't know. Not until your brother came to the island to bargain with my parents."

Words from my mother's last letter to my father flashed in my mind. *He knows what you are. He's going to gather the family and hunt you down. Thomas, he intends to kill you.*

"My blood didn't change you because it's not all human," I said slowly. "My father was a vampire, wasn't he?"

His arms tightened around me. "Your father was like me and my parents. He never made the final change. It's why he came here after he married your mother. He was one of our trainers. He survived the attack on our caravan, and was taken to the caves with us. He must have escaped some time that night. My parents didn't see him again until he came to Lost Lake with your mother."

I understood why he hadn't wanted to tell me this last part. My brothers and I were part vampire, part vampire-hunter. That was the last of the family secrets, and maybe the worst of all, but I didn't feel crushed. Despite their differences, their natures, and even their fates, my mother and father had found each other. They'd married, and had a family. They'd chosen hope over hatred. Faith over fear. Love over death.

Just as Jesse and I had.

"If Rose and Thomas could make a life together," I told my dark boy, "then so can we."

Acknowledgments

I would like to thank those who in so many ways contributed their time and knowledge to help me with the writing of this novel:

My daughter, Katherine, who first requested the story, and who remained on-call as my primary consultant for the entire time I was writing it. I know how annoying I can be, honey, and I appreciate your patience. Now you have to read it.

Hayley Brown, who generously served as both story consultant and manuscript reader whenever I needed. Hayley, you are a treasure and a true friend.

James Davis, who provided much expertise and insight about high school football and student athletes, and helped me understand that it is so much more than just a game. I wish you all the best, James.

Corie Robbins, whose friendship, training, and enormous love for horses provided so much material for this story. We miss you and think of you often.

Last but not least, I'd like to thank Brian Farrey, Sandy Sullivan, and all the terrific folks at Flux for working with me on *After Midnight*. You've made this experience one of the best I've ever had as a novelist, and that I will always remember with a smile.

About the Author

New York Times bestselling author Lynn Viehl has published over forty-seven novels in six genres. On the internet, she hosts Paperback Writer, a popular publishing industry weblog and writers' free online resource. When she's not writing or reading, Lynn lives a quiet life with her family in the country, where she spends her spare time collecting great books, sewing traditional quilts, painting terrible watercolors, and rescuing lost farm dogs, wayward baby birds, and the occasional runaway horse.